First-Person in Russia's Golden Age

Notes from the Underground
Diary of a Madman
Diary of a Superfluous Man
Lucerne

First-Person in Russia's Golden Age

Notes from the Underground
Diary of a Madman
Diary of a Superfluous Man
Lucerne

Dostoyevsky, Gogol, Turgenev and Tolstoy

Translated by
Claud Field
Constance Garnett
Nathan Haskell Dole

Edited with an Introduction by
Sherman Sutherland

Sabino Falls
Tucson

Published by
Sabino Falls Publishing
Tucson

Library of Congress Control Number: 2012944398
Cataloging-in-Publication Data
Sutherland, Sherman.
    First-person in russia's golden age : notes from the underground,
    diary of a madman, diary of a superfluous man, and
    lucerne / Sherman Sutherland.—1st ed.
        p. cm.
    ISBN 978-0-9857501-9-0   (pbk.)
    1. Russian literature—19th century—Translations into English
I. Title
PG3213.U84 F57 2012
891.7'08'007—dc20   2012944398

Cover design: Tara Hsiao
Cover image: detail of Медный всадник (The Bronze Horseman) by
    Vasily Surikov (1870)

www.SabinoFalls.com

Printed in the United States of America

10 9 8 7 6 5 4 3 2 1

Contents

Introduction

When I was asked to contribute to this Sabino Falls Classics edition, I eagerly agreed. Whether you're an expert in Russian languages, a creative writer looking to hone your craft, or simply someone who loves to read great fiction, you have to appreciate the craftsmanship that went into these stories.

This volume includes four classic works: *Diary of a Madman*, written by Nikolai Gogol in 1835, Ivan Turgenev's *Diary of a Superfluous Man* (1850), Leo Tolstoy's "Lucerne" (1857) and *Notes from the Underground*, written by Fyodor Dostoyevsky in 1864. All four represent work created as their respective authors were rising toward the height of their literary and popular success. These stories also, intentionally or not, betray the growing dissatisfaction that was gradually building throughout nineteenth-century Russia.

Some scholars take exception to the term "Golden Age" to refer to that body of literature produced in Russia between, roughly, 1820 and 1890. Such taxonomy, the argument goes, is vague and fails to consider author's own categorization of his or her work, not to mention shortchanging the literature of the preceding and subsequent eras. And how does one precisely demarcate the beginning and end of the Golden Age? Such arguments, of course, could be made about nearly any literary period. Literary periods in general are, after all, human contrivances—and inexact ones, at that—most often conceived after the fact to explain why one work seems similar to another, and why they both seem to influence still others. Did the postmodern period begin with the end of World War II or with the demolition of the Pruitt-Igoe housing project in St. Louis? Did the ancient Greeks refer to themselves as ancient?

However we choose to classify the literature from nineteenth-century Russia, it is difficult to dispute the quality of work that was produced during this time. A more interesting argument, perhaps, might arise from an attempt to understand how such a body of work came to be. Russia, throughout the nineteenth century, was controlled by a succession of emperors, beginning with Paul I and ending with Nicholas II. Of these, the rule of Nicholas I, from 1825 to 1855, is often considered the most repressive. His reign began with the brutal crushing of the Decembrist revolt on the day he was crowned and was marked, throughout his time in power, by a fervent desire to suppress rebellious ideas before they could take root. By 1833, the ideological doctrine of "Orthodoxy, Autocracy, and Nationality"—endorsement of the Russian Orthodox Church, unquestioned loyalty to the Tsarist regime, and support of the Russian nation—had become the official policy of the State. To implement this "Triad of Official Nationality," censors actively monitored speech and literature for anything that could be perceived as a threat to the monarchy.

Dostoyevsky, Gogol, Turgenev and Tolstoy had all been affected by the repressive actions of the autocratic government. Dostoyevsky was sentenced to four years of hard labor in Siberia after being accused of disseminating literature deemed unfavorable to the Tsarist government of Nicholas I. Turgenev was imprisoned for a month after publishing an obituary for Gogol. During the subsequent reign of Alexander II, Tolstoy's home was raided and thoroughly searched by government authorities who were looking for a printing press. Even Gogol, who supported the Tsarist regime, was forced by censors to edit his work, including changing the title of his most acclaimed book, *Dead Souls*, to *The Adventures of Chichikov*.

Taking human nature into account, it's difficult to argue definitively, even in retrospect, if the great literature of nineteenth-century Russia was produced in spite of, or because of, these repressive governmental policies. We do know that St. Petersburg had become an active city by 1820. During this time, the vast majority of Russia was comprised of rural farmland, making the country's few cities natural places of congregation. For the intelligentsia, this was particularly true of the capital city, St. Petersburg. Many of Russia's artists, thinkers and writers—including those in this volume—had spent considerable time in St. Petersburg, making Russia's nineteenth-century literary community less a diaspora than an interconnected collection of like-minded people.

As this volume's title would suggest, these stories all share a common narrative perspective. Obviously, these weren't the first works of fiction to employ a first-person point of view. Even the diary structure had been utilized before—most famously in the West by Samuel Richardson in his bestselling novel, *Pamela*. But whereas the execution of *Pamela* seems at times to invite parody (and receives it, notably in the form of Fielding's *Shamela*), Gogol's Poprishchin and Turgenev's Tchulkaturin feel real to the end, even when, in Gogol's case, the narrator converses with animals and believes himself to be the ruler of Spain. Narrators of the other stories in this collection seem more sane, but are troubled nonetheless. The angst and ennui of Dostoyevsky's unnamed narrator, in particular, portends not only his own Raskolnikov in *Crime and Punishment*, but also Sartre's Roquentin, Camus' Meursault, and dozens of other characters for the next one and a half centuries.

Dostoyevsky, Gogol, Tolstoy and Turgenev all would go on to inspire and influence scores of writers including Anton Chekhov, James Joyce, Ernest Hemingway and Vladimir Nabokov. Indeed, any writer influenced by our twentieth-century modernists must count the writers of this volume as influences as well. The stories in this collection show us where it began, and where it will continue for generations to come.

The works in this volume all represent revised editions of the translations by Claud Field, Constance Garnett and Nathan Haskell Dole. The goal was to remain true to the excellent original translations while presenting more accessible interpretations that reflect the emotional energy of each author's unique work. To that end, spellings and obsolete colloquialisms have been updated and translations that would be misleading for today's reader have been revised.

Fyodor Dostoyevsky
(1809-52)

Notes from the Underground
Translated from the Russian by Constance Garnett

Part I
Underground *

I

I am a sick man. . . . I am a spiteful man. I am an unattractive man. I believe my liver is diseased. However, I know nothing at all about my disease, and do not know for certain what ails me. I don't consult a doctor for it, and never have, though I have a respect for medicine and doctors. Besides, I am extremely superstitious, sufficiently so to respect medicine, anyway (I am well-educated enough not to be superstitious, but I am superstitious). No, I refuse to consult a doctor from

---

* The author of the diary and the diary itself are, of course, imaginary. Nevertheless it is clear that such persons as the writer of these notes not only may, but positively must, exist in our society, when we consider the circumstances in the midst of which our society is formed. I have tried to expose to the view of the public more distinctly than is commonly done, one of the characters of the recent past. He is one of the representatives of a generation still living. In this fragment, entitled "Underground," this person introduces himself and his views, and, as it were, tries to explain the causes owing to which he has made his appearance and was bound to make his appearance in our midst. In the second fragment there are added the actual notes of this person concerning certain events in his life.—Author's note.

spite. That you probably will not understand. Well, I understand it, though. Of course, I can't explain who it is precisely that I am mortifying in this case by my spite: I am perfectly well aware that I cannot "pay out" the doctors by not consulting them; I know better than anyone that by all this I am only injuring myself and no one else. But still, if I don't consult a doctor it is from spite. My liver is bad, well—let it get worse!

I have been going on like that for a long time—twenty years. Now I am forty. I used to be in the government service, but am no longer. I was a spiteful official. I was rude and took pleasure in being so. I did not take bribes, you see, so I was bound to find a recompense in that, at least. (A poor jest, but I will not scratch it out. I wrote it thinking it would sound very witty; but now that I have seen myself that I only wanted to show off in a despicable way, I will not scratch it out on purpose!)

When petitioners used to come for information to the table at which I sat, I used to grind my teeth at them, and felt intense enjoyment when I succeeded in making anybody unhappy. I almost did succeed. For the most part they were all timid people—of course, they were petitioners. But of the uppish ones there was one officer in particular I could not endure. He simply would not be humble, and clanked his sword in a disgusting way. I carried on a feud with him for eighteen months over that sword. At last I got the better of him. He left off clanking it. That happened in my youth, though.

But do you know, gentlemen, what was the chief point about my spite? Why, the whole point, the real sting of it lay in the fact that continually, even in the moment of the acutest spleen, I was inwardly conscious with shame that I was not only not a spiteful but not even an embittered man, that I was simply scaring sparrows at random and amusing myself by it. I might foam at the mouth, but bring me a doll to play with, give me a cup of tea with sugar in it, and maybe I should be appeased. I might even be genuinely touched, though probably I should grind my teeth at myself afterwards and lie awake at night with shame for months after. That was my way.

I was lying when I said just now that I was a spiteful official. I was lying from spite. I was simply amusing myself with the petitioners and with the officer, and in reality I never could become spiteful. I was conscious every moment in myself of many, very many elements absolutely opposite to that. I felt them positively swarming in me, these opposite elements. I knew that they had been swarming in me all my life and craving some outlet from me, but I would not let them, would not let them, purposely would not let them come out. They tormented me till I was ashamed: they drove me to convulsions and—sickened me, at last, how they sickened me! Now, are not you fancying, gentlemen, that I am expressing remorse for something now, that I am asking your forgiveness for something? I am sure you are fancying that . . . However, I assure you I do not care if you are. . . .

It was not only that I could not become spiteful, I did not know how to become anything; neither spiteful nor kind, neither a rascal nor an honest man, neither a hero nor an insect. Now, I am living out my life in my corner, taunting myself with the spiteful and useless consolation that an intelligent man cannot become anything seriously, and it is only the fool who becomes anything. Yes, a man in the nineteenth century must and morally ought to be pre-eminently a characterless creature; a man of character, an active man is pre-eminently a limited creature. That is my conviction of forty years. I am forty years old now, and you know forty years is a whole lifetime; you know it is extreme old age. To live longer than forty years is bad manners, is vulgar, immoral. Who does live beyond forty? Answer that, sincerely and honestly I will tell you who do: fools and worthless fellows. I tell all old men that to their face, all these venerable old men, all these silver-haired and reverend seniors! I tell the whole world that to its face! I have a right to say so, for I shall go on living to sixty myself. To seventy! To eighty! . . . Stay, let me take breath . . .

You imagine no doubt, gentlemen, that I want to amuse you. You are mistaken in that, too. I am by no means such a mirthful person as you imagine, or as you may imagine; however, irritated by all this babble (and I feel that you are irritated) you think fit to ask me who I am—then my answer is, I am a collegiate assessor. I was in the service that I might have something to eat (and solely for that reason), and when last year a distant relation left me six thousand rubles in his will I immediately retired from the service and settled down in my corner. I used to live in this corner before, but now I have settled down in it. My room is a wretched, horrid one in the outskirts of the town. My servant is an old country-woman, ill-natured from stupidity, and, moreover, there is always a nasty smell about her. I am told that the Petersburg climate is bad for me, and that with my small means it is very expensive to live in Petersburg. I know all that better than all these sage and experienced counsellors and monitors. . . . But I am remaining in Petersburg; I am not going away from Petersburg! I am not going away because . . . ech! Why, it is absolutely no matter whether I am going away or not going away.

But what can a decent man speak of with most pleasure?

Answer: Of himself.

Well, so I will talk about myself.

II

I want now to tell you, gentlemen, whether you care to hear it or not, why I could not even become an insect. I tell you solemnly, that I have many times tried to become an insect. But I was not equal even to that. I swear, gentlemen, that to be too conscious is an illness—a real thorough-going illness. For man's everyday needs, it would have been quite enough to have the ordinary human consciousness, that is, half or a quarter of the amount which falls to the lot of a cultivated man of our unhappy nineteenth century, especially one who has the fatal ill-luck to inhabit Petersburg, the most theoretical and intentional town on the whole terrestrial globe. (There are intentional and unintentional towns.) It would have been quite enough, for instance, to have the consciousness by which all so-called direct persons and men of action live. I bet you think I am writing all this from affectation, to be witty at the expense of men of action; and what is more, that from ill-bred affectation, I am clanking a sword like my officer. But, gentlemen, whoever can pride himself on his diseases and even swagger over them?

Though, after all, everyone does do that; people do pride themselves on their diseases, and I do, may be, more than anyone. We will not dispute it; my contention was absurd. But yet I am firmly persuaded that a great deal of consciousness, every sort of consciousness, in fact, is a disease. I stick to that. Let us leave that, too, for a minute. Tell me this: why does it happen that at the very, yes, at the very moments when I am most capable of feeling every refinement of all that is "sublime and beautiful," as they used to say at one time, it would, as though of design, happen to me not only to feel but to do such ugly things, such that . . . Well, in short, actions that all, perhaps, commit; but which, as though purposely, occurred to me at the very time when I was most conscious that they ought not to be committed. The more conscious I was of goodness and of all that was "sublime and beautiful," the more deeply I sank into my mire and the more ready I was to sink in it altogether. But the chief point was that all this was, as it were, not accidental in me, but as though it were bound to be so. It was as though it were my most normal condition, and not in the least disease or depravity, so that at last all desire in me to struggle against this depravity passed. It ended by my almost believing (perhaps actually believing) that this was perhaps my normal condition. But at first, in the beginning, what agonies I endured in that struggle! I did not believe it was the same with other people, and all my life I hid this fact about myself as a secret. I was ashamed (even now, perhaps, I am ashamed): I got to the point of feeling a sort of secret abnormal, despicable enjoyment in returning home to my corner on some disgusting Petersburg night, acutely conscious that that day I had committed a loathsome action again, that what was done could never be undone, and secretly, inwardly gnawing, gnawing at myself for it, tearing and consuming myself till at last the bitterness turned into a sort of shameful accursed sweetness, and at last—into positive real enjoyment! Yes, into enjoyment, into enjoyment! I insist upon that. I have spoken of this because I keep wanting to know for a fact whether other people feel such enjoyment? I will explain; the enjoyment was just from the too intense consciousness of one's own degradation; it was from feeling oneself that one had reached the last barrier, that it was horrible, but that it could not be otherwise; that there was no escape for you; that you never could become a different man; that even if time and faith were still left you to change into something different you would most likely not wish to change; or if you did wish to, even then you would do nothing; because perhaps in reality there was nothing for you to change into.

And the worst of it was, and the root of it all, that it was all in accord with the normal fundamental laws of over-acute consciousness, and with the inertia that was the direct result of those laws, and that consequently one was not only unable to change but could do absolutely nothing. Thus it would follow, as the result of acute consciousness, that one is not to blame in being a scoundrel; as though that were any consolation to the scoundrel once he has come to realize that he actually is a scoundrel. But enough. . . . Ech, I have talked a lot of nonsense, but what have I explained? How is enjoyment in this to be explained? But I will explain it. I will get to the bottom of it! That is why I have taken up my pen. . . .

I, for instance, have a great deal of *amour propre*. I am as suspicious and prone to take offence as a humpback or a dwarf. But upon my word I sometimes have had moments when if I had happened to be slapped in the face I should, perhaps, have been positively glad of it. I say, in earnest, that I should probably have been able to discover even in that a peculiar sort of enjoyment—the enjoyment, of course, of despair; but in despair there are the most intense enjoyments, especially when one is very acutely conscious of the hopelessness of one's position. And when one is slapped in the face— why then the consciousness of being rubbed into a pulp would positively overwhelm one. The worst of it is, look at it which way one will, it still turns out that I was always the most to blame in everything. And what is most humiliating of all, to blame for no fault of my own but, so to say, through the laws of nature. In the first place, to blame because I am cleverer than any of the people surrounding me. (I have always considered myself cleverer than any of the people surrounding me, and sometimes, would you believe it, have been positively ashamed of it. At any rate, I have all my life, as it were, turned my eyes away and never could look people straight in the face.) To blame, finally, because even if I had had magnanimity, I should only have had more suffering from the sense of its uselessness. I should certainly have never been able to do anything from being magnanimous—neither to forgive, for my assailant would perhaps have slapped me from the laws of nature, and one cannot forgive the laws of nature; nor to forget, for even if it were owing to the laws of nature, it is insulting all the same. Finally, even if I had wanted to be anything but magnanimous, had desired on the contrary to revenge myself on my assailant, I could not have revenged myself on any one for anything because I should certainly never have made up my mind to do anything, even if I had been able to. Why should I not have made up my mind? About that in particular I want to say a few words.

III

With people who know how to revenge themselves and to stand up for themselves in general, how is it done? Why, when they are possessed, let us suppose, by the feeling of revenge, then for the time there is nothing else but that feeling left in their whole being. Such a gentleman simply dashes straight for his object like an infuriated bull with its horns down, and nothing but a wall will stop him. (By the way: facing the wall, such gentlemen—that is, the "direct" persons and men of action—are genuinely nonplussed. For them a wall is not an evasion, as for us people who think and consequently do nothing; it is not an excuse for turning aside, an excuse for which we are always very glad, though we scarcely believe in it ourselves, as a rule. No, they are nonplussed in all sincerity. The wall has for them something tranquillizing, morally soothing, final—maybe even something mysterious . . . but of the wall later.)

Well, such a direct person I regard as the real normal man, as his tender mother nature wished to see him when she graciously brought him into being on the earth. I envy such a man till I am green in the face. He is stupid. I am not disputing that, but perhaps the normal man should be stupid, how do you know? Perhaps it is very beautiful, in fact. And I am the more persuaded of that suspicion, if one can call it so, by the fact that if you take, for instance, the antithesis of the normal man, that is, the man of acute consciousness, who has come, of course, not out of the lap of nature but out of a retort (this is almost mysticism, gentlemen, but I suspect this, too), this retort-made man is sometimes so nonplussed in the presence of his antithesis that with all his exaggerated consciousness he genuinely thinks of himself as a mouse and not a man. It may be an acutely conscious mouse, yet it is a mouse, while the other is a man, and therefore, et cetera, et cetera. And the worst of it is, he himself, his very own self, looks on himself as a mouse; no one asks him to do so; and that is an important point. Now let us look at this mouse in action. Let us suppose, for instance, that it feels insulted, too (and it almost always does feel insulted), and wants to revenge itself, too. There may even be a greater accumulation of spite in it than in *l'homme de la nature et de la vérité*. The base and nasty desire to vent that spite on its assailant rankles perhaps even more nastily in it than in *l'homme de la nature et de la vérité*. For through his innate stupidity the latter looks upon his revenge as justice pure and simple; while in consequence of his acute consciousness the mouse does not believe in the justice of it. To come at last to the deed itself, to the very act of revenge. Apart from the one fundamental nastiness the luckless mouse succeeds in creating around it so many other nastinesses in the form of doubts and questions, adds to the one question so many unsettled questions that there inevitably works up around it a sort of fatal brew, a stinking mess, made up of its doubts, emotions, and of the contempt spat upon it by the direct men of action who stand solemnly about it as judges and arbitrators, laughing at it till their healthy sides ache. Of course the only thing left for it is to dismiss all that with a wave of its paw, and, with a smile of assumed contempt in which it does not even itself believe, creep ignominiously into its mouse-hole. There in its nasty, stinking, underground home our insulted, crushed and ridiculed mouse promptly becomes absorbed in cold, malignant and, above all, everlasting spite. For forty years together it will remember its injury down to the smallest, most ignominious details, and every time will add, of itself, details still more ignominious, spitefully teasing and tormenting itself with its own imagination. It will itself be ashamed of its imaginings, but yet it will recall it all, it will go over and over every detail, it will invent unheard of things against itself, pretending that those things might happen, and will forgive nothing. Maybe it will begin to revenge itself, too, but, as it were, piecemeal, in trivial ways, from behind the stove, incognito, without believing either in its own right to vengeance, or in the success of its revenge, knowing that from all its efforts at revenge it will suffer a hundred times more than he on whom it revenges itself, while he, I daresay, will not even scratch himself. On its deathbed it will recall it all over again, with interest accumulated over all the years and . . .

But it is just in that cold, abominable half despair, half belief, in that conscious burying oneself alive for grief in the underworld for forty years, in that acutely recognized and yet partly doubtful hopelessness of one's position, in that hell of unsatisfied desires turned inward, in that fever of oscillations, of resolutions determined for ever and repented of again a minute later—that the savor of that strange enjoyment of which I have spoken lies. It is so subtle, so difficult of analysis, that persons who are a little limited, or even simply persons of strong nerves, will not understand a single atom of it. "Possibly," you will add on your own account with a grin, "people will not understand it either who have never received a slap in the face," and in that way you will politely hint to me that I, too, perhaps, have had the experience of a slap in the face in my life, and so I speak as one who knows. I bet that you are thinking that. But set your minds at rest, gentlemen, I have not received a slap in the face, though it is absolutely a matter of indifference to me what you may think about it. Possibly, I even regret, myself, that I have given so few slaps in the face during my life. But enough . . . not another word on that subject of such extreme interest to you.

I will continue calmly concerning persons with strong nerves who do not understand a certain refinement of enjoyment. Though in certain circumstances these gentlemen bellow their loudest like bulls, though this, let us suppose, does them the greatest credit, yet, as I have said already, confronted with the impossible they subside at once. The impossible means the stone wall! What stone wall? Why, of course, the laws of nature, the deductions of natural science, mathematics.

As soon as they prove to you, for instance, that you are descended from a monkey, then it is no use scowling, accept it for a fact. When they prove to you that in reality one drop of your own fat must be dearer to you than a hundred thousand of your fellow-creatures, and that this conclusion is the final solution of all so-called virtues and duties and all such prejudices and fancies, then you have just to accept it, there is no help for it, for twice two is a law of mathematics. Just try refuting it.

"Upon my word, they will shout at you, it is no use protesting: it is a case of twice two makes four! Nature does not ask your permission, she has nothing to do with your wishes, and whether you like her laws or dislike them, you are bound to accept her as she is, and consequently all her conclusions. A wall, you see, is a wall . . . and so on, and so on."

Merciful Heavens! but what do I care for the laws of nature and arithmetic, when, for some reason I dislike those laws and the fact that twice two makes four? Of course I cannot break through the wall by battering my head against it if I really have not the strength to knock it down, but I am not going to be reconciled to it simply because it is a stone wall and I have not the strength.

As though such a stone wall really were a consolation, and really did contain some word of conciliation, simply because it is as true as twice two makes four. Oh, absurdity of absurdities! How much better it is to understand it all, to recognize it all, all the impossibilities and the stone wall; not to be reconciled to one of those impossibilities and stone walls if it disgusts you to be reconciled to it; by the way of the most inevitable, logical combinations to reach the most revolting conclusions on the everlasting theme, that even for the stone wall you are yourself somehow to blame, though again it is as clear as day you are not to blame in the least, and therefore grinding your teeth in silent impotence to sink into luxurious inertia, brooding on the fact that there is no one even for you

Fyodor Dostoyevsky

to feel vindictive against, that you have not, and perhaps never will have, an object for your spite, that it is a sleight of
hand, a bit of juggling, a card-sharper's trick, that it is simply
a mess, no knowing what and no knowing who, but in spite
of all these uncertainties and jugglings, still there is an ache in
you, and the more you do not know, the worse the ache.

IV

"Ha, ha, ha! You will be finding enjoyment in toothache
next," you cry, with a laugh.

"Well, even in toothache there is enjoyment," I answer. I
had toothache for a whole month and I know there is. In that
case, of course, people are not spiteful in silence, but moan;
but they are not candid moans, they are malignant moans,
and the malignancy is the whole point. The enjoyment of the
sufferer finds expression in those moans; if he did not feel
enjoyment in them he would not moan. It is a good example,
gentlemen, and I will develop it. Those moans express in the
first place all the aimlessness of your pain, which is so humiliating to your consciousness; the whole legal system of nature
on which you spit disdainfully, of course, but from which you
suffer all the same while she does not. They express the consciousness that you have no enemy to punish, but that you
have pain; the consciousness that in spite of all possible
Wagenheims you are in complete slavery to your teeth; that if
someone wishes it, your teeth will leave off aching, and if he
does not, they will go on aching another three months; and
that finally if you are still contumacious and still protest, all
that is left you for your own gratification is to thrash yourself
or beat your wall with your fist as hard as you can, and absolutely nothing more. Well, these mortal insults, these jeers on
the part of someone unknown, end at last in an enjoyment
which sometimes reaches the highest degree of voluptuous-
ness. I ask you, gentlemen, listen sometimes to the moans of
an educated man of the nineteenth century suffering from

toothache, on the second or third day of the attack, when he is beginning to moan, not as he moaned on the first day, that is, not simply because he has toothache, not just as any coarse peasant, but as a man affected by progress and European civilization, a man who is "divorced from the soil and the national elements," as they express it now-a-days. His moans become nasty, disgustingly malignant, and go on for whole days and nights. And of course he knows himself that he is doing himself no sort of good with his moans; he knows better than anyone that he is only lacerating and harassing himself and others for nothing; he knows that even the audience before whom he is making his efforts, and his whole family, listen to him with loathing, do not put a ha'porth of faith in him, and inwardly understand that he might moan differently, more simply, without trills and flourishes, and that he is only amusing himself like that from ill-humor, from malignancy. Well, in all these recognitions and disgraces it is that there lies a voluptuous pleasure. As though he would say: "I am worrying you, I am lacerating your hearts, I am keeping everyone in the house awake. Well, stay awake then, you, too, feel every minute that I have toothache. I am not a hero to you now, as I tried to seem before, but simply a nasty person, an impostor. Well, so be it, then! I am very glad that you see through me. It is nasty for you to hear my despicable moans: well, let it be nasty; here I will let you have a nastier flourish in a minute. . . ." You do not understand even now, gentlemen? No, it seems our development and our consciousness must go further to understand all the intricacies of this pleasure. You laugh? Delighted. My jests, gentlemen, are of course in bad taste, jerky, involved, lacking self-confidence. But of course that is because I do not respect myself. Can a man of perception respect himself at all?

V

Come, can a man who attempts to find enjoyment in the very feeling of his own degradation possibly have a spark of respect for himself? I am not saying this now from any mawkish kind of remorse. And, indeed, I could never endure saying, "Forgive me, Papa, I won't do it again," not because I am incapable of saying that—on the contrary, perhaps just because I have been too capable of it, and in what a way, too. As though of design I used to get into trouble in cases when I was not to blame in any way. That was the nastiest part of it. At the same time I was genuinely touched and penitent, I used to shed tears and, of course, deceived myself, though I was not acting in the least and there was a sick feeling in my heart at the time. . . . For that one could not blame even the laws of nature, though the laws of nature have continually all my life offended me more than anything. It is loathsome to remember it all, but it was loathsome even then. Of course, a minute or so later I would realize wrathfully that it was all a lie, a revolting lie, an affected lie, that is, all this penitence, this emotion, these vows of reform. You will ask why did I worry myself with such antics: answer, because it was very dull to sit with one's hands folded, and so one began cutting capers. That is really it. Observe yourselves more carefully, gentlemen, then you will understand that it is so. I invented adventures for myself and made up a life, so as at least to live in some way. How many times it has happened to me—well, for instance, to take offence simply on purpose, for nothing; and one knows oneself, of course, that one is offended at nothing; that one is putting it on, but yet one brings oneself at last to the point of being really offended. All my life I have had an impulse to play such pranks, so that in the end I could not control it in myself. Another time, twice, in fact, I tried hard to be in love. I suffered, too, gentlemen, I assure you. In the depth of my heart there was no faith in my suffering, only a faint stir of mockery, but yet I did suffer, and in the real, orthodox way; I was jealous, beside myself . . . and it was all from *ennui*, gentlemen, all from *ennui*; inertia overcame me. You know the direct, legitimate fruit of consciousness is inertia, that is, conscious sitting-with-the-hands-folded. I have referred to this already. I repeat, I repeat with emphasis: all "direct" persons and men of action are active just because they are stupid and limited. How explain that? I will tell you: in consequence of their limitation they take immediate and secondary causes for primary ones, and in that way persuade themselves more quickly and easily than other people do that they have found an infallible foundation for their activity, and their minds are at ease and you know that is the chief thing. To begin to act, you know, you must first have your mind completely at ease and no trace of doubt left in it. Why, how am I, for example, to set my mind at rest? Where are the primary causes on which I am to build? Where are my foundations? Where am I to get them from? I exercise myself in reflection, and consequently with me every primary cause at once draws after itself another still more primary, and so on to infinity. That is just the essence of every sort of consciousness and reflection. It must be a case of the laws of nature again. What is the result of it in the end? Why, just the same. Remember I spoke just now of vengeance. (I am sure you did not take it in.) I said that a man revenges himself because he sees justice in it. Therefore he has found a primary cause, that is, justice. And so he is at rest on all sides, and consequently he carries out his revenge calmly and successfully, being persuaded that he is doing a just and honest thing. But I see no justice in it, I find no sort of virtue in it either, and consequently if I attempt to revenge myself, it is only out of spite. Spite, of course, might overcome everything, all my doubts, and so might serve quite successfully in place of a primary cause, precisely because it is not a cause. But what is to be done if I have not even spite (I began with that just now, you know). In consequence again of those accursed laws of consciousness, anger in me is subject to chemical disintegration. You look into it, the object flies off into air, your reasons evaporate, the criminal is not to be found, the wrong becomes not a wrong but a phantom, something like the toothache, for which no one is to blame, and consequently there is only the same outlet left again—that is, to beat the wall as hard as you can. So you give it up with a wave of the hand because you have not found a fundamental cause. And try letting yourself be carried away by your feelings, blindly, without reflection, without a primary cause, repelling consciousness at least for a time; hate or love, if only not to sit with your hands folded. The day after tomorrow, at the latest, you will begin despising yourself for having knowingly deceived yourself. Result: a soap-bubble and inertia. Oh, gentlemen, do you know, perhaps I consider myself an intelligent man, only because all my life I have been able neither to begin nor to finish anything. Granted I am a babbler, a harmless vexatious babbler, like all of us. But what is to be done if the direct and sole vocation of every intelligent man is babble, that is, the intentional pouring of water through a sieve?

VI

Oh, if I had done nothing simply from laziness! Heavens, how I should have respected myself, then. I should have respected myself because I should at least have been capable of being lazy; there would at least have been one quality, as it were, positive in me, in which I could have believed myself. Question: What is he? Answer: A sluggard; how very pleasant it would have been to hear that of oneself! It would mean that I was positively defined, it would mean that there was something to say about me. "Sluggard"—why, it is a calling and vocation, it is a career. Do not jest, it is so. I should then be a member of the best club by right, and should find my occupation in continually respecting myself. I knew a gentleman who prided himself all his life on being a connoisseur of

Lafitte. He considered this as his positive virtue, and never doubted himself. He died, not simply with a tranquil, but with a triumphant conscience, and he was quite right, too. Then I should have chosen a career for myself, I should have been a sluggard and a glutton, not a simple one, but, for instance, one with sympathies for everything sublime and beautiful. How do you like that? I have long had visions of it. That "sublime and beautiful" weighs heavily on my mind at forty But that is at forty; then—oh, then it would have been different! I should have found for myself a form of activity in keeping with it, to be precise, drinking to the health of everything "sublime and beautiful." I should have snatched at every opportunity to drop a tear into my glass and then to drain it to all that is "sublime and beautiful." I should then have turned everything into the sublime and the beautiful; in the nastiest, unquestionable trash, I should have sought out the sublime and the beautiful. I should have exuded tears like a wet sponge. An artist, for instance, paints a picture worthy of Gay. At once I drink to the health of the artist who painted the picture worthy of Gay, because I love all that is "sublime and beautiful." An author has written *as you will*: at once I drink to the health of "anyone you will" because I love all that is "sublime and beautiful."

I should claim respect for doing so. I should persecute anyone who would not show me respect. I should live at ease, I should die with dignity, why, it is charming, perfectly charming! And what a good round belly I should have grown, what a treble chin I should have established, what a ruby nose I should have colored for myself, so that everyone would have said, looking at me: "Here is an asset! Here is something real and solid!" And, say what you like, it is very agreeable to hear such remarks about oneself in this negative age.

VII

But these are all golden dreams. Oh, tell me, who was it first announced, who was it first proclaimed, that man only does nasty things because he does not know his own interests; and that if he were enlightened, if his eyes were opened to his real normal interests, man would at once cease to do nasty things, would at once become good and noble because, being enlightened and understanding his real advantage, he would see his own advantage in the good and nothing else, and we all know that not one man can, consciously, act against his own interests, consequently, so to say, through necessity, he would begin doing good? Oh, the babe! Oh, the pure, innocent child! Why, in the first place, when in all these thousands of years has there been a time when man has acted only from his own interest? What is to be done with the millions of facts that bear witness that men, *consciously*, that is fully understanding their real interests, have left them in the background and have rushed headlong on another path, to meet peril and danger, compelled to this course by nobody and by nothing, but, as it were, simply disliking the beaten track, and have obstinately, willfully, struck out another difficult, absurd way, seeking it almost in the darkness. So, I suppose, this obstinacy and perversity were pleasanter to them than any advantage. . . . Advantage! What is advantage? And will you take it upon yourself to define with perfect accuracy in what the advantage of man consists? And what if it so happens that a man's advantage, *sometimes*, not only may, but even must, consist in his desiring in certain cases what is harmful to himself and not advantageous. And if so, if there can be such a case, the whole principle falls into dust. What do you think— are there such cases? You laugh; laugh away, gentlemen, but only answer me: have man's advantages been reckoned up with perfect certainty? Are there not some which not only have not been included but cannot possibly be included under any classification? You see, you gentlemen have, to the best of my knowledge, taken your whole register of human advantages from the averages of statistical figures and politico-economical formulas. Your advantages are prosperity, wealth, freedom, peace—and so on, and so on. So that the man who should, for instance, go openly and knowingly in opposition to all that list would to your thinking, and indeed mine, too, of course, be an obscurantist or an absolute madman: would not he? But, you know, this is what is surprising: why does it so happen that all these statisticians, sages and lovers of humanity, when they reckon up human advantages invariably leave out one? They don't even take it into their reckoning in the form in which it should be taken, and the whole reckoning depends upon that. It would be no greater matter, they would simply have to take it, this advantage, and add it to the list. But the trouble is, that this strange advantage does not fall under any classification and is not in place in any list. I have a friend for instance . . . Ech! gentlemen, but of course he is your friend, too; and indeed there is no one, no one to whom he is not a friend! When he prepares for any undertaking this gentleman immediately explains to you, elegantly and clearly, exactly how he must act in accordance with the laws of reason and truth. What is more, he will talk to you with excitement and passion of the true normal interests of man; with irony he will upbraid the short-sighted fools who do not understand their own interests, nor the true significance of virtue; and, within a quarter of an hour, without any sudden outside provocation, but simply through something inside him which is stronger than all his interests, he will go off on quite a different tack—that is, act in direct opposition to what he has just been saying about himself, in opposition to the laws of reason, in opposition to his own advantage, in fact in opposition to everything . . . I warn you that my friend is a compound personality and therefore it is difficult to blame him as an individual. The fact is, gentlemen, it seems there must really exist something that is dearer to almost every man than his greatest advantages, or (not to be illogical) there is a most advantageous advantage (the very one omitted of which we spoke just now) which is more important and more advantageous than all other advantages, for the sake of which a man if necessary is ready to act in opposition to all laws; that is, in opposition to reason, honour, peace, prosperity—in fact, in opposition to all those excellent and useful things if only he can attain that fundamental, most advantageous advantage which is dearer to him than all. "Yes, but it's advantage all the same," you will retort. But excuse me, I'll make the point clear, and it is not a case of playing upon words. What matters is, that this advantage is remarkable from the very fact that it breaks down all our classifications, and continually shatters every system constructed by lovers of mankind for the benefit of mankind. In fact, it upsets everything. But before I mention this advantage to you, I want to compromise myself personally, and therefore I boldly declare that all these fine systems, all these theories for explaining to mankind their real normal interests, in order that inevitably striving to pursue these interests they may at once become good and noble—are, in my opinion, so far, mere logical exercises! Yes, logical exercises. Why, to maintain this theory of the regeneration of mankind by means of the pursuit of his own advantage is to my mind almost the same thing . . . as to affirm, for instance, following Buckle, that through civilization mankind becomes softer, and consequently less bloodthirsty and less fitted for warfare. Logically it does seem to follow from his arguments. But man has such a predilection for systems and abstract deductions that he is ready to distort the truth intentionally, he is ready to deny the evidence of his senses only to justify his logic. I take this example because it is the most glaring instance of it. Only look about you: blood is being spilt in streams, and in the merriest way, as though it were champagne. Take the whole of the nineteenth century in which Buckle lived. Take Napoleon—the Great and also the present one. Take North America—the eternal union. Take the farce of Schleswig-Holstein. . . . And what is it that civilization softens in us? The only gain of civilization for mankind is the greater capacity for variety of sensations—and absolutely nothing more. And through the development of this many-sidedness man may come to finding enjoyment in bloodshed. In fact, this has already happened to him. Have you noticed that it is the most civilized gentlemen who have been the sub-tlest slaughterers, to whom the Attilas and Stenka Razins could not hold a candle, and if they are not so conspicuous as the Attilas and Stenka Razins it is simply because they are so often met with, are so ordinary and have become so familiar to us. In any case civilization has made mankind if not more bloodthirsty, at least more vilely, more loathsomely blood-thirsty. In old days he saw justice in bloodshed and with his conscience at peace exterminated those he thought proper. Now we do think bloodshed abominable and yet we engage in this abomination, and with more energy than ever. Which is worse? Decide that for yourselves. They say that Cleopatra (excuse an instance from Roman history) was fond of sticking gold pins into her slave-girls' breasts and derived gratification from their screams and writhings. You will say that that was in the comparatively barbarous times; that these are barbarous times too, because also, comparatively speaking, pins are stuck in even now; that though man has now learned to see more clearly than in barbarous ages, he is still far from having learnt to act as reason and science would dictate. But yet you are fully convinced that he will be sure to learn when he gets rid of certain old bad habits, and when common sense and sci-ence have completely re-educated human nature and turned it in a normal direction. You are confident that then man will cease from *intentional* error and will, so to say, be compelled not to want to set his will against his normal interests. That is not all; then, you say, science itself will teach man (though to my mind it's a superfluous luxury) that he never has really had any caprice or will of his own, and that he himself is something of the nature of a piano-key or the stop of an organ, and that there are, besides, things called the laws of nature; so that everything he does is not done by his willing it, but is done of itself, by the laws of nature. Consequently we have only to discover these laws of nature, and man will no longer have to answer for his actions and life will become exceedingly easy for him. All human actions will then, of course, be tabulated according to these laws, mathematically, like tables of logarithms up to 108,000, and entered in an index; or, better still, there would be published certain edifying works of the nature of encyclopedic lexicons, in which everything will be so clearly calculated and explained that there will be no more incidents or adventures in the world.

Then—this is all what you say—new economic relations will be established, all ready-made and worked out with mathematical exactitude, so that every possible question will vanish in the twinkling of an eye, simply because every possible answer to it will be provided. Then the "Palace of Crystal" will be built. Then . . . In fact, those will be halcyon days. Of course there is no guaranteeing (this is my comment) that it will not be, for instance, frightfully dull then (for what will one have to do when everything will be calculated and tabulated), but on the other hand everything will be extraordinarily rational. Of course boredom may lead you to anything. It is boredom sets one sticking golden pins into people, but all that would not matter. What is bad (this is my comment again) is that I dare say people will be thankful for the gold pins then. Man is stupid, you know, phenomenally stupid; or rather he is not at all stupid, but he is so ungrateful that you could not find another like him in all creation. I, for instance, would not be in the least surprised if all of a sudden, apropos of nothing, in the midst of general prosperity a gentleman with an ignoble, or rather with a reactionary and ironical, countenance were to arise and, putting his arms akimbo, say to us all: "I say, gentleman, hadn't we better kick over the whole show and scatter rationalism to the winds, simply to send these logarithms to the devil, and to enable us to live once more at our own sweet foolish will!" That again would not matter, but what is annoying is that he would be sure to find followers—such is the nature of man. And all that for the most foolish reason, which, one would think, was hardly worth mentioning: that is, that man everywhere and at all times, whoever he may be, has preferred to act as he chose and not in the least as his reason and advantage dictated. And one may choose what is contrary to one's own interests, and sometimes one *positively ought* (that is my idea). One's own free unfettered choice, one's own caprice, however wild it may be, one's own fancy worked up at times to frenzy—is that very "most advantageous advantage" which we have overlooked, which comes under no classification and against which all systems and theories are continually being shattered to atoms. And how do these wiseacres know that man wants a normal, a virtuous choice? What has made them conceive that man must want a rationally advantageous choice? What man wants is simply *independent* choice, whatever that independence may cost and wherever it may lead. And choice, of course, the devil only knows what choice.

VIII

"Ha! ha! ha! But you know there is no such thing as choice in reality, say what you like," you will interpose with a chuckle. "Science has succeeded in so far analyzing man that we know already that choice and what is called freedom of will is nothing else than—"

Stay, gentlemen, I meant to begin with that myself I confess, I was rather frightened. I was just going to say that the devil only knows what choice depends on, and that perhaps that was a very good thing, but I remembered the teaching of science . . . and pulled myself up. And here you have begun upon it. Indeed, if there really is some day discovered a formula for all our desires and caprices—that is, an explanation of what they depend upon, by what laws they arise, how they develop, what they are aiming at in one case and in another and so on, that is a real mathematical formula—then, most likely, man will at once cease to feel desire, indeed, he will be certain to. For who would want to choose by rule? Besides, he will at once be transformed from a human being into an organ-stop or something of the sort; for what is a man without desires, without free will and without choice, if not a stop in an organ? What do you think? Let us reckon the chances—can such a thing happen or not?

"H'm!" you decide. "Our choice is usually mistaken from a false view of our advantage. We sometimes choose absolute nonsense because in our foolishness we see in that nonsense the easiest means for attaining a supposed advantage. But when all that is explained and worked out on paper (which is perfectly possible, for it is contemptible and senseless to suppose that some laws of nature man will never understand), then certainly so-called desires will no longer exist. For if a desire should come into conflict with reason we shall then reason and not desire, because it will be impossible retaining our reason to be *senseless* in our desires, and in that way knowingly act against reason and desire to injure ourselves. And as all choice and reasoning can be really calculated—because there will some day be discovered the laws of our so-called free will—so, joking apart, there may one day be something like a table constructed of them, so that we really shall choose in accordance with it. If, for instance, some day they calculate and prove to me that I made a long nose at someone because I could not help making a long nose at him and that I had to do it in that particular way, what *freedom* is left me, especially if I am a learned man and have taken my degree somewhere? Then I should be able to calculate my whole life for thirty years beforehand. In short, if this could be arranged there would be nothing left for us to do; anyway, we should have to understand that. And, in fact, we ought unwearyingly to repeat to ourselves that at such and such a time and in such and such circumstances nature does not ask our leave; that we have got to take her as she is and not fashion her to suit our fancy, and if we really aspire to formulas and tables of rules, and well, even . . . to the chemical retort, there's no help for it, we must accept the retort too, or else it will be accepted without our consent. . . ."

Yes, but here I come to a stop! Gentlemen, you must excuse me for being over-philosophical; it's the result of forty years underground! Allow me to indulge my fancy. You see, gentlemen, reason is an excellent thing, there's no disputing that, but reason is nothing but reason and satisfies only the rational side of man's nature, while will is a manifestation of the whole life, that is, of the whole human life including reason and all the impulses. And although our life, in this manifestation of it, is often worthless, yet it is life and not simply extracting square roots. Here I, for instance, quite naturally want to live, in order to satisfy all my capacities for life, and not simply my capacity for reasoning, that is, not simply one twentieth of my capacity for life. What does reason know? Reason only knows what it has succeeded in learning (some things, perhaps, it will never learn; this is a poor comfort, but why not say so frankly?) and human nature acts as a whole, with everything that is in it, consciously or unconsciously, and, even if it goes wrong, it lives. I suspect, gentlemen, that you are looking at me with compassion; you tell me again that an enlightened and developed man, such, in short, as the future man will be, cannot consciously desire anything disadvantageous to himself, that that can be proved mathematically. I thoroughly agree, it can—by mathematics. But I repeat for the hundredth time, there is one case, one only, when man may consciously, purposely, desire what is injurious to himself, what is stupid, very stupid—simply in order to have the right to desire for himself even what is very stupid and not to be bound by an obligation to desire only what is sensible. Of course, this very stupid thing, this caprice of ours, may be in reality, gentlemen, more advantageous for us than anything else on earth, especially in certain cases. And in particular it may be more advantageous than any advantage even when it does us obvious harm, and contradicts the soundest conclusions of our reason concerning our advantage—for in any circumstances it preserves for us what is most precious and most important—that is, our personality, our individuality. Some, you see, maintain that this really is the most precious thing for mankind; choice can, of course, if it chooses, be in agreement with reason; and especially if this be not abused but kept within bounds. It is profitable and sometimes even praiseworthy. But very often, and even most often, choice is utterly and stubbornly opposed to reason . . . and . . . and . . . do you know that that, too, is profitable, sometimes even praiseworthy? Gentlemen, let us suppose that man is not stupid. (Indeed one cannot refuse to suppose that, if only from the one consideration, that, if man is stupid, then who is wise?) But if he is not stupid, he is monstrously ungrateful! Phenomenally ungrateful. In fact, I believe that the best definition of man is the ungrateful biped. But that is not all, that is not his worst defect; his worst defect is his perpetual moral obliquity, perpetual—from the days of the Flood to the Schleswig-Holstein period. Moral obliquity and consequently lack of good sense; for it has long been accepted that lack of good sense is due to no other cause than moral obliquity. Put it to the test and cast your eyes upon the history of mankind. What will you see? Is it a grand spectacle? Grand, if you like. Take the Colossus of Rhodes, for instance, that's worth something. With good reason Mr. Anaevsky testifies of it that some say that it is the work of man's hands, while others maintain that it has been created by nature herself. Is it many-colored? May be it is many-colored, too: if one takes the dress uniforms, military and civilian, of all peoples in all ages—that alone is worth something, and if you take the undress uniforms you will never get to the end of it; no historian would be equal to the job. Is it monotonous? May be it's monotonous too: it's fighting and fighting; they are fighting now, they fought first and they fought last—you will admit, that it is almost too monotonous. In short, one may say anything about the history of the world—anything that might enter the most disordered imagination. The only thing one can't say is that it's rational. The very word sticks in one's throat. And, indeed, this is the odd thing that is continually happening: there are continually turning up in life moral and rational persons, sages and lovers of humanity who make it their object to live all their lives as morally and rationally as possible, to be, so to speak, a light to their neighbors simply in order to show them that it is possible to live morally and rationally in this world. And yet we all know that those very people sooner or later have been false to themselves, playing some queer trick, often a most unseemly one. Now I ask you: what can be expected of man since he is a being endowed with strange qualities? Shower upon him every earthly blessing, drown him in a sea of happiness, so that nothing but bubbles of bliss can be seen on the surface; give him economic prosperity, such that he should have nothing else to do but sleep, eat cakes and busy himself with the continuation of his species, and even then out of sheer ingratitude, sheer spite, man would play you some nasty trick. He would even risk his cakes and would deliberately desire the most fatal rubbish, the most uneconomical absurdity, simply to introduce into all this positive good sense his fatal fantastic element. It is just his fantastic dreams, his vulgar folly that he will desire to retain, simply in order to prove to himself—as though that were so necessary—that men still are men and not the keys of a piano, which the laws of nature threaten to control so completely that soon one will be able to desire nothing but by the calendar. And that is not all: even if man really were nothing but a piano-key, even if this were proved to him by natural science and mathematics, even then he would not become reasonable, but would purposely do something perverse out of simple ingratitude, simply to gain his point. And if he does not find means he will contrive destruction and chaos, will contrive sufferings of all sorts, only to gain his point! He will launch a curse upon the world, and as only man can curse (it is his privilege, the primary distinction between him and other animals), may be by his curse alone he will attain his object—that is, convince himself that he is a man and not a piano-key! If you say that all this, too, can be calculated and tabulated—chaos and darkness and curses, so that the mere possibility of calculating it all beforehand would stop it all, and reason would reassert itself, then man would purposely go mad in order to be rid of reason and gain his point! I believe in it, I answer for it, for the whole work of man really seems to consist in nothing but proving to himself every minute that he is a man and not a piano-key! It may be at the cost of his skin, it may be by cannibalism! And this being so, can one help being tempted to rejoice that it has not yet come off, and that desire still depends on something we don't know?

You will scream at me (that is, if you condescend to do so) that no one is touching my free will, that all they are concerned with is that my will should of itself, of its own free will, coincide with my own normal interests, with the laws of nature and arithmetic.

Good heavens, gentlemen, what sort of free will is left when we come to tabulation and arithmetic, when it will all be a case of twice two make four? Twice two makes four without my will. As if free will meant that!

IX

Gentlemen, I am joking, and I know myself that my jokes are not brilliant, but you know one can take everything as a joke. I am, perhaps, jesting against the grain. Gentlemen, I am tormented by questions; answer them for me. You, for instance, want to cure men of their old habits and reform their will in accordance with science and good sense. But how do you know, not only that it is possible, but also that it is *desirable* to reform man in that way? And what leads you to the conclusion that man's inclinations *need* reforming? In short, how do you know that such a reformation will be a benefit to man? And to go to the root of the matter, why are you so positively convinced that not to act against his real normal interests guaranteed by the conclusions of reason and arithmetic is certainly always advantageous for man and must always be a law for mankind? So far, you know, this is only your supposition. It may be the law of logic, but not the law of humanity. You think, gentlemen, perhaps that I am mad? Allow me to defend myself. I agree that man is pre-eminently a creative animal, predestined to strive consciously for an object and to engage in engineering—that is, incessantly and eternally to make new roads, *wherever they may lead*. But the reason why he wants sometimes to go off at a tangent may just be that he is *predestined* to make the road, and perhaps, too, that however stupid the "direct" practical man may be, the thought sometimes will occur to him that the road almost always does lead *somewhere*, and that the destination it leads to is less important than the process of making it, and that the chief thing is to save the well-conducted child from despising engineering, and so giving way to the fatal idleness, which, as we all know, is the mother of all the vices. Man likes to make roads and to create, that is a fact beyond dispute. But why has he such a passionate love for destruction and chaos also? Tell me that! But on that point I want to say a couple of words myself. May it not be that he loves chaos and destruction (there can be no disputing that he does sometimes love it) because he is instinctively afraid of attaining his object and completing the edifice he is constructing? Who knows, perhaps he only loves that edifice from a distance, and is by no means in love with it at close quarters; perhaps he only loves building it and does not want to live in it, but will leave it, when completed, for the use of *les animaux domestiques*—such as the ants, the sheep, and so on. Now the ants have quite a different taste. They have a marvelous edifice of that pattern which endures for ever—the ant-heap.

With the ant-heap the respectable race of ants began and with the ant-heap they will probably end, which does the greatest credit to their perseverance and good sense. But man is a frivolous and incongruous creature, and perhaps, like a chess player, loves the process of the game, not the end of it. And who knows (there is no saying with certainty), perhaps the only goal on earth to which mankind is striving lies in this incessant process of attaining, in other words, in life itself, and not in the thing to be attained, which must always be expressed as a formula, as positive as twice two makes four, and such positiveness is not life, gentlemen, but is the beginning of death. Anyway, man has always been afraid of this mathematical certainty, and I am afraid of it now. Granted that man does nothing but seek that mathematical certainty, he traverses oceans, sacrifices his life in the quest, but to succeed, really to find it, dreads, I assure you. He feels that when he has found it there will be nothing for him to look for. When workmen have finished their work they do at least receive their pay, they go to the tavern, then they are taken to the police-station—and there is occupation for a week. But where can man go? Anyway, one can observe a certain awkwardness about him when he has attained such objects. He loves the process of attaining, but does not quite like to have attained, and that, of course, is very absurd. In fact, man is a comical creature; there seems to be a kind of jest in it all. But yet mathematical certainty is after all, something insufferable. Twice two makes four seems to me simply a piece of insolence. Twice two makes four is a pert coxcomb who stands with arms akimbo barring your path and spitting. I admit that twice two makes four is an excellent thing, but if we are to give everything its due, twice two makes five is sometimes a very charming thing too.

And why are you so firmly, so triumphantly, convinced that only the normal and the positive—in other words, only what is conducive to welfare—is for the advantage of man? Is not reason in error as regards advantage? Does not man, perhaps, love something besides well-being? Perhaps he is just as fond of suffering? Perhaps suffering is just as great a benefit to him as well-being? Man is sometimes extraordinarily, passionately, in love with suffering, and that is a fact. There is no need to appeal to universal history to prove that; only ask yourself, if you are a man and have lived at all. As far as my personal opinion is concerned, to care only for well-being seems to me positively ill-bred. Whether it's good or bad, it is sometimes very pleasant, too, to smash things. I hold no brief for suffering nor for well-being either. I am standing for . . . my caprice, and for its being guaranteed to me when necessary. Suffering would be out of place in vaudevilles, for instance; I know that. In the "Palace of Crystal" it is unthinkable; suffering means doubt, negation, and what would be the good of a "palace of crystal" if there could be any doubt about it? And yet I think man will never renounce real suffering, that is, destruction and chaos. Why, suffering is the sole origin of consciousness. Though I did lay it down at the beginning that consciousness is the greatest misfortune for man, yet I know man prizes it and would not give it up for any satisfaction. Consciousness, for instance, is infinitely superior to twice two makes four. Once you have mathematical certainty there is nothing left to do or to understand. There will be nothing left but to bottle up your five senses and plunge into contemplation. While if you stick to consciousness, even though the same result is attained, you can at least flog your-

self at times, and that will, at any rate, liven you up. Reactionary as it is, corporal punishment is better than nothing.

X

You believe in a palace of crystal that can never be destroyed—a palace at which one will not be able to put out
one's tongue or make a long nose on the sly. And perhaps
that is just why I am afraid of this edifice, that it is of crystal
and can never be destroyed and that one cannot put one's
tongue out at it even on the sly.

You see, if it were not a palace, but a hen-house, I might
creep into it to avoid getting wet, and yet I would not call the
hen-house a palace out of gratitude to it for keeping me dry.
You laugh and say that in such circumstances a hen-house is
as good as a mansion. Yes, I answer, if one had to live simply
to keep out of the rain.

But what is to be done if I have taken it into my head that
that is not the only object in life, and that if one must live one
had better live in a mansion? That is my choice, my desire.
You will only eradicate it when you have changed my preference. Well, do change it, allure me with something else, give
me another ideal. But meanwhile I will not take a hen-house
for a mansion. The palace of crystal may be an idle dream, it
may be that it is inconsistent with the laws of nature and that
I have invented it only through my own stupidity, through
the old-fashioned irrational habits of my generation. But
what does it matter to me that it is inconsistent? That makes
no difference since it exists in my desires, or rather exists as
long as my desires exist. Perhaps you are laughing again?
Laugh away; I will put up with any mockery rather than pretend that I am satisfied when I am hungry. I know, anyway,
that I will not be put off with a compromise, with a recurring
zero, simply because it is consistent with the laws of nature
and actually exists. I will not accept as the crown of my desires a block of buildings with tenements for the poor on a

lease of a thousand years, and perhaps with a sign-board of a dentist hanging out. Destroy my desires, eradicate my ideals, show me something better, and I will follow you. You will say, perhaps, that it is not worth your trouble; but in that case I can give you the same answer. We are discussing things seriously; but if you won't deign to give me your attention, I will drop your acquaintance. I can retreat into my underground hole.

But while I am alive and have desires I would rather my hand were withered off than bring one brick to such a building! Don't remind me that I have just rejected the palace of crystal for the sole reason that one cannot put out one's tongue at it. I did not say because I am so fond of putting my tongue out. Perhaps the thing I resented was, that of all your edifices there has not been one at which one could not put out one's tongue. On the contrary, I would let my tongue be cut off out of gratitude if things could be so arranged that I should lose all desire to put it out. It is not my fault that things cannot be so arranged, and that one must be satisfied with model flats. Then why am I made with such desires? Can I have been constructed simply in order to come to the conclusion that all my construction is a cheat? Can this be my whole purpose? I do not believe it.

But do you know what: I am convinced that we underground folk ought to be kept on a curb. Though we may sit forty years underground without speaking, when we do come out into the light of day and break out we talk and talk and talk. . . .

XI

The long and the short of it is, gentlemen, that it is better to do nothing! Better conscious inertia! And so hurrah for underground! Though I have said that I envy the normal man to the last drop of my bile, yet I should not care to be in his place such as he is now (though I shall not cease envying him).

No, no; anyway the underground life is more advantageous. There, at any rate, one can . . . Oh, but even now I am lying! I am lying because I know myself that it is not underground that is better, but something different, quite different, for which I am thirsting, but which I cannot find! Damn underground!

I will tell you another thing that would be better, and that is, if I myself believed in anything of what I have just written. I swear to you, gentlemen, there is not one thing, not one word of what I have written that I really believe. That is, I believe it, perhaps, but at the same time I feel and suspect that I am lying like a cobbler.

"Then why have you written all this?" you will say to me. "I ought to put you underground for forty years without anything to do and then come to you in your cellar, to find out what stage you have reached! How can a man be left with nothing to do for forty years?"

"Isn't that shameful, isn't that humiliating?" you will say, perhaps, wagging your heads contemptuously. "You thirst for life and try to settle the problems of life by a logical tangle. And how persistent, how insolent are your sallies, and at the same time what a scare you are in! You talk nonsense and are pleased with it; you say impudent things and are in continual alarm and apologising for them. You declare that you are afraid of nothing and at the same time try to ingratiate yourself in our good opinion. You declare that you are gnashing your teeth and at the same time you try to be witty so as to amuse us. You know that your witticisms are not witty, but you are evidently well satisfied with their literary value. You may, perhaps, have really suffered, but you have no respect for your own suffering. You may have sincerity, but you have no modesty; out of the pettiest vanity you expose your sincerity to publicity and ignominy. You doubtlessly mean to say something, but hide your last word through fear, because you have not the resolution to utter it, and only have a cowardly impudence. You boast of consciousness, but you are not sure of your ground, for though your mind works, yet your heart is darkened and corrupt, and you cannot have a full, genuine consciousness without a pure heart. And how intrusive you are, how you insist and grimace! Lies, lies, lies!"

Of course I have myself made up all the things you say. That, too, is from underground. I have been for forty years listening to you through a crack under the floor. I have invented them myself, there was nothing else I could invent. It is no wonder that I have learned it by heart and it has taken a literary form. . . .

But can you really be so credulous as to think that I will print all this and give it to you to read too? And another problem: why do I call you "gentlemen," why do I address you as though you really were my readers? Such confessions as I intend to make are never printed nor given to other people to read. Anyway, I am not strong-minded enough for that, and I don't see why I should be. But you see a fancy has occurred to me and I want to realize it at all costs. Let me explain.

Every man has reminiscences which he would not tell to everyone, but only to his friends. He has other matters in his mind which he would not reveal even to his friends, but only to himself, and that in secret. But there are other things which a man is afraid to tell even to himself, and every decent man has a number of such things stored away in his mind. The more decent he is, the greater the number of such things in his mind. Anyway, I have only lately determined to remember some of my early adventures. Till now I have always avoided them, even with a certain uneasiness. Now, when I am not only recalling them, but have actually decided to write an account of them, I want to try the experiment whether one can, even with oneself, be perfectly open and not take fright at the whole truth. I will observe, in parenthesis, that Heine says that a true autobiography is almost an impossibility, and that man is bound to lie about himself. He considers that

Rousseau certainly told lies about himself in his confessions, and even intentionally lied, out of vanity. I am convinced that Heine is right; I quite understand how sometimes one may, out of sheer vanity, attribute regular crimes to oneself, and indeed I can very well conceive that kind of vanity. But Heine judged of people who made their confessions to the public. I write only for myself, and I wish to declare once and for all that if I write as though I were addressing readers, that is simply because it is easier for me to write in that form. It is a form, an empty form—I shall never have readers. I have made this plain already . . .

I don't wish to be hampered by any restrictions in the compilation of my notes. I shall not attempt any system or method. I will jot things down as I remember them.

But here, perhaps, someone will catch at the word and ask me: if you really don't reckon on readers, why do you make such compacts with yourself—and on paper too—that is, that you won't attempt any system or method, that you jot things down as you remember them, and so on, and so on? Why are you explaining? Why do you apologize?

Well, there it is, I answer.

There is a whole psychology in all this, though. Perhaps it is simply that I am a coward. And perhaps that I purposely imagine an audience before me in order that I may be more dignified while I write. There are perhaps thousands of reasons. Again, what is my object precisely in writing? If it is not for the benefit of the public why should I not simply recall these incidents in my own mind without putting them on paper?

Quite so; but yet it is more imposing on paper. There is something more impressive in it; I shall be better able to criticize myself and improve my style. Besides, I shall perhaps obtain actual relief from writing. Today, for instance, I am particularly oppressed by one memory of a distant past. It came back vividly to my mind a few days ago, and has remained haunting me like an annoying tune that one cannot get rid of. And yet I must get rid of it somehow. I have hundreds of such reminiscences; but at times some one stands out from the hundred and oppresses me. For some reason I believe that if I write it down I should get rid of it. Why not try?

Besides, I am bored, and I never have anything to do. Writing will be a sort of work. They say work makes man kind-hearted and honest. Well, here is a chance for me, anyway.

Snow is falling today, yellow and dingy. It fell yesterday, too, and a few days ago. I fancy it is the wet snow that has reminded me of that incident which I cannot shake off now. And so let it be a story *apropos* of the falling snow.

Part II
Apropos of the Wet Snow

When from dark error's subjugation
My words of passionate exhortation
  Had wrenched thy fainting spirit free;
And writhing prone in thine affliction
Thou didst recall with malediction
  The vice that had encompassed thee:
And when thy slumbering conscience, fretting
  By recollection's torturing flame,
Thou didst reveal the hideous setting
  Of thy life's current ere I came:
When suddenly I saw thee sicken,
  And weeping, hide thine anguished face,
Revolted, maddened, horror-stricken,
  At memories of foul disgrace.

NEKRASSOV
(translated by Juliet Soskice).

I

At that time I was only twenty-four. My life was even then gloomy, ill-regulated, and as solitary as that of a savage. I made friends with no one and positively avoided talking, and buried myself more and more in my hole. At work in the office I never looked at anyone, and was perfectly well aware that my companions looked upon me, not only as a queer fellow, but even looked upon me—I always fancied this—with a sort of loathing. I sometimes wondered why it was that nobody except me fancied that he was looked upon with aversion? One of the clerks had a most repulsive, pock-marked face, which looked positively villainous. I believe I should not have dared to look at anyone with such an unsightly countenance. Another had such a very dirty old uniform that there was an unpleasant odor in his proximity. Yet not one of these gentlemen showed the slightest self-consciousness—either about their clothes or their countenance or their character in any way. Neither of them ever imagined that they were looked at with repulsion; if they had imagined it they would not have minded—so long as their superiors did not look at them in that way. It is clear to me now that, owing to my unbounded vanity and to the high standard I set for myself, I often looked at myself with furious discontent, which verged on loathing, and so I inwardly attributed the same feeling to everyone. I hated my face, for instance: I thought it disgusting, and even suspected that there was something base in my expression, and so every day when I turned up at the office I tried to behave as independently as possible, and to assume a lofty expression, so that I might not be suspected of being abject. "My face may be ugly," I thought, "but let it be lofty, expressive, and, above all, *extremely* intelligent." But I was positively and painfully certain that it was impossible for my countenance ever to express those qualities. And what was worst of all, I thought it actually stupid looking, and I would have been quite satisfied if I could have looked intelligent. In fact, I would even have put up with looking base if, at the same time, my face could have been thought strikingly intelligent.

Of course, I hated my fellow clerks one and all, and I despised them all, yet at the same time I was, as it were, afraid of them. In fact, it happened at times that I thought more highly of them than of myself. It somehow happened quite suddenly that I alternated between despising them and thinking them superior to myself. A cultivated and decent man cannot be vain without setting a fearfully high standard for himself, and without despising and almost hating himself at certain moments. But whether I despised them or thought them superior I dropped my eyes almost every time I met anyone. I

even made experiments whether I could face so and so's looking at me, and I was always the first to drop my eyes. This
worried me to distraction. I had a sickly dread, too, of being
ridiculous, and so had a slavish passion for the conventional
in everything external. I loved to fall into the common rut,
and had a whole-hearted terror of any kind of eccentricity in
myself. But how could I live up to it? I was morbidly sensitive
as a man of our age should be. They were all stupid, and as
like one another as so many sheep. Perhaps I was the only one
in the office who fancied that I was a coward and a slave, and
I fancied it just because I was more highly developed. But it
was not only that I fancied it, it really was so. I was a coward
and a slave. I say this without the slightest embarrassment.
Every decent man of our age must be a coward and a slave.
That is his normal condition. Of that I am firmly persuaded.
He is made and constructed to that very end. And not only at
the present time owing to some casual circumstances, but always, at all times, a decent man is bound to be a coward and a
slave. It is the law of nature for all decent people all over the
earth. If anyone of them happens to be valiant about something, he need not be comforted nor carried away by that; he
would show the white feather just the same before something
else. That is how it invariably and inevitably ends. Only don-
keys and mules are valiant, and they only till they are pushed
up to the wall. It is not worth while to pay attention to them
for they really are of no consequence.

Another circumstance, too, worried me in those days: that
there was no one like me and I was unlike anyone else. "I am
alone and they are *everyone*," I thought—and pondered.

From that it is evident that I was still a youngster.

The very opposite sometimes happened. It was loathsome
sometimes to go to the office; things reached such a point
that I often came home ill. But all at once, *a propos* of nothing,
there would come a phase of skepticism and indifference
(everything happened in phases to me), and I would laugh

myself at my intolerance and fastidiousness, I would reproach myself with being *romantic*. At one time I was unwilling to speak to anyone, while at other times I would not only talk, but go to the length of contemplating making friends with them. All my fastidiousness would suddenly, for no rhyme or reason, vanish. Who knows, perhaps I never had really had it, and it had simply been affected, and got out of books. I have not decided that question even now. Once I quite made friends with them, visited their homes, played preference, drank vodka, talked of promotions. . . . But here let me make a digression.

We Russians, speaking generally, have never had those foolish transcendental "romantics"—German, and still more French—on whom nothing produces any effect; if there were an earthquake, if all France perished at the barricades, they would still be the same, they would not even have the decency to affect a change, but would still go on singing their transcendental songs to the hour of their death, because they are fools. We, in Russia, have no fools; that is well known. That is what distinguishes us from foreign lands. Consequently these transcendental natures are not found amongst us in their pure form. The idea that they are is due to our "realistic" journalists and critics of that day, always on the look out for Kostanzhoglos and Uncle Pyotr Ivanitchs and foolishly accepting them as our ideal; they have slandered our romantics, taking them for the same transcendental sort as in Germany or France. On the contrary, the characteristics of our "romantics" are absolutely and directly opposed to the transcendental European type, and no European standard can be applied to them. (Allow me to make use of this word "romantic"—an old-fashioned and much respected word which has done good service and is familiar to all.) The characteristics of our romantic are to understand everything, *to see everything and to see it often incomparably more clearly than our most realistic minds see it*; to refuse to accept anyone or anything, but at the same time not to despise anything; to give way, to yield, from policy; never to lose sight of a useful practical object (such as rent-free quarters at the government expense, pensions, decorations), to keep their eye on that object through all the enthusiasms and volumes of lyrical poems, and at the same time to preserve "the sublime and the beautiful" inviolate within them to the hour of their death, and to preserve themselves also, incidentally, like some precious jewel wrapped in cotton wool if only for the benefit of "the sublime and the beautiful." Our "romantic" is a man of great breadth and the greatest rogue of all our rogues, I assure you. . . . I can assure you from experience, indeed. Of course, that is, if he is intelligent. But what am I saying! The romantic is always intelligent, and I only meant to observe that although we have had foolish romantics they don't count, and they were only so because in the flower of their youth they degenerated into Germans, and to preserve their precious jewel more comfortably, settled somewhere out there—by preference in Weimar or the Black Forest.

I, for instance, genuinely despised my official work and did not openly abuse it simply because I was in it myself and got a salary for it. Anyway, take note, I did not openly abuse it. Our romantic would rather go out of his mind—a thing, however, which very rarely happens—than take to open abuse, unless he had some other career in view; and he is never kicked out. At most, they would take him to the lunatic asylum as "the King of Spain" if he should go very mad. But it is only the thin, fair people who go out of their minds in Russia. Innumerable "romantics" attain later in life to considerable rank in the service. Their many-sidedness is remarkable! And what a faculty they have for the most contradictory sensations! I was comforted by this thought even in those days, and I am of the same opinion now. That is why there are so many "broad natures" among us who never lose their ideal even in the depths of degradation; and though they never stir a finger for their ideal, though they are arrant thieves and knaves, yet they tearfully cherish their first ideal and are extraordinarily honest at heart. Yes, it is only among us that the most incorrigible rogue can be absolutely and loftily honest at heart without in the least ceasing to be a rogue. I repeat, our romantics, frequently, become such accomplished rascals (I use the term "rascals" affectionately), suddenly display such a sense of reality and practical knowledge that their bewildered superiors and the public generally can only ejaculate in amazement.

Their many-sidedness is really amazing, and goodness knows what it may develop into later on, and what the future has in store for us. It is not a poor material! I do not say this from any foolish or boastful patriotism. But I feel sure that you are again imagining that I am joking. Or perhaps it's just the contrary and you are convinced that I really think so. Anyway, gentlemen, I shall welcome both views as an honor and a special favor. And do forgive my digression.

I did not, of course, maintain friendly relations with my comrades and soon was at loggerheads with them, and in my youth and inexperience I even gave up bowing to them, as though I had cut off all relations. That, however, only happened to me once. As a rule, I was always alone.

In the first place I spent most of my time at home, reading. I tried to stifle all that was continually seething within me by means of external impressions. And the only external means I had was reading. Reading, of course, was a great help—exciting me, giving me pleasure and pain. But at times it bored me fearfully. One longed for movement in spite of everything, and I plunged all at once into dark, underground, loathsome vice of the pettiest kind. My wretched passions were acute, smarting, from my continual, sickly irritability I had hysterical impulses, with tears and convulsions. I had no resource except reading, that is, there was nothing in my surroundings which I could respect and which attracted me. I was overwhelmed with depression, too; I had an hysterical craving for incongruity and for contrast, and so I took to vice. I have not said all this to justify myself. . . . But, no! I am lying. I did want to justify myself. I make that little observation for my own benefit, gentlemen. I don't want to lie. I vowed to myself I would not.

And so, furtively, timidly, in solitude, at night, I indulged in filthy vice, with a feeling of shame which never deserted me, even at the most loathsome moments, and which at such moments nearly made me curse. Already even then I had my underground world in my soul. I was fearfully afraid of being seen, of being met, of being recognized. I visited various obscure haunts.

One night as I was passing a tavern I saw through a lighted window some gentlemen fighting with billiard cues, and saw one of them thrown out of the window. At other times I should have felt very much disgusted, but I was in such a mood at the time, that I actually envied the gentleman thrown out of the window—and I envied him so much that I even went into the tavern and into the billiard-room. "Perhaps," I thought, "I'll have a fight, too, and they'll throw me out of the window."

I was not drunk—but what is one to do—depression will drive a man to such a pitch of hysteria? But nothing happened. It seemed that I was not even equal to being thrown out of the window and I went away without having my fight.

An officer put me in my place from the first moment.

I was standing by the billiard-table and in my ignorance blocking up the way, and he wanted to pass; he took me by the shoulders and without a word—without a warning or explanation—moved me from where I was standing to another spot and passed by as though he had not noticed me. I could have forgiven blows, but I could not forgive his having moved me without noticing me.

Devil knows what I would have given for a real regular quarrel—a more decent, a more *literary* one, so to speak. I had been treated like a fly. This officer was over six foot, while I was a spindly little fellow. But the quarrel was in my hands. I had only to protest and I certainly would have been thrown out of the window. But I changed my mind and preferred to beat a resentful retreat.

I went out of the tavern straight home, confused and troubled, and the next night I went out again with the same lewd intentions, still more furtively, abjectly and miserably than before, as it were, with tears in my eyes—but still I did go out again. Don't imagine, though, it was cowardice made me slink away from the officer; I never have been a coward at heart, though I have always been a coward in action. Don't be in a hurry to laugh—I assure you I can explain it all.

Oh, if only that officer had been one of the sort who would consent to fight a duel! But no, he was one of those gentlemen (alas, long extinct!) who preferred fighting with cues or, like Gogol's Lieutenant Pirogov, appealing to the police. They did not fight duels and would have thought a duel with a civilian like me an utterly unseemly procedure in any case—and they looked upon the duel altogether as something impossible, something free-thinking and French. But they were quite ready to bully, especially when they were over six foot.

I did not slink away through cowardice, but through an unbounded vanity. I was afraid not of his six foot, not of getting a sound thrashing and being thrown out of the window; I should have had physical courage enough, I assure you; but I had not the moral courage. What I was afraid of was that everyone present, from the insolent marker down to the lowest little stinking, pimply clerk in a greasy collar, would jeer at me and fail to understand when I began to protest and to address them in literary language. For of the point of honor—not of honor, but of the point of honor (*point d'honneur*)—one cannot speak among us except in literary language. You can't allude to the "point of honor" in ordinary language. I was fully convinced (the sense of reality, in spite of all my romanticism!) that they would all simply split their sides with laughter, and that the officer would not simply beat me, that is, without insulting me, but would certainly prod me in the back with his knee, kick me round the billiard-table, and only then perhaps have pity and drop me out of the window.

Of course, this trivial incident could not with me end in that. I often met that officer afterwards in the street and noticed him very carefully. I am not quite sure whether he recognized me, I imagine not; I judge from certain signs. But I—I stared at him with spite and hatred and so it went on . . . for several years! My resentment grew even deeper with years. At first I began making stealthy inquiries about this officer. It was difficult for me to do so, for I knew no one. But one day I heard someone shout his surname in the street as I was following him at a distance, as though I were tied to him—and so I learnt his surname. Another time I followed him to his flat, and for ten kopecks learned from the porter where he lived, on which storey, whether he lived alone or with others, and so on—in fact, everything one could learn from a porter. One morning, though I had never tried my hand with the pen, it suddenly occurred to me to write a satire on this officer in the form of a novel which would unmask his villainy. I wrote the novel with relish. I did unmask his villainy, I even exaggerated it; at first I so altered his surname that it could easily be recognized, but on second thoughts I changed it, and sent the story to the *Otetchestvenniya Zapiski*. But at that time such attacks were not the fashion and my story was not printed. That was a great vexation to me.

Sometimes I was positively choked with resentment. At last I determined to challenge my enemy to a duel. I composed a splendid, charming letter to him, imploring him to apologize to me, and hinting rather plainly at a duel in case of refusal. The letter was so composed that if the officer had had the least understanding of the sublime and the beautiful he would certainly have flung himself on my neck and have offered me his friendship. And how fine that would have been! How we should have got on together! "He could have shielded me with his higher rank, while I could have improved his mind with my culture, and, well . . . my ideas, and all sorts of things might have happened." Only fancy, this was two years after his insult to me, and my challenge would have been a ridiculous anachronism, in spite of all the ingenuity of my letter in disguising and explaining away the anachronism. But, thank God (to this day I thank the Almighty with tears in my eyes) I did not send the letter to him. Cold shivers run down my back when I think of what might have happened if I had sent it.

And all at once I revenged myself in the simplest way, by a stroke of genius! A brilliant thought suddenly dawned upon me. Sometimes on holidays I used to stroll along the sunny side of the Nevsky about four o'clock in the afternoon. Though it was hardly a stroll so much as a series of innumerable miseries, humiliations and resentments; but no doubt that was just what I wanted. I used to wriggle along in a most unseemly fashion, like an eel, continually moving aside to make way for generals, for officers of the guards and the hussars, or for ladies. At such minutes there used to be a convulsive twinge at my heart, and I used to feel hot all down my back at the mere thought of the wretchedness of my attire, of the wretchedness and abjectness of my little scurrying figure. This was a regular martyrdom, a continual, intolerable humiliation at the thought, which passed into an incessant and direct sensation, that I was a mere fly in the eyes of all this world, a nasty, disgusting fly—more intelligent, more highly developed, more refined in feeling than any of them, of course—but a fly that was continually making way for everyone, insulted and injured by everyone. Why I inflicted this torture upon myself, why I went to the Nevsky, I don't know. I felt simply drawn there at every possible opportunity.

Already then I began to experience a rush of the enjoyment of which I spoke in the first chapter. After my affair with the officer I felt even more drawn there than before: it was on the Nevsky that I met him most frequently, there I could admire him. He, too, went there chiefly on holidays, He, too, turned out of his path for generals and persons of high rank, and he too, wriggled between them like an eel; but people, like me, or even better dressed than me, he simply walked over; he made straight for them as though there was nothing but empty space before him, and never, under any circumstances, turned aside. I gloated over my resentment watching him and . . . always resentfully made way for him. It exasperated me that even in the street I could not be on an even footing with him.

"Why must you invariably be the first to move aside?" I kept asking myself in hysterical rage, waking up sometimes at three o'clock in the morning. "Why is it you and not he? There's no regulation about it; there's no written law. Let the making way be equal as it usually is when refined people meet; he moves half-way and you move half-way; you pass with mutual respect."

But that never happened, and I always moved aside, while he did not even notice my making way for him. And lo and behold a bright idea dawned upon me! "What," I thought, "if I meet him and don't move on one side? What if I don't move aside on purpose, even if I knock up against him? How would that be?" This audacious idea took such a hold on me that it gave me no peace. I was dreaming of it continually, horribly, and I purposely went more frequently to the Nevsky in order to picture more vividly how I should do it when I did do it. I was delighted. This intention seemed to me more and more practical and possible.

"Of course I shall not really push him," I thought, already more good-natured in my joy. "I will simply not turn aside, will run up against him, not very violently, but just shouldering each other—just as much as decency permits. I will push against him just as much as he pushes against me." At last I made up my mind completely. But my preparations took a great deal of time. To begin with, when I carried out my plan I should need to be looking rather more decent, and so I had to think of my get-up. "In case of emergency, if, for instance, there were any sort of public scandal (and the public there is of the most *recherche*: the Countess walks there; Prince D. walks there; all the literary world is there), I must be well dressed; that inspires respect and of itself puts us on an equal footing in the eyes of the society."

With this object I asked for some of my salary in advance, and bought at Tchurkin's a pair of black gloves and a decent hat. Black gloves seemed to me both more dignified and *bon ton* than the lemon-colored ones which I had contemplated at first. "The color is too gaudy, it looks as though one were trying to be conspicuous," and I did not take the lemon-colored ones. I had got ready long beforehand a good shirt, with white bone studs; my overcoat was the only thing that held me back. The coat in itself was a very good one, it kept me warm; but it was wadded and it had a raccoon collar which was the height of vulgarity. I had to change the collar at any sacrifice, and to have a beaver one like an officer's. For this purpose I began visiting the Gostiny Dvor and after several attempts I pitched upon a piece of cheap German beaver. Though these German beavers soon grow shabby and look wretched, yet at first they look exceedingly well, and I only needed it for the occasion. I asked the price; even so, it was too expensive. After thinking it over thoroughly I decided to sell my raccoon collar. The rest of the money—a considerable sum for me, I decided to borrow from Anton Antonitch Syetotchkin, my immediate superior, an unassuming person, though grave and judicious. He never lent money to anyone, but I had, on entering the service, been specially recommended to him by an important personage who had got me my berth. I was horribly worried. To borrow from Anton Antonitch seemed to me monstrous and shameful. I did not sleep for two or three nights. Indeed, I did not sleep well at that time, I was in a fever; I had a vague sinking at my heart or else a sudden throbbing, throbbing, throbbing! Anton Antonitch was surprised at first, then he frowned, then he reflected, and did after all lend me the money, receiving from me a written authorization to take from my salary a fortnight later the sum that he had lent me.

In this way everything was at last ready. The handsome beaver replaced the mean-looking raccoon, and I began by degrees to get to work. It would never have done to act off-hand, at random; the plan had to be carried out skillfully, by degrees. But I must confess that after many efforts I began to despair: we simply could not run into each other. I made every preparation, I was quite determined—it seemed as though we should run into one another directly—and before I knew what I was doing I had stepped aside for him again and he had passed without noticing me. I even prayed as I approached him that God would grant me determination. One time I had made up my mind thoroughly, but it ended in my stumbling and falling at his feet because at the very last instant when I was six inches from him my courage failed me. He very calmly stepped over me, while I flew on one side like a ball. That night I was ill again, feverish and delirious.

And suddenly it ended most happily. The night before I had made up my mind not to carry out my fatal plan and to abandon it all, and with that object I went to the Nevsky for the last time, just to see how I would abandon it all. Suddenly, three paces from my enemy, I unexpectedly made up my mind—I closed my eyes, and we ran full tilt, shoulder to shoulder, against one another! I did not budge an inch and passed him on a perfectly equal footing! He did not even look round and pretended not to notice it; but he was only pretending, I am convinced of that. I am convinced of that to this day! Of course, I got the worst of it—he was stronger, but that was not the point. The point was that I had attained my object, I had kept up my dignity, I had not yielded a step, and had put myself publicly on an equal social footing with him. I returned home feeling that I was fully avenged for everything. I was delighted. I was triumphant and sang Italian arias. Of course, I will not describe to you what happened to me three days later; if you have read my first chapter you can guess for yourself. The officer was afterwards transferred; I have not seen him now for fourteen years. What is the dear fellow doing now? Whom is he walking over?

II

But the period of my dissipation would end and I always felt very sick afterwards. It was followed by remorse—I tried to drive it away; I felt too sick. By degrees, however, I grew used to that too. I grew used to everything, or rather I voluntarily resigned myself to enduring it. But I had a means of escape that reconciled everything—that was to find refuge in "the sublime and the beautiful," in dreams, of course. I was a terrible dreamer, I would dream for three months on end, tucked away in my corner, and you may believe me that at those moments I had no resemblance to the gentleman who, in the perturbation of his chicken heart, put a collar of German beaver on his great-coat. I suddenly became a hero. I would not have admitted my six-foot lieutenant even if he had called on me. I could not even picture him before me then. What were my dreams and how I could satisfy myself with them—it is hard to say now, but at the time I was satisfied with them. Though, indeed, even now, I am to some extent satisfied with them. Dreams were particularly sweet and vivid after a spell of dissipation; they came with remorse and with tears, with curses and transports. There were moments of such positive intoxication, of such happiness, that there was not the faintest trace of irony within me, on my honour. I had faith, hope, love. I believed blindly at such times that by some miracle, by some external circumstance, all this would suddenly open out, expand; that suddenly a vista of suitable activity—beneficent, good, and, above all, *ready made* (what sort of activity I had no idea, but the great thing was that it should be all ready for me)—would rise up before me—and I should come out into the light of day, almost riding a white horse and crowned with laurel. Anything but the foremost place I could not conceive for myself, and for that very reason I quite contentedly occupied the lowest in reality. Either to be a hero or to grovel in the mud—there was nothing between. That was my ruin, for when I was in the mud I comforted myself with the thought that at other times I was a hero, and the hero was a cloak for the mud: for an ordinary man it was shameful to defile himself, but a hero was too lofty to be utterly defiled, and so he might defile himself. It is worth noting that these attacks of the "sublime and the beautiful" visited me even during the period of dissipation and just at the times when I was touching the bottom. They came in separate spurts, as though reminding me of themselves, but did not banish the dissipation by their appearance. On the contrary, they seemed to add a zest to it by contrast, and were only sufficiently present to serve as an appetizing sauce. That sauce was made up of contradictions and sufferings, of agonizing inward analysis, and all these pangs and pin-pricks gave a certain piquancy, even a significance to my dissipation—in fact, completely answered the purpose of an appetizing sauce. There was a certain depth of meaning in it. And I could hardly have resigned myself to the simple, vulgar, direct debauchery of a clerk and have endured all the filthiness of it. What could have allured me about it then and have drawn me at night into the street? No, I had a lofty way of getting out of it all.

And what loving-kindness, oh Lord, what loving-kindness I felt at times in those dreams of mine! in those "flights into the sublime and the beautiful"; though it was fantastic love, though it was never applied to anything human in reality, yet there was so much of this love that one did not feel afterwards even the impulse to apply it in reality; that would have been superfluous. Everything, however, passed satisfactorily by a lazy and fascinating transition into the sphere of art, that is, into the beautiful forms of life, lying ready, largely stolen from the poets and novelists and adapted to all sorts of needs and uses. I, for instance, was triumphant over everyone; everyone, of course, was in dust and ashes, and was forced spontaneously to recognize my superiority, and I forgave them all. I was a poet and a grand gentleman, I fell in love; I came in for countless millions and immediately devoted them to humanity, and at the same time I confessed before all the people my shameful deeds, which, of course, were not merely shameful, but had in them much that was "sublime and beautiful" something in the Manfred style. Everyone would kiss me and weep (what idiots they would be if they did not), while I should go barefoot and hungry preaching new ideas and fighting a victorious Austerlitz against the obscurantists. Then the band would play a march, an amnesty would be declared, the Pope would agree to retire from Rome to Brazil; then there would be a ball for the whole of Italy at the Villa Borghese on the shores of Lake Como, Lake Como being for that purpose transferred to the neighborhood of Rome; then would come a scene in the bushes, and so on, and so on—as though you did not know all about it? You will say that it is vulgar and contemptible to drag all this into public after all the tears and transports which I have myself confessed. But why is it contemptible? Can you imagine that I am ashamed of it all, and that it was stupider than anything in your life, gentlemen? And I can assure you that some of these fancies were by no means badly composed. . . . It did not all happen on the shores of Lake Como. And yet you are right—it really is vulgar and contemptible. And most contemptible of all it is that now I am attempting to justify myself to you. And even more contemptible than that is my making this remark now. But that's enough, or there will be no end to it; each step will be more contemptible than the last. . . .

I could never stand more than three months of dreaming at a time without feeling an irresistible desire to plunge into society. To plunge into society meant to visit my superior at the office, Anton Antonitch Syetotchkin. He was the only permanent acquaintance I have had in my life, and I wonder at the fact myself now. But I only went to see him when that phase came over me, and when my dreams had reached such a point of bliss that it became essential at once to embrace my fellows and all mankind; and for that purpose I needed, at least, one human being, actually existing. I had to call on Anton Antonitch, however, on Tuesday—his at-home day; so I had always to time my passionate desire to embrace humanity so that it might fall on a Tuesday.

This Anton Antonitch lived on the fourth storey in a house in Five Corners, in four low-pitched rooms, one smaller than the other, of a particularly frugal and sallow appearance. He had two daughters and their aunt, who used to pour out the tea. Of the daughters one was thirteen and another fourteen, they both had snub noses, and I was awfully shy of them because they were always whispering and giggling together. The master of the house usually sat in his study on a leather couch in front of the table with some grey-headed gentleman, usually a colleague from our office or some other department. I never saw more than two or three visitors there, always the same. They talked about the excise duty; about business in the senate, about salaries, about promotions, about His Excellency, and the best means of pleasing him, and so on. I had the patience to sit like a fool beside these people for four hours at a stretch, listening to them without knowing what to say to them or venturing to say a word. I became stupefied, several times I felt myself perspiring, I was overcome by a sort of paralysis; but this was pleasant and good for me. On returning home I deferred for a time my desire to embrace all mankind.

I had however one other acquaintance of a sort, Simonov, who was an old schoolfellow. I had a number of schoolfellows, indeed, in Petersburg, but I did not associate with them and had even given up nodding to them in the street. I believe I had transferred into the department I was in simply to avoid their company and to cut off all connection with my hateful childhood. Curses on that school and all those terrible years of penal servitude! In short, I parted from my schoolfellows as soon as I got out into the world. There were two or three left to whom I nodded in the street. One of them was Simonov, who had in no way been distinguished at school, was of a quiet and equable disposition; but I discovered in him a certain independence of character and even honesty I don't even suppose that he was particularly stupid. I had at one time spent some rather soulful moments with him, but these had not lasted long and had somehow been suddenly clouded over. He was evidently uncomfortable at these reminiscences, and was, I fancy, always afraid that I might take up the same tone again. I suspected that he had an aversion for me, but still I went on going to see him, not being quite certain of it.

And so on one occasion, unable to endure my solitude and knowing that as it was Thursday Anton Antonitch's door would be closed, I thought of Simonov. Climbing up to his fourth storey I was thinking that the man disliked me and that it was a mistake to go and see him. But as it always happened that such reflections impelled me, as though purposely, to put myself into a false position, I went in. It was almost a year since I had last seen Simonov.

III

I found two of my old schoolfellows with him. They seemed to be discussing an important matter. All of them took scarcely any notice of my entrance, which was strange, for I had not met them for years. Evidently they looked upon me as something on the level of a common fly. I had not been treated like that even at school, though they all hated me. I knew, of course, that they must despise me now for my lack of success in the service, and for my having let myself sink so low, going about badly dressed and so on—which seemed to them a sign of my incapacity and insignificance. But I had not expected such contempt. Simonov was positively surprised at my turning up. Even in old days he had always seemed surprised at my coming. All this disconcerted me: I sat down, feeling rather miserable, and began listening to what they were saying.

They were engaged in warm and earnest conversation about a farewell dinner which they wanted to arrange for the next day to a comrade of theirs called Zverkov, an officer in the army, who was going away to a distant province. This Zverkov had been all the time at school with me too. I had begun to hate him particularly in the upper forms. In the lower forms he had simply been a pretty, playful boy whom everybody liked. I had hated him, however, even in the lower forms, just because he was a pretty and playful boy. He was always bad at his lessons and got worse and worse as he went on; however, he left with a good certificate, as he had powerful interests. During his last year at school he came in for an estate of two hundred serfs, and as almost all of us were poor he took up a swaggering tone among us. He was vulgar in the extreme, but at the same time he was a good-natured fellow, even in his swaggering. In spite of superficial, fantastic and sham notions of honor and dignity, all but very few of us positively groveled before Zverkov, and the more so the more he swaggered. And it was not from any interested motive that they groveled, but simply because he had been favored by the gifts of nature. Moreover, it was, as it were, an accepted idea among us that Zverkov was a specialist in regard to tact and the social graces. This last fact particularly infuriated me. I hated the abrupt self-confident tone of his voice, his admiration of his own witticisms, which were often frightfully stupid, though he was bold in his language; I hated his handsome, but stupid face (for which I would, however, have gladly exchanged my intelligent one), and the free-and-easy military manners in fashion in the "'forties." I hated the way in which he used to talk of his future conquests of women (he did not venture to begin his attack upon women until he had the epaulettes of an officer, and was looking forward to them with impatience), and boasted of the duels he would constantly be fighting. I remember how I, invariably so taciturn, suddenly fastened upon Zverkov, when one day talking at a leisure moment with his schoolfellows of his future relations with the fair sex, and growing as sportive as a puppy in the sun, he all at once declared that he would not leave a single village girl on his estate unnoticed, that that was his *droit de seigneur*, and that if the peasants dared to protest he would have them all flogged and double the tax on them, the bearded rascals. Our servile rabble applauded, but I attacked him, not from compassion for the girls and their fathers, but simply because they were applauding such an insect. I got the better of him on that occasion, but though Zverkov was stupid he was lively and impudent, and so laughed it off, and in such a way that my victory was not really complete; the laugh was on his side. He got the better of me on several occasions afterwards, but without malice, jestingly, casually. I remained angrily and contemptuously silent and would not answer him. When we left school he made advances to me; I did not rebuff them, for I was flattered, but we soon parted and quite naturally. Afterwards I heard of his barrack-room success as a lieutenant, and of the fast life he was leading. Then there came other rumours—of his successes in the service. By then he had taken to cutting me in the street, and I suspected that he was afraid of compromising himself by greeting a personage as insignificant as me. I saw him once in the theatre, in the third tier of boxes. By then he was wearing shoulder-straps. He was twisting and twirling about, ingratiating himself with the daughters of an ancient General. In three years he had gone off considerably, though he was still rather handsome and adroit. One could see that by the time he was thirty he would be corpulent. So it was to this Zverkov that my schoolfellows were going to give a dinner on his departure. They had kept up with him for those three years, though privately they did not consider themselves on an equal footing with him, I am convinced of that.

Of Simonov's two visitors, one was Ferfitchkin, a Russianized German—a little fellow with the face of a monkey, a blockhead who was always deriding everyone, a very bitter enemy of mine from our days in the lower forms—a vulgar, impudent, swaggering fellow, who affected a most sensitive feeling of personal honor, though, of course, he was a wretched little coward at heart. He was one of those worshippers of Zverkov who made up to the latter from interested motives, and often borrowed money from him. Simonov's other visitor, Trudolyubov, was a person in no way remarkable—a tall young fellow, in the army, with a cold face, fairly honest, though he worshipped success of every sort, and was only capable of thinking of promotion. He was some sort of distant relation of Zverkov's, and this, foolish as it seems, gave him a certain importance among us. He always thought me of no consequence whatever; his behavior to me, though not quite courteous, was tolerable.

"Well, with seven rubles each," said Trudolyubov, "twenty-one rubles between the three of us, we ought to be able to get a good dinner. Zverkov, of course, won't pay."

"Of course not, since we are inviting him," Simonov decided.

"Can you imagine," Ferfitchkin interrupted hotly and conceitedly, like some insolent flunkey boasting of his master the

General's decorations, "can you imagine that Zverkov will let us pay alone? He will accept from delicacy, but he will order half a dozen bottles of champagne."

"Do we want half a dozen for the four of us?" observed Trudolyubov, taking notice only of the half dozen.

"So the three of us, with Zverkov for the fourth, twenty-one rubles, at the Hotel de Paris at five o'clock tomorrow," Simonov, who had been asked to make the arrangements, concluded finally.

"How twenty-one rubles?" I asked in some agitation, with a show of being offended; "if you count me it will not be twenty-one, but twenty-eight rubles."

It seemed to me that to invite myself so suddenly and unexpectedly would be positively graceful, and that they would all be conquered at once and would look at me with respect.

"Do you want to join, too?" Simonov observed, with no appearance of pleasure, seeming to avoid looking at me. He knew me through and through.

It infuriated me that he knew me so thoroughly.

"Why not? I am an old schoolfellow of his, too, I believe, and I must own I feel hurt that you have left me out," I said, boiling over again.

"And where were we to find you?" Ferfitchkin put in roughly.

"You never were on good terms with Zverkov," Trudolyubov added, frowning.

But I had already clutched at the idea and would not give it up.

"It seems to me that no one has a right to form an opinion upon that," I retorted in a shaking voice, as though something tremendous had happened. "Perhaps that is just my reason for wishing it now, that I have not always been on good terms with him."

"Oh, there's no making you out . . . with these refinements," Trudolyubov jeered.

"We'll put your name down," Simonov decided, addressing me. "Tomorrow at five-o'clock at the Hotel de Paris."

"What about the money?" Ferfitchkin began in an undertone, indicating me to Simonov, but he broke off, for even Simonov was embarrassed.

"That will do," said Trudolyubov, getting up. "If he wants to come so much, let him."

"But it's a private thing, between us friends," Ferfitchkin said crossly, as he, too, picked up his hat. "It's not an official gathering."

"We do not want at all, perhaps . . ."

They went away. Ferfitchkin did not greet me in any way as he went out, Trudolyubov barely nodded. Simonov, with whom I was left *tete-a-tete*, was in a state of vexation and perplexity, and looked at me queerly. He did not sit down and did not ask me to.

"H'm . . . yes . . . tomorrow, then. Will you pay your subscription now? I just ask so as to know," he muttered in embarrassment.

I flushed crimson, as I did so I remembered that I had owed Simonov fifteen rubles for ages—which I had, indeed, never forgotten, though I had not paid it.

"You will understand, Simonov, that I could have no idea when I came here. . . . I am very much vexed that I have forgotten. . . ."

"All right, all right, that doesn't matter. You can pay tomorrow after the dinner. I simply wanted to know. . . . Please don't. . ."

He broke off and began pacing the room still more vexed. As he walked he began to stamp with his heels.

"Am I keeping you?" I asked, after two minutes of silence.

"Oh!" he said, starting, "that is—to be truthful—yes. I have to go and see someone . . . not far from here," he added in an apologetic voice, somewhat abashed.

"My goodness, why didn't you say so?" I cried, seizing my cap, with an astonishingly free-and-easy air, which was the last thing I should have expected of myself.

"It's close by . . . not two paces away," Simonov repeated, accompanying me to the front door with a fussy air which did not suit him at all. "So five o'clock, punctually, tomorrow," he called down the stairs after me. He was very glad to get rid of me. I was in a fury.

"What possessed me, what possessed me to force myself upon them?" I wondered, grinding my teeth as I strode along the street, "for a scoundrel, a pig like that Zverkov! Of course I had better not go; of course, I must just snap my fingers at them. I am not bound in any way. I'll send Simonov a note by tomorrow's post. . . ."

But what made me furious was that I knew for certain that I should go, that I should make a point of going; and the more tactless, the more unseemly my going would be, the more certainly I would go.

And there was a positive obstacle to my going: I had no money. All I had was nine rubles, I had to give seven of that to my servant, Apollon, for his monthly wages. That was all I paid him—he had to keep himself.

Not to pay him was impossible, considering his character. But I will talk about that fellow, about that plague of mine, another time.

However, I knew I should go and should not pay him his wages.

That night I had the most hideous dreams. No wonder; all the evening I had been oppressed by memories of my miserable days at school, and I could not shake them off. I was sent to the school by distant relations, upon whom I was dependent and of whom I have heard nothing since—they sent me there a forlorn, silent boy, already crushed by their reproaches, already troubled by doubt, and looking with savage distrust at everyone. My schoolfellows met me with spiteful and merciless jibes because I was not like any of them. But I could not endure their taunts; I could not give in to them with the ignoble readiness with which they gave in to one another. I hated them from the first, and shut myself away from everyone in timid, wounded and disproportionate pride. Their coarseness revolted me. They laughed cynically at my face, at my clumsy figure; and yet what stupid faces they had themselves. In our school the boys' faces seemed in a special way to degenerate and grow stupider. How many fine-looking boys came to us! In a few years they became repulsive. Even at sixteen I wondered at them morosely; even then I was struck by the pettiness of their thoughts, the stupidity of their pursuits, their games, their conversations. They had no understanding of such essential things, they took no interest in such striking, impressive subjects, that I could not help considering them inferior to myself. It was not wounded vanity that drove me to it, and for God's sake do not thrust upon me your hackneyed remarks, repeated to nausea, that "I was only a dreamer," while they even then had an understanding of life. They understood nothing, they had no idea of real life, and I swear that that was what made me most indignant with them. On the contrary, the most obvious, striking reality they accepted with fantastic stupidity and even at that time were accustomed to respect success. Everything that was just, but oppressed and looked down upon, they laughed at heartlessly and shamefully. They took rank for intelligence; even at sixteen they were already talking about a snug berth. Of course, a great deal of it was due to their stupidity, to the bad examples with which they had always been surrounded in their childhood and boyhood. They were monstrously depraved. Of course a great deal of that, too, was superficial and an assumption of cynicism; of course there were glimpses of youth and freshness even in their depravity; but even that freshness was not attractive, and showed itself in a certain rakishness. I hated them horribly, though perhaps I was worse than any of them. They repaid me in the same way, and did not conceal their aversion for me. But by then I did not desire their affection: on the contrary, I continually longed for their humiliation. To escape from their derision I purposely began to make all the progress I could with my studies and forced my way to the very top. This impressed them. Moreover, they all began by degrees to grasp that I had already read books none of them could read, and understood things (not forming part of our school curriculum) of which they had not even heard. They took a savage and sarcastic view of it, but were morally impressed, especially as the teachers began to notice me on those grounds. The mockery ceased, but the hostility remained, and cold and strained relations became permanent between us. In the end I could not put up with it: with years a craving for society, for friends, developed in me. I attempted to get on friendly terms with some of my schoolfellows; but somehow or other my intimacy with them was always strained and soon ended of itself. Once, indeed, I did have a friend. But I was already a tyrant at heart; I wanted to exercise unbounded sway over him; I tried to instil into him a contempt for his surroundings; I required of him a disdainful and complete break with those surroundings. I frightened him with my passionate affection; I reduced him to tears, to hysterics. He was a simple and devoted soul; but when he devoted himself to me entirely I began to hate him immediately and repulsed him—as though all I needed him for was to win a victory over him, to subjugate him and nothing else. But I could not subjugate all of them; my friend was not at all like them either, he was, in fact, a rare exception. The first thing I did on leaving school was to give up the special job for which I had been destined so as to break all ties, to curse my past and shake the dust from off my feet. . . . And goodness knows why, after all that, I should go trudging off to Simonov's!

Early next morning I roused myself and jumped out of bed with excitement, as though it were all about to happen at once. But I believed that some radical change in my life was coming, and would inevitably come that day. Owing to its rarity, perhaps, any external event, however trivial, always made me feel as though some radical change in my life were at hand. I went to the office, however, as usual, but sneaked away home two hours earlier to get ready. The great thing, I thought, is not to be the first to arrive, or they will think I am overjoyed at coming. But there were thousands of such great points to consider, and they all agitated and overwhelmed me. I polished my boots a second time with my own hands; nothing in the world would have induced Apollon to clean them twice a day, as he considered that it was more than his duties required of him. I stole the brushes to clean them from the passage, being careful he should not detect it, for fear of his contempt. Then I minutely examined my clothes and thought that everything looked old, worn and threadbare. I had let myself get too slovenly. My uniform, perhaps, was tidy, but I could not go out to dinner in my uniform. The worst of it was that on the knee of my trousers was a big yellow stain. I had a foreboding that that stain would deprive me of nine-tenths of my personal dignity. I knew, too, that it was very poor to think so. "But this is no time for thinking: now I am in for the real thing," I thought, and my heart sank. I knew, too, perfectly well even then, that I was monstrously exaggerating the facts. But how could I help it? I could not control myself and was already shaking with fever. With despair I pictured to myself how coldly and disdainfully that "scoundrel" Zverkov would meet me; with what dull-witted, invincible contempt the blockhead Trudolyubov would look at me; with what impudent rudeness the insect Ferfitchkin would snigger at me in order to curry favor with Zverkov; how completely Simonov would take it all in, and how he would despise me for the abjectness of my vanity and lack of spirit—and, worst of all, how paltry, *unliterary*, commonplace it would all be. Of course, the best thing would be not to go at all. But that was most impossible of all: if I feel impelled to do anything, I seem to be pitchforked into it. I should have jeered at myself ever afterwards: "So you funked it, you funked it, you funked the *real thing!*" On the contrary, I passionately longed to show all that "rabble" that I was by no means such a spiritless creature as I seemed to myself. What is more, even in the acutest paroxysm of this cowardly fever, I dreamed of getting the upper hand, of dominating them, carrying them away, making them like me—if only for my "elevation of thought and unmistakable wit." They would abandon Zverkov, he would sit on one side, silent and ashamed, while I should crush him. Then, perhaps, we would be reconciled and drink to our everlasting friendship; but what was most bitter and humiliating for me was that I knew even then, knew fully and for certain, that I needed nothing of all this really, that I did not really want to crush, to subdue, to attract them, and that I did not care a straw really for the result, even if I did achieve it. Oh, how I prayed for the day to pass quickly! In unutterable anguish I went to the window, opened the movable pane and looked out into the troubled darkness of the thickly falling wet snow. At last my wretched little clock hissed out five. I seized my hat and, trying not to look at Apollon, who had been all day expecting his month's wages, but in his foolishness was unwilling to be the first to speak about it, I slipped between him and the door and, jumping into a high-class sledge, on which I spent my last half ruble, I drove up in grand style to the Hotel de Paris.

IV

I had been certain the day before that I should be the first to arrive. But it was not a question of being the first to arrive. Not only were they not there, but I had difficulty in finding our room. The table was not laid even. What did it mean? After a good many questions I elicited from the waiters that the dinner had been ordered not for five, but for six o'clock.

This was confirmed at the buffet too. I felt really ashamed to go on questioning them. It was only twenty-five minutes past five. If they changed the dinner hour they ought at least to have let me know—that is what the post is for, and not to have put me in an absurd position in my own eyes and . . . and even before the waiters. I sat down; the servant began laying the table; I felt even more humiliated when he was present. Towards six o'clock they brought in candles, though there were lamps burning in the room. It had not occurred to the waiter, however, to bring them in at once when I arrived. In the next room two gloomy, angry-looking persons were eating their dinners in silence at two different tables. There was a great deal of noise, even shouting, in a room further away; one could hear the laughter of a crowd of people, and nasty little shrieks in French: there were ladies at the dinner. It was sickening, in fact. I rarely passed more unpleasant moments, so much so that when they did arrive all together punctually at six I was overjoyed to see them, as though they were my deliverers, and even forgot that it was incumbent upon me to show resentment.

Zverkov walked in at the head of them; evidently he was the leading spirit. He and all of them were laughing; but, seeing me, Zverkov drew himself up a little, walked up to me deliberately with a slight, rather jaunty bend from the waist. He shook hands with me in a friendly, but not over-friendly, fashion, with a sort of circumspect courtesy like that of a General, as though in giving me his hand he were warding off something. I had imagined, on the contrary, that on coming in he would at once break into his habitual thin, shrill laugh and fall to making his insipid jokes and witticisms. I had been preparing for them ever since the previous day, but I had not expected such condescension, such high-official courtesy. So, then, he felt himself ineffably superior to me in every respect! If he only meant to insult me by that high-official tone, it would not matter, I thought—I could pay him back for it one way or another. But what if, in reality, without the least desire to be offensive, that sheepshead had a notion in earnest that he was superior to me and could only look at me in a patronizing way? The very supposition made me gasp.

"I was surprised to hear of your desire to join us," he began, lisping and drawling, which was something new. "You and I seem to have seen nothing of one another. You fight shy of us. You shouldn't. We are not such terrible people as you think. Well, anyway, I am glad to renew our acquaintance."

And he turned carelessly to put down his hat on the window.

"Have you been waiting long?" Trudolyubov inquired.

"I arrived at five o'clock as you told me yesterday," I answered aloud, with an irritability that threatened an explosion.

"Didn't you let him know that we had changed the hour?" said Trudolyubov to Simonov.

"No, I didn't. I forgot," the latter replied, with no sign of regret, and without even apologizing to me he went off to order the *hors d'oeuvre*.

"So you've been here a whole hour? Oh, poor fellow!" Zverkov cried ironically, for to his notions this was bound to be extremely funny. That rascal Ferfitchkin followed with his nasty little snigger like a puppy yapping. My position struck him, too, as exquisitely ludicrous and embarrassing.

"It isn't funny at all!" I cried to Ferfitchkin, more and more irritated. "It wasn't my fault, but other people's. They neglected to let me know. It was . . . it was . . . it was simply absurd."

"It's not only absurd, but something else as well," muttered Trudolyubov, naively taking my part. "You are not hard enough upon it. It was simply rudeness—unintentional, of course. And how could Simonov . . . h'm!"

"If a trick like that had been played on me," observed Ferfitchkin, "I should . . ."

"But you should have ordered something for yourself," Zverkov interrupted, "or simply asked for dinner without waiting for us."

"You will allow that I might have done that without your permission," I rapped out. "If I waited, it was . . ."

"Let us sit down, gentlemen," cried Simonov, coming in. "Everything is ready; I can answer for the champagne; it is capitally frozen. . . . You see, I did not know your address, where was I to look for you?" he suddenly turned to me, but again he seemed to avoid looking at me. Evidently he had something against me. It must have been what happened yesterday.

All sat down; I did the same. It was a round table. Trudolyubov was on my left, Simonov on my right, Zverkov was sitting opposite, Ferfitchkin next to him, between him and Trudolyubov.

"Tell me, are you . . . in a government office?" Zverkov went on attending to me. Seeing that I was embarrassed he seriously thought that he ought to be friendly to me, and, so to speak, cheer me up.

"Does he want me to throw a bottle at his head?" I thought, in a fury. In my novel surroundings I was unnaturally ready to be irritated.

"In the N—— office," I answered jerkily, with my eyes on my plate.

"And ha-ave you a go-od berth? I say, what ma-a-de you leave your original job?"

"What ma-a-de me was that I wanted to leave my original job," I drawled more than he, hardly able to control myself. Ferfitchkin went off into a guffaw. Simonov looked at me ironically. Trudolyubov left off eating and began looking at me with curiosity.

Zverkov winced, but he tried not to notice it.

"And the remuneration?"

"What remuneration?"

"I mean, your sa-a-lary?"

"Why are you cross-examining me?" However, I told him at once what my salary was. I turned horribly red.

"It is not very handsome," Zverkov observed majestically.

"Yes, you can't afford to dine at cafes on that," Ferfitchkin added insolently.

"To my thinking it's very poor," Trudolyubov observed gravely.

"And how thin you have grown! How you have changed!" added Zverkov, with a shade of venom in his voice, scanning me and my attire with a sort of insolent compassion.

"Oh, spare his blushes," cried Ferfitchkin, sniggering.

"My dear sir, allow me to tell you I am not blushing," I broke out at last; "do you hear? I am dining here, at this cafe, at my own expense, not at other people's—note that, Mr. Ferfitchkin."

"Wha-at? Isn't everyone here dining at his own expense? You would seem to be . . ." Ferfitchkin flew out at me, turning as red as a lobster, and looking me in the face with fury.

"Tha-at," I answered, feeling I had gone too far, "and I imagine it would be better to talk of something more intelligent."

"You intend to show off your intelligence, I suppose?"

"Don't disturb yourself, that would be quite out of place here."

"Why are you clacking away like that, my good sir, eh? Have you gone out of your wits in your office?"

"Enough, gentlemen, enough!" Zverkov cried, authoritatively.

"How stupid it is!" muttered Simonov.

"It really is stupid. We have met here, a company of friends, for a farewell dinner to a comrade and you carry on an altercation," said Trudolyubov, rudely addressing himself to me alone. "You invited yourself to join us, so don't disturb the general harmony."

"Enough, enough!" cried Zverkov. "Give over, gentlemen, it's out of place. Better let me tell you how I nearly got married the day before yesterday. . . ."

And then followed a burlesque narrative of how this gentleman had almost been married two days before. There was not a word about the marriage, however, but the story was adorned with generals, colonels and kammer-junkers, while Zverkov almost took the lead among them. It was greeted with approving laughter; Ferfitchkin positively squealed.

No one paid any attention to me, and I sat crushed and humiliated.

"Good Heavens, these are not the people for me!" I thought. "And what a fool I have made of myself before them! I let Ferfitchkin go too far, though. The brutes imagine they are doing me an honor in letting me sit down with them. They don't understand that it's an honor to them and not to me! I've grown thinner! My clothes! Oh, damn my trousers! Zverkov noticed the yellow stain on the knee as soon as he came in. . . . But what's the use! I must get up at once, this very minute, take my hat and simply go without a word . . . with contempt! And tomorrow I can send a challenge. The scoundrels! As though I cared about the seven rubles. They may think. . . . Damn it! I don't care about the seven rubles. I'll go this minute!"

Of course I remained. I drank sherry and Lafitte by the glassful in my discomfiture. Being unaccustomed to it, I was quickly affected. My annoyance increased as the wine went to my head. I longed all at once to insult them all in a most flagrant manner and then go away. To seize the moment and show what I could do, so that they would say, "He's clever, though he is absurd," and . . . and . . . in fact, damn them all!

I scanned them all insolently with my drowsy eyes. But they seemed to have forgotten me altogether. They were noisy, vociferous, cheerful. Zverkov was talking all the time. I began listening. Zverkov was talking of some exuberant lady whom he had at last led on to declaring her love (of course, he was lying like a horse), and how he had been helped in this affair by an intimate friend of his, a Prince Kolya, an officer in the hussars, who had three thousand serfs.

"And yet this Kolya, who has three thousand serfs, has not put in an appearance here tonight to see you off," I cut in suddenly.

For one minute everyone was silent. "You are drunk already." Trudolyubov deigned to notice me at last, glancing contemptuously in my direction. Zverkov, without a word, examined me as though I were an insect. I dropped my eyes. Simonov made haste to fill up the glasses with champagne.

Trudolyubov raised his glass, as did everyone else but me.

"Your health and good luck on the journey!" he cried to Zverkov. "To old times, to our future, hurrah!"

They all tossed off their glasses, and crowded round Zverkov to kiss him. I did not move; my full glass stood untouched before me.

"Why, aren't you going to drink it?" roared Trudolyubov, losing patience and turning menacingly to me.

"I want to make a speech separately, on my own account . . . and then I'll drink it, Mr. Trudolyubov."

"Spiteful brute!" muttered Simonov. I drew myself up in my chair and feverishly seized my glass, prepared for something extraordinary, though I did not know myself precisely what I was going to say.

"*Silence!*" cried Ferfitchkin. "Now for a display of wit!"

Zverkov waited very gravely, knowing what was coming.

"Mr. Lieutenant Zverkov," I began, "let me tell you that I hate phrases, phrasemongers and men in corsets . . . that's the first point, and there is a second one to follow it."

There was a general stir.

"The second point is: I hate ribaldry and ribald talkers. Especially ribald talkers! The third point: I love justice, truth and honesty." I went on almost mechanically, for I was beginning to shiver with horror myself and had no idea how I came to be talking like this. "I love thought, Monsieur Zverkov; I love true comradeship, on an equal footing and not . . . H'm . . . I love . . . But, however, why not? I will drink your health, too, Mr. Zverkov. Seduce the Circassian girls, shoot the enemies of the fatherland and . . . and . . . to your health, Monsieur Zverkov!"

Zverkov got up from his seat, bowed to me and said:

"I am very much obliged to you." He was frightfully offended and turned pale.

"Damn the fellow!" roared Trudolyubov, bringing his fist down on the table.

"Well, he wants a punch in the face for that," squealed Ferfitchkin.

"We ought to turn him out," muttered Simonov.

"Not a word, gentlemen, not a movement!" cried Zverkov solemnly, checking the general indignation. "I thank you all, but I can show him for myself how much value I attach to his words."

"Mr. Ferfitchkin, you will give me satisfaction tomorrow for your words just now!" I said aloud, turning with dignity to Ferfitchkin.

"A duel, you mean? Certainly," he answered. But probably I was so ridiculous as I challenged him and it was so out of keeping with my appearance that everyone including Ferfitchkin was prostrate with laughter.

"Yes, let him alone, of course! He is quite drunk," Trudolyubov said with disgust.

"I shall never forgive myself for letting him join us," Simonov muttered again.

"Now is the time to throw a bottle at their heads," I thought to myself. I picked up the bottle . . . and filled my glass. . . . "No, I'd better sit on to the end," I went on thinking; "you would be pleased, my friends, if I went away. Nothing will induce me to go. I'll go on sitting here and drinking to the end, on purpose, as a sign that I don't think you of the slightest consequence. I will go on sitting and drinking, because this is a public-house and I paid my entrance money. I'll sit here and drink, for I look upon you as so many pawns, as inanimate pawns. I'll sit here and drink . . . and sing if I want to, yes, sing, for I have the right to . . . to sing . . . H'm!"

But I did not sing. I simply tried not to look at any of them. I assumed most unconcerned attitudes and waited with impatience for them to speak first. But alas, they did not address me! And oh, how I wished, how I wished at that moment to be reconciled to them! It struck eight, at last nine. They moved from the table to the sofa. Zverkov stretched himself on a lounge and put one foot on a round table. Wine was brought there. He did, as a fact, order three bottles on his own account. I, of course, was not invited to join them. They all sat round him on the sofa. They listened to him, almost with reverence. It was evident that they were fond of him. "What for? What for?" I wondered. From time to time they were moved to drunken enthusiasm and kissed each other. They talked of the Caucasus, of the nature of true passion, of snug berths in the service, of the income of an hussar called Podharzhevsky, whom none of them knew personally, and rejoiced in the largeness of it, of the extraordinary grace and beauty of a Princess D., whom none of them had ever seen; then it came to Shakespeare's being immortal.

I smiled contemptuously and walked up and down the other side of the room, opposite the sofa, from the table to the stove and back again. I tried my very utmost to show them that I could do without them, and yet I purposely made a noise with my boots, thumping with my heels. But it was all in vain. They paid no attention. I had the patience to walk up and down in front of them from eight o'clock till eleven, in the same place, from the table to the stove and back again. "I walk up and down to please myself and no one can prevent me." The waiter who came into the room stopped, from time to time, to look at me. I was somewhat giddy from turning round so often; at moments it seemed to me that I was in delirium. During those three hours I was three times soaked with sweat and dry again. At times, with an intense, acute pang I was stabbed to the heart by the thought that ten years, twenty years, forty years would pass, and that even in forty years I would remember with loathing and humiliation those filthiest, most ludicrous, and most awful moments of my life. No one could have gone out of his way to degrade himself more shamelessly, and I fully realized it, fully, and yet I went on pacing up and down from the table to the stove. "Oh, if you only knew what thoughts and feelings I am capable of, how cultured I am!" I thought at moments, mentally addressing the sofa on which my enemies were sitting. But my enemies behaved as though I were not in the room. Once—only once—they turned towards me, just when Zverkov was talking about Shakespeare, and I suddenly gave a contemptuous laugh. I laughed in such an affected and disgusting way that they all at once broke off their conversation, and silently and gravely for two minutes watched me walking up and down from the table to the stove, *taking no notice of them.* But nothing came of it: they said nothing, and two minutes later they ceased to notice me again. It struck eleven.

"Friends," cried Zverkov getting up from the sofa, "let us all be off now, *there!*"

"Of course, of course," the others assented. I turned sharply to Zverkov. I was so harassed, so exhausted, that I would have cut my throat to put an end to it. I was in a fever; my hair, soaked with perspiration, stuck to my forehead and temples.

"Zverkov, I beg your pardon," I said abruptly and resolutely. "Ferfitchkin, yours too, and everyone's, everyone's: I have insulted you all!"

"Aha! A duel is not in your line, old man," Ferfitchkin hissed venomously.

It sent a sharp pang to my heart.

"No, it's not the duel I am afraid of, Ferfitchkin! I am ready to fight you tomorrow, after we are reconciled. I insist upon it, in fact, and you cannot refuse. I want to show you that I am not afraid of a duel. You shall fire first and I shall fire into the air."

"He is comforting himself," said Simonov.

"He's simply raving," said Trudolyubov.

"But let us pass. Why are you barring our way? What do you want?" Zverkov answered disdainfully.

They were all flushed, their eyes were bright: they had been drinking heavily.

"I ask for your friendship, Zverkov; I insulted you, but . . ."

"Insulted? *you* insulted *me*? Understand, sir, that you never, under any circumstances, could possibly insult *me*."

"And that's enough for you. Out of the way!" concluded Trudolyubov.

"Olympia is mine, friends, that's agreed!" cried Zverkov.

"We won't dispute your right, we won't dispute your right," the others answered, laughing.

I stood as though spat upon. The party went noisily out of the room. Trudolyubov struck up some stupid song. Simonov remained behind for a moment to tip the waiters. I suddenly went up to him.

"Simonov! give me six rubles!" I said, with desperate resolution.

He looked at me in extreme amazement, with vacant eyes. He, too, was drunk.

"You don't mean you are coming with us?"

"Yes."

"I've no money," he snapped out, and with a scornful laugh he went out of the room.

I clutched at his overcoat. It was a nightmare.

"Simonov, I saw you had money. Why do you refuse me? Am I a scoundrel? Beware of refusing me: if you knew, if you knew why I am asking! My whole future, my whole plans depend upon it!"

Simonov pulled out the money and almost flung it at me.

"Take it, if you have no sense of shame!" he pronounced pitilessly, and ran to overtake them.

I was left for a moment alone. Disorder, the remains of dinner, a broken wine-glass on the floor, spilt wine, cigarette ends, fumes of drink and delirium in my brain, an agonising misery in my heart and finally the waiter, who had seen and heard all and was looking inquisitively into my face.

"I am going there!" I cried. "Either they shall all go down on their knees to beg for my friendship, or I will give Zverkov a slap in the face!"

V

"So this is it, this is it at last—contact with real life," I muttered as I ran headlong downstairs. "This is very different from the Pope's leaving Rome and going to Brazil, very different from the ball on Lake Como!"

"You are a scoundrel," a thought flashed through my mind, "if you laugh at this now."

"No matter!" I cried, answering myself. "Now everything is lost!"

There was no trace to be seen of them, but that made no difference—I knew where they had gone.

At the steps was standing a solitary night sledge-driver in a rough peasant coat, powdered over with the still falling, wet, and as it were warm, snow. It was hot and steamy. The little shaggy piebald horse was also covered with snow and coughing, I remember that very well. I made a rush for the roughly made sledge; but as soon as I raised my foot to get into it, the recollection of how Simonov had just given me six rubles seemed to double me up and I tumbled into the sledge like a sack.

"No, I must do a great deal to make up for all that," I cried. "But I will make up for it or perish on the spot this very night. Start!"

We set off. There was a perfect whirl in my head.

"They won't go down on their knees to beg for my friendship. That is a mirage, cheap mirage, revolting, romantic and fantastical—that's another ball on Lake Como. And so I am bound to slap Zverkov's face! It is my duty to. And so it is settled; I am flying to give him a slap in the face. Hurry up!"

The driver tugged at the reins.

"As soon as I go in I'll give it him. Ought I before giving him the slap to say a few words by way of preface? No. I'll simply go in and give it him. They will all be sitting in the drawing-room, and he with Olympia on the sofa. That damned Olympia! She laughed at my looks on one occasion and refused me. I'll pull Olympia's hair, pull Zverkov's ears! No, better one ear, and pull him by it round the room. Maybe they will all begin beating me and will kick me out. That's most likely, indeed. No matter! Anyway, I shall first slap him; the initiative will be mine; and by the laws of honor that is everything: he will be branded and cannot wipe off the slap by any blows, by nothing but a duel. He will be forced to fight. And let them beat me now. Let them, the ungrateful wretches! Trudolyubov will beat me hardest, he is so strong; Ferfitchkin will be sure to catch hold sideways and tug at my hair. But no matter, no matter! That's what I am going for. The blockheads will be forced at last to see the tragedy of it all! When they drag me to the door I shall call out to them that in reality they are not worth my little finger. Get on, driver, get on!" I cried to the driver. He started and flicked his whip, I shouted so savagely.

"We shall fight at daybreak, that's a settled thing. I've done with the office. Ferfitchkin made a joke about it just now. But where can I get pistols? Nonsense! I'll get my salary in advance and buy them. And powder, and bullets? That's the second's business. And how can it all be done by daybreak? and where am I to get a second? I have no friends. Nonsense!" I cried, lashing myself up more and more. "It's of no consequence! The first person I meet in the street is bound to be my second, just as he would be bound to pull a drowning man out of water. The most eccentric things may happen. Even if I were to ask the director himself to be my second tomorrow, he would be bound to consent, if only from a feeling of chivalry, and to keep the secret! Anton Antonitch. . . ."

The fact is, that at that very minute the disgusting absurdity of my plan and the other side of the question was clearer and more vivid to my imagination than it could be to anyone on earth. But . . . .

"Get on, driver, get on, you rascal, get on!"

"Ugh, sir!" said the son of toil.

Cold shivers suddenly ran down me. Wouldn't it be better . . . to go straight home? My God, my God! Why did I invite myself to this dinner yesterday? But no, it's impossible. And my walking up and down for three hours from the table to the stove? No, they, they and no one else must pay for my walking up and down! They must wipe out this dishonour! Drive on!

And what if they give me into custody? They won't dare! They'll be afraid of the scandal. And what if Zverkov is so contemptuous that he refuses to fight a duel? He is sure to; but in that case I'll show them . . . I will turn up at the posting station when he's setting off tomorrow, I'll catch him by the leg, I'll pull off his coat when he gets into the carriage. I'll get my teeth into his hand, I'll bite him. "See what lengths you can drive a desperate man to!" He may hit me on the head and they may belabor me from behind. I will shout to the assembled multitude: "Look at this young puppy who is driving off to captivate the Circassian girls after letting me spit in his face!"

Of course, after that everything will be over! The office will have vanished off the face of the earth. I shall be arrested, I shall be tried, I shall be dismissed from the service, thrown in prison, sent to Siberia. Never mind! In fifteen years when they let me out of prison I will trudge off to him, a beggar, in rags. I shall find him in some provincial town. He will be married and happy. He will have a grown-up daughter. . . . I shall say to him: "Look, monster, at my hollow cheeks and my rags! I've lost everything—my career, my happiness, art, science, *the woman I loved*, and all through you. Here are pistols. I have come to discharge my pistol and . . . and I . . . forgive you. Then I shall fire into the air and he will hear nothing more of me. . . ."

I was actually on the point of tears, though I knew perfectly well at that moment that all this was out of Pushkin's *Silvio* and Lermontov's *Masquerade*. And all at once I felt horribly ashamed, so ashamed that I stopped the horse, got out of the sledge, and stood still in the snow in the middle of the street. The driver gazed at me, sighing and astonished.

What was I to do? I could not go on there—it was evidently stupid, and I could not leave things as they were, because that would seem as though . . . Heavens, how could I leave things! And after such insults! "No!" I cried, throwing myself into the sledge again. "It is ordained! It is fate! Drive on, drive on!"

And in my impatience I punched the sledge-driver on the back of the neck.

"What are you up to? What are you hitting me for?" the peasant shouted, but he whipped up his nag so that it began kicking.

The wet snow was falling in big flakes; I unbuttoned myself, regardless of it. I forgot everything else, for I had finally decided on the slap, and felt with horror that it was going to happen *now, at once*, and that *no force could stop it*. The deserted street lamps gleamed sullenly in the snowy darkness like torches at a funeral. The snow drifted under my great-coat, under my coat, under my cravat, and melted there. I did not wrap myself up—all was lost, anyway.

At last we arrived. I jumped out, almost unconscious, ran up the steps and began knocking and kicking at the door. I felt fearfully weak, particularly in my legs and knees. The door was opened quickly as though they knew I was coming. As a fact, Simonov had warned them that perhaps another gentleman would arrive, and this was a place in which one had to give notice and to observe certain precautions. It was one of those "millinery establishments" which were abolished by the police a good time ago. By day it really was a shop; but at night, if one had an introduction, one might visit it for other purposes.

I walked rapidly through the dark shop into the familiar drawing-room, where there was only one candle burning, and stood still in amazement: there was no one there. "Where are they?" I asked somebody. But by now, of course, they had separated. Before me was standing a person with a stupid smile, the "madam" herself, who had seen me before. A minute later a door opened and another person came in.

Taking no notice of anything I strode about the room, and, I believe, I talked to myself. I felt as though I had been saved from death and was conscious of this, joyfully, all over: I should have given that slap, I should certainly, certainly have given it! But now they were not here and . . . everything had vanished and changed! I looked round. I could not realize my condition yet. I looked mechanically at the girl who had come in: and had a glimpse of a fresh, young, rather pale face, with straight, dark eyebrows, and with grave, as it were wondering, eyes that attracted me at once; I should have hated her if she had been smiling. I began looking at her more intently and, as it were, with effort. I had not fully collected my thoughts. There was something simple and good-natured in her face, but something strangely grave. I am sure that this stood in her way here, and no one of those fools had noticed her. She could not, however, have been called a beauty, though she was tall, strong-looking, and well built. She was very simply dressed. Something loathsome stirred within me. I went straight up to her.

I chanced to look into the glass. My harassed face struck me as revolting in the extreme, pale, angry, abject, with disheveled hair. "No matter, I am glad of it," I thought; "I am glad that I shall seem repulsive to her; I like that."

VI

. . . Somewhere behind a screen a clock began wheezing, as though oppressed by something, as though someone were strangling it. After an unnaturally prolonged wheezing there followed a shrill, nasty, and as it were unexpectedly rapid, chime—as though someone were suddenly jumping forward. It struck two. I woke up, though I had indeed not been asleep but lying half-conscious.

It was almost completely dark in the narrow, cramped, low-pitched room, cumbered up with an enormous wardrobe and piles of cardboard boxes and all sorts of frippery and litter. The candle end that had been burning on the table was going out and gave a faint flicker from time to time. In a few minutes there would be complete darkness.

I was not long in coming to myself; everything came back to my mind at once, without an effort, as though it had been in ambush to pounce upon me again. And, indeed, even while I was unconscious a point seemed continually to remain in my memory unforgotten, and round it my dreams moved drearily. But strange to say, everything that had happened to me in that day seemed to me now, on waking, to be in the far, far away past, as though I had long, long ago lived all that down.

My head was full of fumes. Something seemed to be hovering over me, rousing me, exciting me, and making me restless. Misery and spite seemed surging up in me again and seeking an outlet. Suddenly I saw beside me two wide open eyes scrutinizing me curiously and persistently. The look in those eyes was coldly detached, sullen, as it were utterly remote; it weighed upon me.

A grim idea came into my brain and passed all over my body, as a horrible sensation, such as one feels when one goes into a damp and moldy cellar. There was something unnatural in those two eyes, beginning to look at me only now. I recalled, too, that during those two hours I had not said a single word to this creature, and had, in fact, considered it utterly superfluous; in fact, the silence had for some reason gratified me. Now I suddenly realized vividly the hideous idea—revolting as a spider—of vice, which, without love, grossly and shamelessly begins with that in which true love finds its consummation. For a long time we gazed at each other like that, but she did not drop her eyes before mine and her expression did not change, so that at last I felt uncomfortable.

"What is your name?" I asked abruptly, to put an end to it.

"Liza," she answered almost in a whisper, but somehow far from graciously, and she turned her eyes away.

I was silent.

"What weather! The snow . . . it's disgusting!" I said, almost to myself, putting my arm under my head despondently, and gazing at the ceiling.

She made no answer. This was horrible.

"Have you always lived in Petersburg?" I asked a minute later, almost angrily, turning my head slightly towards her.

"No."

"Where do you come from?"

"From Riga," she answered reluctantly.

"Are you a German?"

"No, Russian."

"Have you been here long?"

"Where?"

"In this house?"

"A fortnight."

She spoke more and more jerkily. The candle went out; I could no longer distinguish her face.

"Have you a father and mother?"

"Yes . . . no . . . I have."

"Where are they?"

"There . . . in Riga."

"What are they?"

"Oh, nothing."

"Nothing? Why, what class are they?"

"Tradespeople."

"Have you always lived with them?"

"Yes."

"How old are you?"

"Twenty."

"Why did you leave them?"

"Oh, for no reason."

That answer meant "Let me alone; I feel sick, sad."

We were silent.

God knows why I did not go away. I felt myself more and more sick and dreary. The images of the previous day began of themselves, apart from my will, flitting through my memory in confusion. I suddenly recalled something I had seen that morning when, full of anxious thoughts, I was hurrying to the office.

"I saw them carrying a coffin out yesterday and they nearly dropped it," I suddenly said aloud, not that I desired to open the conversation, but as it were by accident.

"A coffin?"

"Yes, in the Haymarket; they were bringing it up out of a cellar."

"From a cellar?"

"Not from a cellar, but a basement. Oh, you know . . . down below . . . from a house of ill-fame. It was filthy all round . . . Egg-shells, litter . . . a stench. It was loathsome."

Silence.

"A nasty day to be buried," I began, simply to avoid being silent.

"Nasty, in what way?"

"The snow, the wet." (I yawned.)

"It makes no difference," she said suddenly, after a brief silence.

"No, it's horrid." (I yawned again). "The gravediggers must have sworn at getting drenched by the snow. And there must have been water in the grave."

"Why water in the grave?" she asked, with a sort of curiosity, but speaking even more harshly and abruptly than before.

I suddenly began to feel provoked.

"Why, there must have been water at the bottom a foot deep. You can't dig a dry grave in Volkovo Cemetery."

"Why?"

"Why? Why, the place is waterlogged. It's a regular marsh. So they bury them in water. I've seen it myself . . . many times."

(I had never seen it once, indeed I had never been in Volkovo, and had only heard stories of it.)

"Do you mean to say, you don't mind how you die?"

"But why should I die?" she answered, as though defending herself.

"Why, some day you will die, and you will die just the same as that dead woman. She was . . . a girl like you. She died of consumption."

"A wench would have died in hospital . . ." (She knows all about it already: she said "wench," not "girl.")

"She was in debt to her madam," I retorted, more and more provoked by the discussion; "and went on earning money for her up to the end, though she was in consumption. Some sledge-drivers standing by were talking about her to some soldiers and telling them so. No doubt they knew her.

They were laughing. They were going to meet in a pot-house to drink to her memory."

A great deal of this was my invention. Silence followed, profound silence. She did not stir.

"And is it better to die in a hospital?"

"Isn't it just the same? Besides, why should I die?" she added irritably.

"If not now, a little later."

"Why a little later?"

"Why, indeed? Now you are young, pretty, fresh, you fetch a high price. But after another year of this life you will be very different—you will go off."

"In a year?"

"Anyway, in a year you will be worth less," I continued malignantly. "You will go from here to something lower, another house; a year later—to a third, lower and lower, and in seven years you will come to a basement in the Haymarket. That will be if you were lucky. But it would be much worse if you got some disease, consumption, say . . . and caught a chill, or something or other. It's not easy to get over an illness in your way of life. If you catch anything you may not get rid of it. And so you would die."

"Oh, well, then I shall die," she answered, quite vindictively, and she made a quick movement.

"But one is sorry."

"Sorry for whom?"

"Sorry for life." Silence.

"Have you been engaged to be married? Eh?"

"What's that to you?"

"Oh, I am not cross-examining you. It's nothing to me. Why are you so cross? Of course you may have had your own troubles. What is it to me? It's simply that I felt sorry."

"Sorry for whom?"

"Sorry for you."

"No need," she whispered hardly audibly, and again made a faint movement.

That incensed me at once. What! I was so gentle with her, and she. . . .

"Why, do you think that you are on the right path?"

"I don't think anything."

"That's what's wrong, that you don't think. Realize it while there is still time. There still is time. You are still young, good-looking; you might love, be married, be happy. . . ."

"Not all married women are happy," she snapped out in the rude abrupt tone she had used at first.

"Not all, of course, but anyway it is much better than the life here. Infinitely better. Besides, with love one can live even without happiness. Even in sorrow life is sweet; life is sweet, however one lives. But here what is there but . . . foulness? Phew!"

I turned away with disgust; I was no longer reasoning coldly. I began to feel myself what I was saying and warmed to the subject. I was already longing to expound the cherished ideas I had brooded over in my corner. Something suddenly flared up in me. An object had appeared before me.

"Never mind my being here, I am not an example for you. I am, perhaps, worse than you are. I was drunk when I came here, though," I hastened, however, to say in self-defense. "Besides, a man is no example for a woman. It's a different thing. I may degrade and defile myself, but I am not anyone's slave. I come and go, and that's an end of it. I shake it off, and I am a different man. But you are a slave from the start. Yes, a slave! You give up everything, your whole freedom. If you want to break your chains afterwards, you won't be able to; you will be more and more fast in the snares. It is an accursed bondage. I know it. I won't speak of anything else, maybe you won't understand, but tell me: no doubt you are in debt to your madam? There, you see," I added, though she made no answer, but only listened in silence, entirely absorbed, "that's a bondage for you! You will never buy your freedom. They will see to that. It's like selling your soul to the devil. . . . And besides . . . perhaps, I too, am just as un-lucky—how do you know—and wallow in the mud on pur-pose, out of misery? You know, men take to drink from grief; well, maybe I am here from grief. Come, tell me, what is there good here? Here you and I . . . came together . . . just now and did not say one word to one another all the time, and it was only afterwards you began staring at me like a wild creature, and I at you. Is that loving? Is that how one human being should meet another? It's hideous, that's what it is!"

"Yes!" she assented sharply and hurriedly.

I was positively astounded by the promptitude of this "Yes." So the same thought may have been straying through her mind when she was staring at me just before. So she, too, was capable of certain thoughts? "Damn it all, this was inter-esting, this was a point of likeness!" I thought, almost rubbing my hands. And indeed it's easy to turn a young soul like that!

It was the exercise of my power that attracted me most.

She turned her head nearer to me, and it seemed to me in the darkness that she propped herself on her arm. Perhaps she was scrutinizing me. How I regretted that I could not see her eyes. I heard her deep breathing.

"Why have you come here?" I asked her, with a note of au-thority already in my voice.

"Oh, I don't know."

"But how nice it would be to be living in your father's house! It's warm and free; you have a home of your own."

"But what if it's worse than this?"

"I must take the right tone," flashed through my mind. "I may not get far with sentimentality." But it was only a mo-mentary thought. I swear she really did interest me. Besides, I was exhausted and moody. And cunning so easily goes hand-in-hand with feeling.

"Who denies it!" I hastened to answer. "Anything may happen. I am convinced that someone has wronged you, and that you are more sinned against than sinning. Of course, I know nothing of your story, but it's not likely a girl like you has come here of her own inclination. . . ."

"A girl like me?" she whispered, hardly audibly; but I heard it.

Damn it all, I was flattering her. That was horrid. But perhaps it was a good thing. . . . She was silent.

"See, Liza, I will tell you about myself. If I had had a home from childhood, I shouldn't be what I am now. I often think that. However bad it may be at home, anyway they are your father and mother, and not enemies, strangers. Once a year at least, they'll show their love of you. Anyway, you know you are at home. I grew up without a home; and perhaps that's why I've turned so . . . unfeeling."

I waited again. "Perhaps she doesn't understand," I thought, "and, indeed, it is absurd—it's moralizing."

"If I were a father and had a daughter, I believe I should love my daughter more than my sons, really," I began indirectly, as though talking of something else, to distract her attention. I must confess I blushed.

"Why so?" she asked.

Ah! so she was listening!

"I don't know, Liza. I knew a father who was a stern, austere man, but used to go down on his knees to his daughter, used to kiss her hands, her feet, he couldn't make enough of her, really. When she danced at parties he used to stand for five hours at a stretch, gazing at her. He was mad over her: I understand that! She would fall asleep tired at night, and he would wake to kiss her in her sleep and make the sign of the cross over her. He would go about in a dirty old coat, he was stingy to everyone else, but would spend his last penny for her, giving her expensive presents, and it was his greatest delight when she was pleased with what he gave her. Fathers always love their daughters more than the mothers do. Some girls live happily at home! And I believe I should never let my daughters marry."

"What next?" she said, with a faint smile.

"I should be jealous, I really should. To think that she should kiss anyone else! That she should love a stranger more than her father! It's painful to imagine it. Of course, that's all nonsense, of course every father would be reasonable at last. But I believe before I should let her marry, I should worry myself to death; I should find fault with all her suitors. But I should end by letting her marry whom she herself loved. The one whom the daughter loves always seems the worst to the father, you know. That is always so. So many family troubles come from that."

"Some are glad to sell their daughters, rather than marrying them honorably."

Ah, so that was it!

"Such a thing, Liza, happens in those accursed families in which there is neither love nor God," I retorted warmly, "and where there is no love, there is no sense either. There are such families, it's true, but I am not speaking of them. You must have seen wickedness in your own family, if you talk like that. Truly, you must have been unlucky. H'm! . . . that sort of thing mostly comes about through poverty."

"And is it any better with the gentry? Even among the poor, honest people who live happily?"

"H'm . . . yes. Perhaps. Another thing, Liza, man is fond of reckoning up his troubles, but does not count his joys. If he counted them up as he ought, he would see that every lot has enough happiness provided for it. And what if all goes well with the family, if the blessing of God is upon it, if the husband is a good one, loves you, cherishes you, never leaves you! There is happiness in such a family! Even sometimes there is happiness in the midst of sorrow; and indeed sorrow is everywhere. If you marry *you will find out for yourself*. But think of the first years of married life with one you love: what happiness, what happiness there sometimes is in it! And indeed it's the ordinary thing. In those early days even quarrels with one's husband end happily. Some women get up quarrels with their husbands just because they love them. Indeed, I knew a woman like that: she seemed to say that because she loved him, she would torment him and make him feel it. You know that you may torment a man on purpose through love. Women are particularly given to that, thinking to themselves 'I will love him so, I will make so much of him afterwards, that it's no sin to torment him a little now.' And all in the house rejoice in the sight of you, and you are happy and gay and peaceful and honorable. . . . Then there are some women who are jealous. If he went off anywhere—I knew one such woman, she couldn't restrain herself, but would jump up at night and run off on the sly to find out where he was, whether he was with some other woman. That's a pity. And the woman knows herself it's wrong, and her heart fails her and she suffers, but she loves—it's all through love. And how sweet it is to make up after quarrels, to own herself in the wrong or to forgive him! And they both are so happy all at once—as though they had met anew, been married over again; as though their love had begun afresh. And no one, no one should know what passes between husband and wife if they love one another. And whatever quarrels there may be between them they ought not to call in their own mother to judge between them and tell tales of one another. They are their own judges. Love is a holy mystery and ought to be hidden from all other eyes, whatever happens. That makes it holier and better. They respect one another more, and much is built on respect. And if once there has been love, if they have been married for love, why should love pass away? Surely one can keep it! It is rare that one cannot keep it. And if the husband is kind and straightforward, why should not love last? The first phase of married love will pass, it is true, but then

there will come a love that is better still. Then there will be
the union of souls, they will have everything in common,
there will be no secrets between them. And once they have
children, the most difficult times will seem to them happy, so
long as there is love and courage. Even toil will be a joy, you
may deny yourself bread for your children and even that will
be a joy, They will love you for it afterwards; so you are laying
by for your future. As the children grow up you feel that you
are an example, a support for them; that even after you die
your children will always keep your thoughts and feelings,
because they have received them from you, they will take on
your semblance and likeness. So you see this is a great duty.
How can it fail to draw the father and mother nearer? People
say it's a trial to have children. Who says that? It is heavenly
happiness! Are you fond of little children, Liza? I am awfully
fond of them. You know—a little rosy baby boy at your bosom, and what husband's heart is not touched, seeing his wife
nursing his child! A plump little rosy baby, sprawling and
snuggling, chubby little hands and feet, clean tiny little nails,
so tiny that it makes one laugh to look at them; eyes that look
as if they understand everything. And while it sucks it clutch-
es at your bosom with its little hand, plays. When its father
comes up, the child tears itself away from the bosom, flings
itself back, looks at its father, laughs, as though it were fearfully funny, and falls to sucking again. Or it will bite its
mother's breast when its little teeth are coming, while it looks
sideways at her with its little eyes as though to say, 'Look, I
am biting!' Is not all that happiness when they are the three
together, husband, wife and child? One can forgive a great
deal for the sake of such moments. Yes, Liza, one must first
learn to live oneself before one blames others!"

"It's by pictures, pictures like that one must get at you," I
thought to myself, though I did speak with real feeling, and
all at once I flushed crimson. "What if she were suddenly to
burst out laughing, what should I do then?" That idea drove

me to fury. Towards the end of my speech I really was excited, and now my vanity was somehow wounded. The silence continued. I almost nudged her.

"Why are you—" she began and stopped. But I understood: there was a quiver of something different in her voice, not abrupt, harsh and unyielding as before, but something soft and shamefaced, so shamefaced that I suddenly felt ashamed and guilty.

"What?" I asked, with tender curiosity.

"Why, you. . ."

"What?"

"Why, you . . . speak somehow like a book," she said, and again there was a note of irony in her voice.

That remark sent a pang to my heart. It was not what I was expecting.

I did not understand that she was hiding her feelings under irony, that this is usually the last refuge of modest and chaste-souled people when the privacy of their soul is coarsely and intrusively invaded, and that their pride makes them refuse to surrender till the last moment and shrink from giving expression to their feelings before you. I ought to have guessed the truth from the timidity with which she had repeatedly approached her sarcasm, only bringing herself to utter it at last with an effort. But I did not guess, and an evil feeling took possession of me.

"Wait a bit!" I thought.

VII

"Oh, hush, Liza! How can you talk about being like a book, when it makes even me, an outsider, feel sick? Though I don't look at it as an outsider, for, indeed, it touches me to the heart. . . . Is it possible, is it possible that you do not feel sick at being here yourself? Evidently habit does wonders! God knows what habit can do with anyone. Can you seriously think that you will never grow old, that you will always be good-looking, and that they will keep you here for ever and ever? I say nothing of the loathsomeness of the life here. . . . Though let me tell you this about it—about your present life, I mean; here though you are young now, attractive, nice, with soul and feeling, yet you know as soon as I came to myself just now I felt at once sick at being here with you! One can only come here when one is drunk. But if you were anywhere else, living as good people live, I should perhaps be more than attracted by you, should fall in love with you, should be glad of a look from you, let alone a word; I should hang about your door, should go down on my knees to you, should look upon you as my betrothed and think it an honor to be allowed to. I should not dare to have an impure thought about you. But here, you see, I know that I have only to whistle and you have to come with me whether you like it or not. I don't consult your wishes, but you mine. The lowest laborer hires himself as a workman, but he doesn't make a slave of himself altogether; besides, he knows that he will be free again presently. But when are you free? Only think what you are giving up here? What is it you are making a slave of? It is your soul, together with your body; you are selling your soul which you have no right to dispose of! You give your love to be outraged by every drunkard! Love! But that's everything, you know, it's a priceless diamond, it's a maiden's treasure, love—why, a man would be ready to give his soul, to face death to gain that love. But how much is your love worth now? You are sold, all of you, body and soul, and there is no need to strive for love when you can have everything without love. And you know there is no greater insult to a girl than that, do you understand? To be sure, I have heard that they comfort you, poor fools, they let you have lovers of your own here. But you know that's simply a farce, that's simply a sham, it's just laughing at you, and you are taken in by it! Why, do you suppose he really loves you, that lover of yours? I don't believe it. How can he love you when he knows you may be called away from him any minute? He would be a low fellow if he did! Will he have a grain of respect for you? What have you in common with him? He laughs at you and robs you—that is all his love amounts to! You are lucky if he does not beat you. Very likely he does beat you, too. Ask him, if you have got one, whether he will marry you. He will laugh in your face, if he doesn't spit in it or give you a blow—though maybe he is not worth a bad halfpenny himself. And for what have you ruined your life, if you come to think of it? For the coffee they give you to drink and the plentiful meals? But with what object are they feeding you up? An honest girl couldn't swallow the food, for she would know what she was being fed for. You are in debt here, and, of course, you will always be in debt, and you will go on in debt to the end, till the visitors here begin to scorn you. And that will soon happen, don't rely upon your youth—all that flies by express train here, you know. You will be kicked out. And not simply kicked out; long before that she'll begin nagging at you, scolding you, abusing you, as though you had not sacrificed your health for her, had not thrown away your youth and your soul for her benefit, but as though you had ruined her, beggared her, robbed her. And don't expect anyone to take your part: the others, your companions, will attack you, too, win her favor, for all are in slavery here, and have lost all conscience and pity here long ago. They have become utterly vile, and nothing on earth is viler, more loathsome, and more insulting than their abuse. And you are laying down everything here, unconditionally, youth and health and beauty and hope, and at twenty-two you will look like a woman of five-and-thirty, and you will be lucky if you are not diseased, pray to God for that! No doubt you are thinking now that you have a gay time and no work to do! Yet there is no work harder or more dreadful in the world or ever has been. One would think that the heart alone would be worn out with tears. And you won't dare to say a word, not half a word when they drive you away from here; you will go away as though you were to blame. You will change to another house, then to a third, then somewhere else, till you come down at last to the Haymarket. There you will be beaten at every turn; that is good manners there, the visitors don't know how to be friendly without beating you. You don't believe that it is so hateful there? Go and look for yourself some time, you can see with your own eyes. Once, one New Year's Day, I saw a woman at a door. They had turned her out as a joke, to give her a taste of the frost because she had been crying so much, and they shut the door behind her. At nine o'clock in the morning she was already quite drunk, disheveled, half-naked, covered with bruises, her face was powdered, but she had a black-eye, blood was trickling from her nose and her teeth; some cabman had just given her a drubbing. She was sitting on the stone steps, a salt fish of some sort was in her hand; she was crying, wailing something about her luck and beating with the fish on the steps, and cabmen and drunken soldiers were crowding in the doorway taunting her. You don't believe that you will ever be like that? I should be sorry to believe it, too, but how do you know; maybe ten years, eight years ago that very woman with the salt fish came here fresh as a cherub, innocent, pure, knowing no evil, blushing at every word. Perhaps she was like you, proud, ready to take offence, not like the others; perhaps she looked like a queen, and knew what happiness was in store for the man who should love her and whom she should love. Do you see how it ended? And what if at that very minute when she was beating on the filthy steps with that fish, drunken and disheveled— what if at that very minute she recalled the pure early days in her father's house, when she used to go to school and the neighbor's son watched for her on the way, declaring that he would love her as long as he lived, that he would devote his life to her, and when they vowed to love one another for ever and be married as soon as they were grown up! No, Liza, it would be happy for you if you were to die soon of consumption in some corner, in some cellar like that woman just now. In the hospital, do you say? You will be lucky if they take you, but what if you are still of use to the madam here? Consumption is a queer disease, it is not like fever. The patient goes on hoping till the last minute and says he is all right. He deludes himself And that just suits your madam. Don't doubt it, that's how it is; you have sold your soul, and what is more you owe money, so you daren't say a word. But when you are dying, all will abandon you, all will turn away from you, for then there will be nothing to get from you. What's more, they will reproach you for cumbering the place, for being so long over dying. However you beg you won't get a drink of water without abuse: 'Whenever are you going off, you nasty hussy, you won't let us sleep with your moaning, you make the gentlemen sick.' That's true, I have heard such things said myself. They will thrust you dying into the filthiest corner in the cellar—in the damp and darkness; what will your thoughts be, lying there alone? When you die, strange hands will lay you out, with grumbling and impatience; no one will bless you, no one will sigh for you, they only want to get rid of you as soon as may be; they will buy a coffin, take you to the grave as they did that poor woman today, and celebrate your memory at the tavern. In the grave, sleet, filth, wet snow—no need to put themselves out for you—'Let her down, Vanuha; it's just like her luck—even here, she is head-foremost, the hussy. Shorten the cord, you rascal.' 'It's all right as it is.' 'All right, is it? Why, she's on her side! She was a fellow-creature, after all! But, never mind, throw the earth on her.' And they won't care to waste much time quarrelling over you. They will scatter the wet blue clay as quick as they can and go off to the tavern . . . and there your memory on earth will end; other women have children to go to their graves, fathers, husbands. While for you neither tear, nor sigh, nor remembrance; no one in the whole world will ever come to you, your name will vanish from the face of the earth—as though you had never existed, never been born at all! Nothing but filth and mud, however you knock at your coffin lid at night, when the dead arise, however you cry: 'Let me out, kind people, to live in the light of day! My life was no life at all; my life has been thrown away like a dish-clout; it was drunk away in the tavern at the Haymarket; let me out, kind people, to live in the world again.'"

And I worked myself up to such a pitch that I began to have a lump in my throat myself, and . . . and all at once I stopped, sat up in dismay and, bending over apprehensively, began to listen with a beating heart. I had reason to be troubled.

I had felt for some time that I was turning her soul upside down and rending her heart, and—and the more I was convinced of it, the more eagerly I desired to gain my object as quickly and as effectually as possible. It was the exercise of my skill that carried me away; yet it was not merely sport. . . .

I knew I was speaking stiffly, artificially, even bookishly, in fact, I could not speak except "like a book." But that did not trouble me: I knew, I felt that I should be understood and that this very bookishness might be an assistance. But now, having attained my effect, I was suddenly panic-stricken. Never before had I witnessed such despair! She was lying on her face, thrusting her face into the pillow and clutching it in both hands. Her heart was being torn. Her youthful body was shuddering all over as though in convulsions. Suppressed sobs rent her bosom and suddenly burst out in weeping and wailing, then she pressed closer into the pillow: she did not want anyone here, not a living soul, to know of her anguish and her tears. She bit the pillow, bit her hand till it bled (I saw that afterwards), or, thrusting her fingers into her disheveled hair, seemed rigid with the effort of restraint, holding her breath and clenching her teeth. I began saying something, begging her to calm herself, but felt that I did not dare; and all at once, in a sort of cold shiver, almost in terror, began fumbling in the dark, trying hurriedly to get dressed to go. It was dark; though I tried my best I could not finish dressing quickly. Suddenly I felt a box of matches and a candlestick with a whole candle in it. As soon as the room was lighted up, Liza sprang up, sat up in bed, and with a contorted face, with a half insane smile, looked at me almost senselessly. I sat down beside her and took her hands; she came to herself, made an impulsive movement towards me, would have caught hold of me, but did not dare, and slowly bowed her head before me.

"Liza, my dear, I was wrong . . . forgive me, my dear," I began, but she squeezed my hand in her fingers so tightly that I felt I was saying the wrong thing and stopped.

"This is my address, Liza, come to me."

"I will come," she answered resolutely, her head still bowed.

"But now I am going, good-bye . . . till we meet again."

I got up; she, too, stood up and suddenly flushed all over, gave a shudder, snatched up a shawl that was lying on a chair and muffled herself in it to her chin. As she did this she gave another sickly smile, blushed and looked at me strangely. I felt wretched; I was in haste to get away—to disappear.

"Wait a minute," she said suddenly, in the passage just at the doorway, stopping me with her hand on my overcoat. She put down the candle in hot haste and ran off; evidently she had thought of something or wanted to show me something. As she ran away she flushed, her eyes shone, and there was a smile on her lips—what was the meaning of it? Against my will I waited: she came back a minute later with an expression that seemed to ask forgiveness for something. In fact, it was not the same face, not the same look as the evening before: sullen, mistrustful and obstinate. Her eyes now were imploring, soft, and at the same time trustful, caressing, timid. The expression with which children look at people they are very fond of, of whom they are asking a favour. Her eyes were a light hazel, they were lovely eyes, full of life, and capable of expressing love as well as sullen hatred.

Making no explanation, as though I, as a sort of higher being, must understand everything without explanations, she held out a piece of paper to me. Her whole face was positively beaming at that instant with naive, almost childish, triumph. I unfolded it. It was a letter to her from a medical student or someone of that sort—a very high-flown and flowery, but extremely respectful, love-letter. I don't recall the words now, but I remember well that through the high-flown phrases there was apparent a genuine feeling, which cannot be feigned. When I had finished reading it I met her glowing, questioning, and childishly impatient eyes fixed upon me. She fastened her eyes upon my face and waited impatiently for what I should say. In a few words, hurriedly, but with a sort of joy and pride, she explained to me that she had been to a dance somewhere in a private house, a family of "very nice people, *who knew nothing*, absolutely nothing, for she had only come here so lately and it had all happened . . . and she hadn't made up her mind to stay and was certainly going away as soon as she had paid her debt. . ." and at that party there had been the student who had danced with her all the evening. He had talked to her, and it turned out that he had known her in old days at Riga when he was a child, they had played together, but a very long time ago—and he knew her parents, but *about this* he knew nothing, nothing whatever, and had no suspicion! And the day after the dance (three days ago) he had sent her that letter through the friend with whom she had gone to the party . . . and . . . well, that was all.

She dropped her shining eyes with a sort of bashfulness as she finished.

The poor girl was keeping that student's letter as a precious treasure, and had run to fetch it, her only treasure, because she did not want me to go away without knowing that she, too, was honestly and genuinely loved; that she, too, was addressed respectfully. No doubt that letter was destined to lie in her box and lead to nothing. But none the less, I am certain that she would keep it all her life as a precious treasure, as her pride and justification, and now at such a minute she had thought of that letter and brought it with naive pride to raise herself in my eyes that I might see, that I, too, might think well of her. I said nothing, pressed her hand and went out. I so longed to get away . . . I walked all the way home, in spite of the fact that the melting snow was still falling in heavy flakes. I was exhausted, shattered, in bewilderment. But behind the bewilderment the truth was already gleaming. The loathsome truth.

VIII

It was some time, however, before I consented to recognize that truth. Waking up in the morning after some hours of heavy, leaden sleep, and immediately realizing all that had happened on the previous day, I was positively amazed at my last night's *sentimentality* with Liza, at all those "outcries of horror and pity." "To think of having such an attack of womanish hysteria, pah!" I concluded. And what did I thrust my address upon her for? What if she comes? Let her come, though; it doesn't matter. . . . But *obviously*, that was not now the chief and the most important matter: I had to make haste and at all costs save my reputation in the eyes of Zverkov and Simonov as quickly as possible; that was the chief business. And I was so taken up that morning that I actually forgot all about Liza.

First of all I had at once to repay what I had borrowed the day before from Simonov. I resolved on a desperate measure: to borrow fifteen rubles straight off from Anton Antonitch. As luck would have it he was in the best of humors that morning, and gave it to me at once, on the first asking. I was so delighted at this that, as I signed the IOU with a swaggering air, I told him casually that the night before "I had been keeping it up with some friends at the Hotel de Paris; we were giving a farewell party to a comrade, in fact, I might say a friend of my childhood, and you know—a desperate rake, fearfully spoilt—of course, he belongs to a good family, and has considerable means, a brilliant career; he is witty, charming, a regular Lovelace, you understand; we drank an extra 'half-dozen' and . . ."

And it went off all right; all this was uttered very easily, unconstrainedly and complacently.

On reaching home I promptly wrote to Simonov.

To this hour I am lost in admiration when I recall the truly gentlemanly, good-humored, candid tone of my letter. With tact and good-breeding, and, above all, entirely without superfluous words, I blamed myself for all that had happened. I defended myself, "if I really may be allowed to defend myself," by alleging that being utterly unaccustomed to wine, I had been intoxicated with the first glass, which I said, I had drunk before they arrived, while I was waiting for them at the Hotel de Paris between five and six o'clock. I begged Simonov's pardon especially; I asked him to convey my explanations to all the others, especially to Zverkov, whom "I seemed to remember as though in a dream" I had insulted. I added that I would have called upon all of them myself, but my head ached, and besides I had not the face to. I was particularly pleased with a certain lightness, almost carelessness (strictly within the bounds of politeness, however), which was apparent in my style, and better than any possible arguments, gave them at once to understand that I took rather an independent view of "all that unpleasantness last night"; that I was by no means so utterly crushed as you, my friends, probably imagine; but on the contrary, looked upon it as a gentleman serenely respecting himself should look upon it. "On a young hero's past no censure is cast!"

"There is actually an aristocratic playfulness about it!" I thought admiringly, as I read over the letter. "And it's all because I am an intellectual and cultivated man! Another man in my place would not have known how to extricate himself, but here I have got out of it and am as jolly as ever again, and all because I am 'a cultivated and educated man of our day.' And, indeed, perhaps, everything was due to the wine yesterday. H'm!" . . . No, it was not the wine. I did not drink anything at all between five and six when I was waiting for them. I had lied to Simonov; I had lied shamelessly; and indeed I wasn't ashamed now. . . . Hang it all though, the great thing was that I was rid of it.

I put six rubles in the letter, sealed it up, and asked Apollon to take it to Simonov. When he learned that there was money in the letter, Apollon became more respectful and agreed to take it. Towards evening I went out for a walk. My head was still aching and giddy after yesterday. But as evening came on and the twilight grew denser, my impressions and, following them, my thoughts, grew more and more different and confused. Something was not dead within me, in the depths of my heart and conscience it would not die, and it showed itself in acute depression. For the most part I jostled my way through the most crowded business streets, along Myeshtchansky Street, along Sadovy Street and in Yusupov Garden. I always liked particularly sauntering along these streets in the dusk, just when there were crowds of working people of all sorts going home from their daily work, with faces looking cross with anxiety. What I liked was just that cheap bustle, that bare prose. On this occasion the jostling of the streets irritated me more than ever, I could not make out what was wrong with me, I could not find the clue, something seemed rising up continually in my soul, painfully, and refusing to be appeased. I returned home completely upset, it was just as though some crime were lying on my conscience.

The thought that Liza was coming worried me continually. It seemed queer to me that of all my recollections of yesterday this tormented me, as it were, especially, as it were, quite separately. Everything else I had quite succeeded in forgetting by the evening; I dismissed it all and was still perfectly satisfied with my letter to Simonov. But on this point I was not satisfied at all. It was as though I were worried only by Liza. "What if she comes," I thought incessantly, "well, it doesn't matter, let her come! H'm! it's horrid that she should see, for instance, how I live. Yesterday I seemed such a hero to her, while now, h'm! It's horrid, though, that I have let myself go so, the room looks like a beggar's. And I brought myself to go out to dinner in such a suit! And my American leather sofa with the stuffing sticking out. And my dressing-gown, which will not cover me, such tatters, and she will see all this and she will see Apollon. That beast is certain to insult her. He will fasten upon her in order to be rude to me. And I, of course, shall be panic-stricken as usual, I shall begin bowing and scraping before her and pulling my dressing-gown round me, I shall begin smiling, telling lies. Oh, the beastliness! And it isn't the beastliness of it that matters most! There is something more important, more loathsome, viler! Yes, viler! And to put on that dishonest lying mask again! . . ."

When I reached that thought I fired up all at once.

"Why dishonest? How dishonest? I was speaking sincerely last night. I remember there was real feeling in me, too. What I wanted was to excite an honorable feeling in her. . . . Her crying was a good thing, it will have a good effect."

Yet I could not feel at ease. All that evening, even when I had come back home, even after nine o'clock, when I calculated that Liza could not possibly come, still she haunted me, and what was worse, she came back to my mind always in the same position. One moment out of all that had happened last night stood vividly before my imagination; the moment when I struck a match and saw her pale, distorted face, with its look of torture. And what a pitiful, what an unnatural, what a distorted smile she had at that moment! But I did not know then, that fifteen years later I should still in my imagination see Liza, always with the pitiful, distorted, inappropriate smile which was on her face at that minute.

Next day I was ready again to look upon it all as nonsense, due to over-excited nerves, and, above all, as *exaggerated*. I was always conscious of that weak point of mine, and sometimes very much afraid of it. "I exaggerate everything, that is where I go wrong," I repeated to myself every hour. But, however, "Liza will very likely come all the same," was the refrain with which all my reflections ended. I was so uneasy that I sometimes flew into a fury: "She'll come, she is certain to come!" I cried, running about the room, "if not today, she will come tomorrow; she'll find me out! The damnable romanticism of these pure hearts! Oh, the vileness—oh, the silliness—oh, the stupidity of these 'wretched sentimental souls!' Why, how fail to understand? How could one fail to understand? . . ."

But at this point I stopped short, and in great confusion, indeed.

And how few, how few words, I thought, in passing, were needed; how little of the idyllic (and affectedly, bookishly, artificially idyllic too) had sufficed to turn a whole human life at once according to my will. That's virginity, to be sure! Freshness of soil!

At times a thought occurred to me, to go to her, "to tell her all," and beg her not to come to me. But this thought stirred such wrath in me that I believed I should have crushed that "damned" Liza if she had chanced to be near me at the time. I should have insulted her, have spat at her, have turned her out, have struck her!

One day passed, however, another and another; she did not come and I began to grow calmer. I felt particularly bold and cheerful after nine o'clock, I even sometimes began dreaming, and rather sweetly: I, for instance, became the salvation of Liza, simply through her coming to me and my talking to her. . . . I develop her, educate her. Finally, I notice that she loves me, loves me passionately. I pretend not to understand (I don't know, however, why I pretend, just for effect, perhaps). At last all confusion, transfigured, trembling and sobbing, she flings herself at my feet and says that I am her saviour, and that she loves me better than anything in the world. I am amazed, but. . . . "Liza," I say, "can you imagine that I have not noticed your love? I saw it all, I divined it, but I did not dare to approach you first, because I had an influence over you and was afraid that you would force yourself, from gratitude, to respond to my love, would try to rouse in your heart a feeling which was perhaps absent, and I did not wish that . . . because it would be tyranny . . . it would be indelicate (in short, I launch off at that point into European, inexplicably lofty subtleties a la George Sand), but now, now you are mine, you are my creation, you are pure, you are good, you are my noble wife.

> 'Into my house come bold and free,
>   Its rightful mistress there to be'."

Then we begin living together, go abroad and so on, and so on. In fact, in the end it seemed vulgar to me myself, and I began putting out my tongue at myself.

Besides, they won't let her out, "the hussy!" I thought. They don't let them go out very readily, especially in the evening (for some reason I fancied she would come in the evening, and at seven o'clock precisely). Though she did say she was not altogether a slave there yet, and had certain rights; so, h'm! Damn it all, she will come, she is sure to come!

It was a good thing, in fact, that Apollon distracted my attention at that time by his rudeness. He drove me beyond all patience! He was the bane of my life, the curse laid upon me by Providence. We had been squabbling continually for years, and I hated him. My God, how I hated him! I believe I had never hated anyone in my life as I hated him, especially at some moments. He was an elderly, dignified man, who worked part of his time as a tailor. But for some unknown reason he despised me beyond all measure, and looked down upon me insufferably. Though, indeed, he looked down upon everyone. Simply to glance at that flaxen, smoothly brushed head, at the tuft of hair he combed up on his forehead and oiled with sunflower oil, at that dignified mouth, compressed into the shape of the letter V, made one feel one was confronting a man who never doubted of himself. He was a pedant, to the most extreme point, the greatest pedant I had met on earth, and with that had a vanity only befitting Alexander of Macedon. He was in love with every button on his coat, every nail on his fingers—absolutely in love with them, and he looked it! In his behavior to me he was a perfect tyrant, he spoke very little to me, and if he chanced to glance at me he gave me a firm, majestically self-confident and invariably ironical look that drove me sometimes to fury. He did his work with the air of doing me the greatest favour, though he did scarcely anything for me, and did not, indeed, consider himself bound to do anything. There could be no doubt that he looked upon me as the greatest fool on earth, and that "he did not get rid of me" was simply that he could get wages from me every month. He consented to do nothing for me for seven rubles a month. Many sins should be forgiven me for what I suffered from him. My hatred reached such a point that sometimes his very step almost threw me into convulsions. What I loathed particularly was his lisp. His tongue must have been a little too long or something of that sort, for he continually lisped, and seemed to be very proud of it, imagining that it greatly added to his dignity. He spoke in a slow, measured tone, with his hands behind his back and his eyes fixed on the ground. He maddened me particularly when he read aloud the psalms to himself behind his partition. Many a battle I waged over that reading! But he was awfully fond of reading aloud in the evenings, in a slow, even, singsong voice, as though over the dead. It is interesting that that is how he has ended: he hires himself out to read the psalms over the dead, and at the same time he kills rats and makes blacking. But at that time I could not get rid of him, it was as though he were chemically combined with my existence. Besides, nothing would have induced him to consent to leave me. I could not live in furnished lodgings: my lodging was my private solitude, my shell, my cave, in which I concealed myself from all mankind, and Apollon seemed to me, for some reason, an integral part of that flat, and for seven years I could not turn him away.

To be two or three days behind with his wages, for instance, was impossible. He would have made such a fuss, I should not have known where to hide my head. But I was so exasperated with everyone during those days, that I made up my mind for some reason and with some object to *punish* Apollon and not to pay him for a fortnight the wages that were owing him. I had for a long time—for the last two years—been intending to do this, simply in order to teach him not to give himself airs with me, and to show him that if I liked I could withhold his wages. I purposed to say nothing to him about it, and was purposely silent indeed, in order to score off his pride and force him to be the first to speak of his wages. Then I would take the seven rubles out of a drawer, show him I have the money put aside on purpose, but that I won't, I won't, I simply won't pay him his wages, I won't just because that is "what I wish," because "I am master, and it is for me to decide," because he has been disrespectful, because he has been rude; but if he were to ask respectfully I might be softened and give it to him, otherwise he might wait another fortnight, another three weeks, a whole month. . . .

But angry as I was, yet he got the better of me. I could not hold out for four days. He began as he always did begin in such cases, for there had been such cases already, there had been attempts (and it may be observed I knew all this beforehand, I knew his nasty tactics by heart). He would begin by fixing upon me an exceedingly severe stare, keeping it up for several minutes at a time, particularly on meeting me or seeing me out of the house. If I held out and pretended not to notice these stares, he would, still in silence, proceed to further tortures. All at once, *apropos* of nothing, he would walk softly and smoothly into my room, when I was pacing up and down or reading, stand at the door, one hand behind his back and one foot behind the other, and fix upon me a stare more than severe, utterly contemptuous. If I suddenly asked him what he wanted, he would make me no answer, but continue staring at me persistently for some seconds, then, with a peculiar compression of his lips and a most significant air, deliberately turn round and deliberately go back to his room. Two hours later he would come out again and again present himself before me in the same way. It had happened that in my fury I did not even ask him what he wanted, but simply raised my head sharply and imperiously and began staring back at him. So we stared at one another for two minutes; at last he turned with deliberation and dignity and went back again for two hours.

If I were still not brought to reason by all this, but persisted in my revolt, he would suddenly begin sighing while he looked at me, long, deep sighs as though measuring by them the depths of my moral degradation, and, of course, it ended at last by his triumphing completely: I raged and shouted, but still was forced to do what he wanted.

This time the usual staring maneuvers had scarcely begun when I lost my temper and flew at him in a fury. I was irritated beyond endurance apart from him.

"Stay," I cried, in a frenzy, as he was slowly and silently turning, with one hand behind his back, to go to his room. "Stay! Come back, come back, I tell you!" and I must have bawled so unnaturally, that he turned round and even looked at me with some wonder. However, he persisted in saying nothing, and that infuriated me.

"How dare you come and look at me like that without being sent for? Answer!"

After looking at me calmly for half a minute, he began turning round again.

"Stay!" I roared, running up to him, "don't stir! There. Answer, now: what did you come in to look at?"

"If you have any order to give me it's my duty to carry it out," he answered, after another silent pause, with a slow, measured lisp, raising his eyebrows and calmly twisting his head from one side to another, all this with exasperating composure.

"That's not what I am asking you about, you torturer!" I shouted, turning crimson with anger. "I'll tell you why you came here myself: you see, I don't give you your wages, you are so proud you don't want to bow down and ask for it, and so you come to punish me with your stupid stares, to worry me and you have no sus-pic-ion how stupid it is—stupid, stupid, stupid, stupid! . . ."

He would have turned round again without a word, but I seized him.

"Listen," I shouted to him. "Here's the money, do you see, here it is," (I took it out of the table drawer); "here's the seven rubles complete, but you are not going to have it, you . . . are . . . not . . . going . . . to . . . have it until you come respectfully with bowed head to beg my pardon. Do you hear?"

"That cannot be," he answered, with the most unnatural self-confidence.

"It shall be so," I said, "I give you my word of honor, it shall be!"

"And there's nothing for me to beg your pardon for," he went on, as though he had not noticed my exclamations at all. "Why, besides, you called me a 'torturer,' for which I can summon you at the police-station at any time for insulting behavior."

"Go, summon me," I roared, "go at once, this very minute, this very second! You are a torturer all the same! a torturer!"

But he merely looked at me, then turned, and regardless of my loud calls to him, he walked to his room with an even step and without looking round.

"If it had not been for Liza nothing of this would have happened," I decided inwardly. Then, after waiting a minute, I went myself behind his screen with a dignified and solemn air, though my heart was beating slowly and violently.

"Apollon," I said quietly and emphatically, though I was breathless, "go at once without a minute's delay and fetch the police-officer."

He had meanwhile settled himself at his table, put on his spectacles and taken up some sewing. But, hearing my order, he burst into a guffaw.

"At once, go this minute! Go on, or else you can't imagine what will happen."

"You are certainly out of your mind," he observed, without even raising his head, lisping as deliberately as ever and threading his needle. "Whoever heard of a man sending for the police against himself? And as for being frightened—you are upsetting yourself about nothing, for nothing will come of it."

"Go!" I shrieked, clutching him by the shoulder. I felt I should strike him in a minute.

But I did not notice the door from the passage softly and slowly open at that instant and a figure come in, stop short, and begin staring at us in perplexity I glanced, nearly swooned with shame, and rushed back to my room. There, clutching at my hair with both hands, I leaned my head against the wall and stood motionless in that position.

Two minutes later I heard Apollon's deliberate footsteps. "There is some woman asking for you," he said, looking at me with peculiar severity. Then he stood aside and let in Liza. He would not go away, but stared at us sarcastically.

"Go away, go away," I commanded in desperation. At that moment my clock began whirring and wheezing and struck seven.

IX

"Into my house come bold and free,
Its rightful mistress there to be."

I stood before her crushed, crestfallen, revoltingly confused, and I believe I smiled as I did my utmost to wrap myself in the skirts of my ragged wadded dressing-gown—exactly as I had imagined the scene not long before in a fit of depression. After standing over us for a couple of minutes Apollon went away, but that did not make me more at ease. What made it worse was that she, too, was overwhelmed with confusion, more so, in fact, than I should have expected. At the sight of me, of course.

"Sit down," I said mechanically, moving a chair up to the table, and I sat down on the sofa. She obediently sat down at once and gazed at me open-eyed, evidently expecting something from me at once. This naiveté of expectation drove me to fury, but I restrained myself.

She ought to have tried not to notice, as though everything had been as usual, while instead of that, she . . . and I dimly felt that I should make her pay dearly for *all this*.

"You have found me in a strange position, Liza," I began, stammering and knowing that this was the wrong way to begin. "No, no, don't imagine anything," I cried, seeing that she had suddenly flushed. "I am not ashamed of my poverty. . . . On the contrary, I look with pride on my poverty. I am poor but honorable. . . . One can be poor and honorable," I muttered. "However . . . would you like tea?. . . ."

"No," she was beginning.

"Wait a minute."

I leapt up and ran to Apollon. I had to get out of the room somehow.

"Apollon," I whispered in feverish haste, flinging down before him the seven rubles which had remained all the time in my clenched fist, "here are your wages, you see I give them to you; but for that you must come to my rescue: bring me tea and a dozen rusks from the restaurant. If you won't go, you'll make me a miserable man! You don't know what this woman is. . . . This is—everything! You may be imagining something. . . . But you don't know what that woman is! . . ."

Apollon, who had already sat down to his work and put on his spectacles again, at first glanced askance at the money without speaking or putting down his needle; then, without paying the slightest attention to me or making any answer, he went on busying himself with his needle, which he had not yet threaded. I waited before him for three minutes with my arms crossed *a la Napoleon*. My temples were moist with sweat. I was pale, I felt it. But, thank God, he must have been moved to pity, looking at me. Having threaded his needle he deliberately got up from his seat, deliberately moved back his chair, deliberately took off his spectacles, deliberately counted the money, and finally asking me over his shoulder: "Shall I get a whole portion?" deliberately walked out of the room. As I was going back to Liza, the thought occurred to me on the way: shouldn't I run away just as I was in my dressing-gown, no matter where, and then let happen what would?

I sat down again. She looked at me uneasily. For some minutes we were silent.

"I will kill him," I shouted suddenly, striking the table with my fist so that the ink spurted out of the inkstand.

"What are you saying!" she cried, starting.

"I will kill him! kill him!" I shrieked, suddenly striking the table in absolute frenzy, and at the same time fully understanding how stupid it was to be in such a frenzy. "You don't know, Liza, what that torturer is to me. He is my torturer. . . . He has gone now to fetch some rusks; he . . ."

And suddenly I burst into tears. It was an hysterical attack. How ashamed I felt in the midst of my sobs; but still I could not restrain them.

She was frightened.

"What is the matter? What is wrong?" she cried, fussing about me.

"Water, give me water, over there!" I muttered in a faint voice, though I was inwardly conscious that I could have got on very well without water and without muttering in a faint voice. But I was, what is called, *putting it on*, to save appearances, though the attack was a genuine one.

She gave me water, looking at me in bewilderment. At that moment Apollon brought in the tea. It suddenly seemed to me that this commonplace, prosaic tea was horribly undignified and paltry after all that had happened, and I blushed crimson. Liza looked at Apollon with positive alarm. He went out without a glance at either of us.

"Liza, do you despise me?" I asked, looking at her fixedly, trembling with impatience to know what she was thinking.

She was confused, and did not know what to answer.

"Drink your tea," I said to her angrily. I was angry with myself, but, of course, it was she who would have to pay for it. A horrible spite against her suddenly surged up in my heart; I believe I could have killed her. To revenge myself on her I swore inwardly not to say a word to her all the time. "She is the cause of it all," I thought.

Our silence lasted for five minutes. The tea stood on the table; we did not touch it. I had got to the point of purposely refraining from beginning in order to embarrass her further; it was awkward for her to begin alone. Several times she glanced at me with mournful perplexity. I was obstinately silent. I was, of course, myself the chief sufferer, because I was fully conscious of the disgusting meanness of my spiteful stupidity, and yet at the same time I could not restrain myself.

"I want to. . . get away . . . from there altogether," she began, to break the silence in some way, but, poor girl, that was just what she ought not to have spoken about at such a stupid moment to a man so stupid as I was. My heart positively ached with pity for her tactless and unnecessary straightforwardness. But something hideous at once stifled all compassion in me; it even provoked me to greater venom. I did not care what happened. Another five minutes passed.

"Perhaps I am in your way," she began timidly, hardly audibly, and was getting up.

But as soon as I saw this first impulse of wounded dignity I positively trembled with spite, and at once burst out.

"Why have you come to me, tell me that, please?" I began, gasping for breath and regardless of logical connection in my words. I longed to have it all out at once, at one burst; I did not even trouble how to begin. "Why have you come? Answer, answer," I cried, hardly knowing what I was doing. "I'll tell you, my good girl, why you have come. You've come because I talked sentimental stuff to you then. So now you are soft as butter and longing for fine sentiments again. So you may as well know that I was laughing at you then. And I am laughing at you now. Why are you shuddering? Yes, I was laughing at you! I had been insulted just before, at dinner, by the fellows who came that evening before me. I came to you, meaning to thrash one of them, an officer; but I didn't succeed, I didn't find him; I had to avenge the insult on someone to get back my own again; you turned up, I vented my spleen on you and laughed at you. I had been humiliated, so I wanted to humiliate; I had been treated like a rag, so I wanted to show my power. . . . That's what it was, and you imagined I had come there on purpose to save you. Yes? You imagined that? You imagined that?"

I knew that she would perhaps be muddled and not take it all in exactly, but I knew, too, that she would grasp the gist of it, very well indeed. And so, indeed, she did. She turned white as a handkerchief, tried to say something, and her lips worked painfully; but she sank on a chair as though she had been felled by an axe. And all the time afterwards she listened to me with her lips parted and her eyes wide open, shuddering with awful terror. The cynicism, the cynicism of my words overwhelmed her. . . .

"Save you!" I went on, jumping up from my chair and running up and down the room before her. "Save you from what? But perhaps I am worse than you myself. Why didn't you throw it in my teeth when I was giving you that sermon: 'But what did you come here yourself for? was it to read us a sermon?' Power, power was what I wanted then, sport was what I wanted, I wanted to wring out your tears, your humiliation, your hysteria—that was what I wanted then! Of course, I couldn't keep it up then, because I am a wretched creature, I was frightened, and, the devil knows why, gave you my address in my folly. Afterwards, before I got home, I was cursing and swearing at you because of that address, I hated you already because of the lies I had told you. Because I only like playing with words, only dreaming, but, do you know, what I really want is that you should all go to hell. That is what I want. I want peace; yes, I'd sell the whole world for a farthing, straight off, so long as I was left in peace. Is the world to go to pot, or am I to go without my tea? I say that the world may go to pot for me so long as I always get my tea. Did you know that, or not? Well, anyway, I know that I am a blackguard, a scoundrel, an egoist, a sluggard. Here I have been shuddering for the last three days at the thought of your coming. And do you know what has worried me particularly for these three days? That I posed as such a hero to you, and now you would see me in a wretched torn dressing-gown, beggarly, loathsome. I told you just now that I was not ashamed of my poverty; so you may as well know that I am ashamed of it; I am more ashamed of it than of anything, more afraid of it than of being found out if I were a thief, because I am as vain as though I had been skinned and the very air blowing on me hurt. Surely by now you must realize that I shall never forgive you for having found me in this wretched dressing-gown, just as I was flying at Apollon like a spiteful cur. The savior, the former hero, was flying like a mangy, unkempt sheep-dog at his lackey, and the lackey was jeering at him! And I shall never forgive you for the tears I could not help shedding before you just now, like some silly woman put to shame! And for what I am confessing to you now, I shall never forgive you either! Yes—you must answer for it all because you turned up like this, because I am a blackguard, because I am the nastiest, stupidest, absurdest and most envious of all the worms on earth, who are not a bit better than I am, but, the devil knows why, are never put to confusion; while I shall always be insulted by every louse, that is my doom! And what is it to me that you don't understand a word of this! And what do I care, what do I care about you, and whether you go to ruin there or not? Do you understand? How I shall hate you now after saying this, for having been here and listening. Why, it's not once in a lifetime a man speaks out like this, and then it is in hysterics! . . . What more do you want? Why do you still stand confronting me, after all this? Why are you worrying me? Why don't you go?"

But at this point a strange thing happened. I was so accustomed to think and imagine everything from books, and to picture everything in the world to myself just as I had made it up in my dreams beforehand, that I could not all at once take in this strange circumstance. What happened was this: Liza, insulted and crushed by me, understood a great deal more than I imagined. She understood from all this what a woman understands first of all, if she feels genuine love, that is, that I was myself unhappy.

The frightened and wounded expression on her face was followed first by a look of sorrowful perplexity. When I began calling myself a scoundrel and a blackguard and my tears flowed (the tirade was accompanied throughout by tears) her whole face worked convulsively. She was on the point of getting up and stopping me; when I finished she took no notice of my shouting: "Why are you here, why don't you go away?" but realized only that it must have been very bitter to me to say all this. Besides, she was so crushed, poor girl; she considered herself infinitely beneath me; how could she feel anger or resentment? She suddenly leapt up from her chair with an irresistible impulse and held out her hands, yearning towards me, though still timid and not daring to stir. . . . At this point there was a revulsion in my heart too. Then she suddenly rushed to me, threw her arms round me and burst into tears. I, too, could not restrain myself, and sobbed as I never had before.

"They won't let me . . . I can't be good!" I managed to articulate; then I went to the sofa, fell on it face downwards, and sobbed on it for a quarter of an hour in genuine hysterics. She came close to me, put her arms round me and stayed motionless in that position. But the trouble was that the hysterics could not go on for ever, and (I am writing the loathsome truth) lying face downwards on the sofa with my face thrust into my nasty leather pillow, I began by degrees to be aware of a far-away, involuntary but irresistible feeling that it would be awkward now for me to raise my head and look Liza straight in the face. Why was I ashamed? I don't know, but I was ashamed. The thought, too, came into my overwrought brain that our parts now were completely changed, that she was now the heroine, while I was just a crushed and humiliated creature as she had been before me that night—four days before. . . . And all this came into my mind during the minutes I was lying on my face on the sofa.

My God! surely I was not envious of her then.

I don't know, to this day I cannot decide, and at the time, of course, I was still less able to understand what I was feeling than now. I cannot get on without domineering and tyrannizing over someone, but . . . there is no explaining anything by reasoning and so it is useless to reason.

I conquered myself, however, and raised my head; I had to do so sooner or later . . . and I am convinced to this day that it was just because I was ashamed to look at her that another feeling was suddenly kindled and flamed up in my heart . . . a feeling of mastery and possession. My eyes gleamed with passion, and I gripped her hands tightly. How I hated her and how I was drawn to her at that minute! The one feeling intensified the other. It was almost like an act of vengeance. At first there was a look of amazement, even of terror on her face, but only for one instant. She warmly and rapturously embraced me.

X

A quarter of an hour later I was rushing up and down the room in frenzied impatience, from minute to minute I went up to the screen and peeped through the crack at Liza. She was sitting on the ground with her head leaning against the bed, and must have been crying. But she did not go away, and that irritated me. This time she understood it all. I had insulted her finally, but . . . there's no need to describe it. She realized that my outburst of passion had been simply revenge, a fresh humiliation, and that to my earlier, almost causeless hatred was added now a *personal hatred*, born of envy. . . . Though I do not maintain positively that she understood all this distinctly; but she certainly did fully understand that I was a despicable man, and what was worse, incapable of loving her.

I know I shall be told that this is incredible—but it is incredible to be as spiteful and stupid as I was; it may be added that it was strange I should not love her, or at any rate, appreciate her love. Why is it strange? In the first place, by then I was incapable of love, for I repeat, with me loving meant tyrannizing and showing my moral superiority. I have never in my life been able to imagine any other sort of love, and have nowadays come to the point of sometimes thinking that love really consists in the right—freely given by the beloved object—to tyrannize over her.

Even in my underground dreams I did not imagine love except as a struggle. I began it always with hatred and ended it with moral subjugation, and afterwards I never knew what to do with the subjugated object. And what is there to wonder at in that, since I had succeeded in so corrupting myself, since I was so out of touch with "real life," as to have actually thought of reproaching her, and putting her to shame for having come to me to hear "fine sentiments"; and did not even guess that she had come not to hear fine sentiments, but to love me, because to a woman all reformation, all salvation from any sort of ruin, and all moral renewal is included in love and can only show itself in that form.

I did not hate her so much, however, when I was running about the room and peeping through the crack in the screen. I was only insufferably oppressed by her being here. I wanted her to disappear. I wanted "peace," to be left alone in my underground world. Real life oppressed me with its novelty so much that I could hardly breathe.

But several minutes passed and she still remained, without stirring, as though she were unconscious. I had the shamelessness to tap softly at the screen as though to remind her. . . . She started, sprang up, and flew to seek her kerchief, her hat, her coat, as though making her escape from me. . . . Two minutes later she came from behind the screen and looked with heavy eyes at me. I gave a spiteful grin, which was forced, however, to *keep up appearances*, and I turned away from her eyes.

"Good-bye," she said, going towards the door.

I ran up to her, seized her hand, opened it, thrust something in it and closed it again. Then I turned at once and dashed away in haste to the other corner of the room to avoid seeing, anyway. . . .

I did mean a moment since to tell a lie—to write that I did this accidentally, not knowing what I was doing through foolishness, through losing my head. But I don't want to lie, and so I will say straight out that I opened her hand and put the money in it . . . from spite. It came into my head to do this while I was running up and down the room and she was sitting behind the screen. But this I can say for certain: though I did that cruel thing purposely, it was not an impulse from the heart, but came from my evil brain. This cruelty was so affected, so purposely made up, so completely a product of the brain, of books, that I could not even keep it up a minute—first I dashed away to avoid seeing her, and then in shame and despair rushed after Liza. I opened the door in the passage and began listening.

"Liza! Liza!" I cried on the stairs, but in a low voice, not boldly. There was no answer, but I fancied I heard her footsteps, lower down on the stairs.

"Liza!" I cried, more loudly.

No answer. But at that minute I heard the stiff outer glass door open heavily with a creak and slam violently; the sound echoed up the stairs.

She had gone. I went back to my room in hesitation. I felt horribly oppressed.

I stood still at the table, beside the chair on which she had sat and looked aimlessly before me. A minute passed, suddenly I started; straight before me on the table I saw. . . . In short, I saw a crumpled blue five-ruble note, the one I had thrust into her hand a minute before. It was the same note; it could be no other, there was no other in the flat. So she had managed to fling it from her hand on the table at the moment when I had dashed into the further corner.

Well! I might have expected that she would do that. Might I have expected it? No, I was such an egoist, I was so lacking in respect for my fellow-creatures that I could not even imagine she would do so. I could not endure it. A minute later I flew like a madman to dress, flinging on what I could at random and ran headlong after her. She could not have got two hundred paces away when I ran out into the street.

It was a still night and the snow was coming down in masses and falling almost perpendicularly, covering the pavement and the empty street as though with a pillow. There was no one in the street, no sound was to be heard. The street lamps gave a disconsolate and useless glimmer. I ran two hundred paces to the cross-roads and stopped short.

Where had she gone? And why was I running after her?

Why? To fall down before her, to sob with remorse, to kiss her feet, to entreat her forgiveness! I longed for that, my whole breast was being rent to pieces, and never, never shall I recall that minute with indifference. But—what for? I thought. Should I not begin to hate her, perhaps, even tomorrow, just because I had kissed her feet today? Should I give her happiness? Had I not recognized that day, for the hundredth time, what I was worth? Should I not torture her?

I stood in the snow, gazing into the troubled darkness and pondered this.

"And will it not be better?" I mused fantastically, afterwards at home, stifling the living pang of my heart with fantastic dreams. "Will it not be better that she should keep the resentment of the insult for ever? Resentment—why, it is purification; it is a most stinging and painful consciousness! Tomorrow I should have defiled her soul and have exhausted her heart, while now the feeling of insult will never die in her heart, and however loathsome the filth awaiting her—the feeling of insult will elevate and purify her . . . by hatred . . . h'm! . . . perhaps, too, by forgiveness. . . . Will all that make things easier for her though? . . ."

And, indeed, I will ask on my own account here, an idle question: which is better—cheap happiness or exalted sufferings? Well, which is better?

So I dreamed as I sat at home that evening, almost dead with the pain in my soul. Never had I endured such suffering and remorse, yet could there have been the faintest doubt when I ran out from my lodging that I should turn back half-way? I never met Liza again and I have heard nothing of her. I will add, too, that I remained for a long time afterwards pleased with the phrase about the benefit from resentment and hatred in spite of the fact that I almost fell ill from misery.

*   *   *   *

Even now, so many years later, all this is somehow a very evil memory. I have many evil memories now, but . . . hadn't I better end my "Notes" here? I believe I made a mistake in beginning to write them, anyway I have felt ashamed all the time I've been writing this story; so it's hardly literature so much as a corrective punishment. Why, to tell long stories, showing how I have spoiled my life through morally rotting in my corner, through lack of fitting environment, through divorce from real life, and rankling spite in my underground world, would certainly not be interesting; a novel needs a hero, and all the traits for an anti-hero are *expressly* gathered together here, and what matters most, it all produces an unpleasant impression, for we are all divorced from life, we are all cripples, every one of us, more or less. We are so divorced from it that we feel at once a sort of loathing for real life, and so cannot bear to be reminded of it. Why, we have come almost to looking upon real life as an effort, almost as hard work, and we are all privately agreed that it is better in books. And why do we fuss and fume sometimes? Why are we perverse and ask for something else? We don't know what ourselves. It would be the worse for us if our petulant prayers were answered. Come, try, give any one of us, for instance, a little more independence, untie our hands, widen the spheres of our activity, relax the control and we . . . yes, I assure you . . . we should be begging to be under control again at once. I know that you will very likely be angry with me for that, and will begin shouting and stamping. Speak for yourself, you will say, and for your miseries in your underground holes, and don't dare to say all of us—excuse me, gentlemen, I am not justifying myself with that "all of us." As for what concerns me in particular I have only in my life carried to an extreme what you have not dared to carry halfway, and what's more, you have taken your cowardice for good sense, and have found comfort in deceiving yourselves. So that perhaps, after all, there is more life in me than in you. Look into it more carefully! Why, we don't even know what living means now, what it is, and what it is called? Leave us alone without books and we shall be lost and in confusion at once. We shall not know what to join on to, what to cling to, what to love and what to hate, what to respect and what to despise. We are oppressed at being men—men with a real individual body and blood, we are ashamed of it, we think it a disgrace and try to contrive to be some sort of impossible generalized man. We are stillborn, and for generations past have been begotten, not by living fathers, and that suits us better and better. We are developing a taste for it. Soon we shall contrive to be born somehow from an idea. But enough; I don't want to write more from "Underground."

[*The notes of this paradoxalist do not end here, however. He could not refrain from going on with them, but it seems to us that we may stop here.*]

—1864

Nikolai Gogol

Nikolai Gogol
(1809-52)

Diary of a Madman
Translated from the Russian by Claud Field

October 3rd.

—Something very strange happened today. I got up fairly late, and when Mavra brought me my clean boots, I asked her how late it was. When she told me it had long struck ten, I dressed as quickly as possible.

To tell the truth, I would have rather not gone to the office at all today, for I knew beforehand that our department-chief would give me a sour look. For some time past he has been in the habit of saying to me, "Look here, my friend; there is something wrong with your head. You often rush about as though you were possessed. Then you make such a mess of your documents that the devil himself couldn't sort them out; you write the title without any capital letters, and add neither the date nor the docket-number." The long-legged scoundrel! He is obviously envious of me because I sit in the director's work-room, and mend His Excellency's quill pens. In short, I only went to the office today because I'd hoped to meet the accountant and convince him to me a meager advance in my pay.

A terrible man, this accountant! As for his advancing anyone's salary—you might sooner expect the skies to fall. You may beg and beseech him, and be on the very verge of ruin—

this grey devil won't budge an inch. At the same time, his own cook at home, as all the world knows, boxes his ears.

I really don't see what good one gets by serving in our department. There are no plums there. In the fiscal and judicial offices, it is quite different. There some ungainly fellow sits in a corner and writes and writes; he has such a shabby coat and such an ugly face that one would like to spit on both of them. But you should see what a splendid country-house he rents. He would not condescend to accept a gift so meager as a gilt porcelain cup. "You can give that to your family doctor," he would say. Nothing less than a pair of thoroughbred horses, a fine carriage, or a beaver-fur coat worth three hundred rubles would be good enough for him. And yet he seems so mild and quiet, and asks so amiably, "Please lend me your penknife; I wish to mend my pen." Nevertheless, he knows how to verbally undress a petitioner until he has only a patch of clothes left on his body.

In our office it must be admitted everything is done in a proper and gentlemanly way; there is more cleanness and elegance than one will ever find in Government offices. The tables are mahogany, and everyone is addressed as "sir." And truly, were it not for this official propriety, I should long ago have sent in my resignation.

I put on my old cloak, and took my umbrella, as a light rain was falling. Few people were on the streets except for some women, who had flung their skirts over their heads. Here and there, a cabman or a shopman passed by with his umbrella up. Of the higher classes, there was only the rare official here and there. One I saw at the street-crossing, and thought to myself, "Ah! my friend, you are not going to the office, but after that young lady who walks in front of you. You are just like the officers who run after every petticoat they see."

As I was thus following the train of my thoughts, I saw a carriage stop before a shop just as I was passing it. I recognized it at once; it was our director's carriage. "He has nothing to do in the shop," I said to myself; "it must be his daughter."

I pressed myself close against the wall. A lackey opened the carriage door, and, as I had expected, she fluttered like a bird out of it. How proudly she looked right and left; how she drew her eyebrows together, and shot lightnings from her eyes—good heavens! I am lost, hopelessly lost!

But why must she come out in such abominable weather? And yet they say women are so mad on their finery!

She did not recognize me. I had wrapped myself as closely as possible in my cloak. It was dirty and old-fashioned, and I would not have liked to have been seen by her wearing it. Now they wear cloaks with long collars, but mine has only a short double collar, and the cloth is of inferior quality.

Her little dog could not get into the shop, and remained outside. I know this dog; its name is "Meggy."

Before I had been standing there a minute, I heard a voice call, "Good day, Meggy!"

Who the devil was that? I looked round and saw two ladies hurrying by under an umbrella—one old, the other fairly young. They were already gone when I heard the same voice again, "For shame, Meggy!"

Who was that? *What* was that? I saw Meggy sniffing at a dog which ran behind the ladies. The deuce! For a moment I thought I must be drunk, since it's so rare to hear dogs speak, but I hadn't had a drop all day.

"No, Fidel, you are wrong," I heard Meggy say quite distinctly. "I was—bow wow!—I was—bow! wow! wow!—very ill."

What an extraordinary dog! I was, to tell the truth, quite amazed to hear it talk human language. But when I considered the matter well, I ceased to be astonished. In fact, such things have already happened in the world. It is said that in England a fish put its head out of water and spoke a few words in such an extraordinary language that learned men have been puzzling over them for three years, and have not succeeded in interpreting them yet. I also read in the paper of two cows who entered a shop and asked for a pound of tea.

Meanwhile what Meggy went on to say seemed to me still more remarkable. She added, "I wrote to you lately, Fidel; perhaps Polkan did not bring you the letter."

Now I am willing to forfeit a whole month's salary if I ever heard of dogs writing before. This has certainly astonished me. For some time now I have been able to hear and see things which no other man has heard and seen.

"I will," I thought, "follow that dog in order to get to the bottom of the matter, Accordingly, I opened my umbrella and went after the two ladies. They went down Bean Street, turned through Citizen Street and Carpenter Street, and finally halted on the Cuckoo Bridge before a large apartment house. I know this house; it is Sverkoff's. What a monster he is! What sort of people live there! How many cooks, how many bagmen! There are fellow officials of mine also there packed on each other like herrings. And I have a friend there, a very fine cornet player."

The ladies mounted to the fifth story. "Very good," thought I; "I will make a note of the number, in order to follow up the matter at the first opportunity."

October 11th.

—Today is Wednesday, and I was as usual in the office. I came early on purpose, sat down, and mended all the pens.

Our director must be a very clever man. The whole room is full of bookcases. I read the titles of some of the books; they were very learned, beyond the comprehension of people of my class, and all in French and German. I look at his face and see how much dignity there is in his eyes. I never hear a single superfluous word from his mouth, except that when he hands over the documents, he asks "What sort of weather is it?"

No, he is not a man of our class; he is a real statesman. I have already noticed that I am a special favorite of his. If now his daughter also—ah! what folly—let me say no more about it!

I have read the *Northern Bee*. What foolish people the French are! By heavens! I should like to tackle them all, and give them a thrashing. I have also read a fine description of a ball given by a landowner of Kursk. The land-owners of Kursk write a fine style.

Then I noticed that it was already half-past twelve, and the director had not yet left his bedroom. But about half-past one something happened which no pen can describe.

The door opened. I thought it was the director; I jumped up with my documents from the seat, and—then—she—herself—came into the room. Ye saints! how beautifully she was dressed. Her garments were whiter than a swan—oh how splendid! And she herself was radiant as the sun, indeed, the real sun!

She greeted me and asked, "Has my father come yet?"

Ah! what a voice. A canary bird! A real canary bird!

"Your Excellency," I wanted to exclaim, "don't have me executed, but if it must be done, then please kill me with your own angelic hand." But, God knows why, I could not bring it out, so I only said, "No, he has not come yet."

She glanced at me, looked at the books, and let her handkerchief fall. Instantly I started up, but slipped on the infernal polished floor, and nearly broke my nose. Still I succeeded in picking up the handkerchief. Ye heavenly choirs, what a handkerchief! So tender and soft, of the finest cambric. It had the scent of a general's rank!

She thanked me, and smiled so amiably that her sugar lips nearly melted. Then she left the room.

After I had sat there about an hour, a flunkey came in and said, "You can go home, Mr. Ivanovitch; the director has already gone out!"

I cannot stand these lackeys! They hang about the vestibules, and scarcely vouchsafe to greet one with a nod. Yes, sometimes it is even worse; once one of these rascals offered me his snuff-box without even getting up from his chair. "Don't you know, you country-bumpkin, that I am an official and of aristocratic birth?"

This time, however, I took my hat and overcoat quietly; these people naturally never think of helping one on with it. I went home, lay a good while on the bed, and wrote some verses in my note :

> 'Tis an hour since I saw thee,
> And it seems a whole long year;
> Without you, I loathe my own existence,
> How can I live on, my dear?

I think they are by Pushkin.

In the evening, I wrapped myself in my cloak, hastened to the director's house, and waited there a long time to see if she would come out and get into the carriage. I only wanted to see her once, but she did not come.

November 6th.

—Our chief clerk has gone mad. When I came to the office today, he called me to his room and began as follows: "Look here, my friend, what wild ideas have got into your head?"

"How! What? None at all," I answered.

"Consider well. You are already past forty; it is quite time to be reasonable. What do you imagine? Do you think I don't know all your tricks? Are you trying to pay court to the director's daughter? Look at yourself and realize what you are! A nonentity, nothing else. I would not give a kopeck for you. Look well in the glass. How can you have such thoughts with such a caricature of a face?"

May the devil take him! Because his own face has a certain resemblance to a medicine-bottle, because he has a curly bush of hair on his head, and sometimes combs it upwards, and sometimes plasters it down in all kinds of queer ways, he thinks that he can do everything. I know well, I know why he is angry with me. He is envious; perhaps he has noticed the tokens of favor which have been graciously shown me. But why should I bother about him? A councillor! What sort of important animal is that? He wears a gold chain with his watch, buys himself boots at thirty rubles a pair; may the devil take him! Am I a tailor's son or some other obscure cabbage? I am a nobleman! I can also work my way up. I am just forty-two—an age when a man's real career generally begins. Wait a bit, my friend! I too may get to a superior's rank; or perhaps, if God is gracious, even to a higher one, I shall make a name which will far outstrip yours. You think there are no able men except yourself? I only need to order a fashionable coat and wear a tie like yours, and you would be quite eclipsed.

But I have no money—that is the worst part of it!

November 8th.
—I was at the theatre. "The Russian House–Fool" was performed. I laughed heartily. There was also a kind of musical comedy which contained amusing hits at barristers. The language was very coarse; I am surprised the censor passed it. Lines in the comedy accuse merchants of cheating; and say their sons lead immoral lives, and behave disrespectfully towards the nobility.

The critics also are criticized; they are said only to be able to find fault, so that authors have to beg the public for protection.

Our modern dramatists certainly write amusing things. I am very fond of the theatre. If I have only a kopeck in my pocket, I always go there. Most of my fellow-officials are uneducated boors, and never enter a theatre unless one throws free tickets at their head.

One actress sang divinely. She made me think of—but silence!

November 9th.

—About eight o'clock I went to the office. The chief clerk pretended not to notice my arrival. I for my part also behaved as though he were not in existence. I read through and collated documents. At four o'clock I left. I passed by the director's house, but no one was to be seen. After dinner I lay for a good while on the bed.

November 11th.

—Today I sat in the director's room, mended twenty-three pens for him and, for Her—for Her Excellence, his daughter—four more.

The director likes to see many pens lying on his table. What a head he must have! He continually wraps himself in silence, but I don't think the smallest trifle escapes his eye. I should like to know what he is generally thinking of, what is really going on in this brain; I should like to get acquainted with the whole manner of life of these gentlemen, and get a closer view of their cunning courtiers' arts, and all the activities of these circles. I have often thought of asking His Excellence about them; but—the devil knows why!—every time my tongue failed me and I could get nothing out but my meteorological report.

I wish I could get a look into the spare room whose door I so often see open. And a second small room behind the spare room excites my curiosity. How splendidly it is fitted up; what a quantity of mirrors and choice china it contains! I should also like to cast a glance into those regions where Her Excellency, the daughter, wields the sceptre. I should like to see how all the scent-bottles and boxes are arranged in her boudoir, and the flowers which exhale so delicious a scent that one is half afraid to breathe. And her clothes lying about which are too ethereal to be called clothes—and her stockings—ah! but I have said too much already. . . .

Today there came to me what seemed a heavenly inspiration. I remembered the conversation between the two dogs which I had overheard on the Nevski Prospect. "Very good," I thought; "now I see my way clear. I must get hold of the correspondence which these two silly dogs have carried on with each other. In it I shall probably find many things explained."

I had already once called Meggy to me and said to her, "Listen, Meggy! Now we are alone together; if you like, I will also shut the door so that no one can see us. Tell me now all that you know about your mistress. I swear to you that I will tell no one."

But the cunning dog drew in its tail, ruffled up its hair, and went quite quietly out of the door, as though it had heard nothing.

I had long been of the opinion that dogs are much cleverer than men. I also believed that they could talk, and that only a certain obstinacy kept them from doing so. They are especially watchful animals, and nothing escapes their observation. Now, cost what it may, I will go tomorrow to Sverkoff's house in order to ask after Fidel, and if I have luck, to get hold of all the letters which Meggy has written to her.

November 12th.
—Today about two o'clock in the afternoon I started in order, by some means or other, to see Fidel and question her.

I cannot stand this smell of Sauerkraut which assails one's olfactory nerves from all the shops in Citizen Street. There also exhales such an odor from under each house door, that one must hold one's nose and pass by quickly. There ascends also so much smoke and soot from the artisans' shops that it is almost impossible to get through it.

When I had climbed up to the sixth story, and had rung the bell, a rather pretty girl with a freckled face came out. I recognized her as the companion of the old lady. She blushed a little and asked "What do you want?"

"I want to have a little conversation with your dog."

She was a simple-minded girl, as I saw at once. The dog came running and barking loudly. I wanted to take hold of it, but the abominable beast nearly caught hold of my nose with its teeth. But in a corner of the room I saw its sleeping-basket. Ah! that was what I wanted. I went to it, rummaged in the straw, and to my great satisfaction drew out a little packet of small pieces of paper. When the hideous little dog saw this, it first bit me in the calf of the leg, and then, as soon as it had become aware of my theft, it began to whimper and to fawn on me; but I said, "No, you little beast; good-bye!" and hastened away.

I believe the girl thought me mad; at any rate, she was thoroughly alarmed.

When I reached my room I wished to get to work at once, and read through the letters by daylight, since I do not see well by candle-light; but the wretched Mavra had got the idea of sweeping the floor. These blockheads of Finnish women are always clean where there is no need to be.

I then went for a little walk and began to think over what had happened. Now at last I could get to the bottom of all facts, ideas and motives! These letters would explain everything. Dogs are clever fellows; they know all about politics, and I will certainly find in the letters all I want, especially the character of the director and all his relationships. And through these letters I will get information about her who—but silence!

Towards evening I came home and lay for a good while on the bed.

November 13th.
—Now let us see! The letter is fairly legible but the handwriting is somewhat doggish.

Dear Fidel!—I cannot get accustomed to your ordinary name, as if they could not have found a better one for you! Fidel! How tasteless! How ordinary! But this is not the time to discuss it. I am very glad that we thought of corresponding with each other.

The letter is quite correctly written. The punctuation and spelling are perfectly right. Even our head clerk does not write so simply and clearly, though he declares he has been at the University. Let us go on.

> I think that it is one of the most refined joys of this world to interchange thoughts, feelings, and impressions.

H'm! This idea comes from some book which has been translated from German. I can't remember the title.

> I speak from experience, although I have not gone farther into the world than just before our front door. Does not my life pass happily and comfortably? My mistress, whom her father calls Sophie, is quite in love with me.

Ah! Ah!—but better be silent!

> Her father also often strokes me. I drink tea and coffee with cream. Yes, my dear, I must confess to you that I find no satisfaction in those large, gnawed-at bones which Polkan devours in the kitchen. Only the bones of wild fowl are good, and that only when the marrow has not been sucked out of them. They taste very nice with a little sauce, but there should be no green stuff in it. But I know nothing worse than the habit of giving dogs balls of bread kneaded up. Someone sits at table, kneads a bread-ball with dirty fingers, calls you and sticks it in your mouth. Good manners forbid your refusing it, and you eat it—with disgust it is true, but you eat it.

The deuce! What is this? What rubbish! As if she could find nothing more suitable to write about! I will see if there is anything more reasonable on the second page.

I am quite willing to inform you of everything that goes on here. I have already mentioned the most important person in the house, whom Sophie calls 'Papa.' He is a very strange man.

Ah! Here we are at last! Yes, I knew it; they have a politician's penetrating eye for all things. Let us see what she says about "Papa."

     ... a strange man. Generally he is silent; he only speaks seldom, but about a week ago he kept on repeating to himself, 'Shall I get it or not?' In one hand he took a sheet of paper; the other he stretched out as though to receive something, and repeated, 'Shall I get it or not?' Once he turned to me with the question, 'What do you think, Meggy?' I did not understand in the least what he meant, sniffed at his boots, and went away. A week later he came home with his face beaming. That morning he was visited by several officers in uniform who congratulated him. At the dinner-table he was in a better humor than I have ever seen him before.

Ah! he is ambitious then! I must make a note of that.

     Pardon, my dear, I hasten to conclude, etc., etc. Tomorrow I will finish the letter.

     Now, good morning; here I am again at your service. Today my mistress Sophie ...

Ah! we will see what she says about Sophie. Let us go on!

     ... was in an unusually excited state. She went to a ball, and I was glad that I could write to you in her absence. She likes going to balls, although she gets dreadfully irritated while dressing. I cannot understand, my dear, what is the pleasure in going to a ball. She comes home from the ball at six o'clock in the early morning, and to judge by her pale and emaciated face, she has had nothing to eat. I could, frankly speaking, not endure such an existence. If I could not get partridge with sauce, or the wing of a roast chicken, I don't know what I should do. Porridge with sauce is also tolerable, but I can get up no enthusiasm for carrots, turnips, and artichokes.

The style is very unequal! One sees at once that it has not been written by a man. The beginning is quite intelligent, but at the end the canine nature breaks out. I will read another letter; it is rather long and there is no date.

Ah, my dear, how delightful is the arrival of spring! My heart beats as though it expected something. There is a perpetual ringing in my ears, so that I often stand with my foot raised, for several minutes at a time, and listen towards the door. In confidence I will tell you that I have many admirers. I often sit on the window-sill and let them pass in review. Ah! if you knew what miscreations there are among them; one, a clumsy house-dog, with stupidity written on his face, walks the street with an important air and imagines that he is an extremely important person, and that the eyes of all the world are fastened on him. I don't pay him the least attention, and pretend not to see him at all.

And what a hideous bulldog has taken up his post opposite my window! If he stood on his hind-legs, as the monster probably cannot, he would be taller by a head than my mistress's papa, who himself has a stately figure. This lout seems, moreover, to be very impudent. I growl at him, but he does not seem to mind that at all. If he at least would only wrinkle his forehead! Instead of that, he stretches out his tongue, droops his big ears, and stares in at the window—this rustic boor! But do you think, my dear, that my heart remains proof against all temptations? Alas no! If you had only seen that gentlemanly dog who crept through the fence of the neighboring house. Treasure is his name. Ah, my dear, what a delightful snout he has!

To the devil with the stuff! What rubbish it is! How can one blacken paper with such absurdities. Give me a man. I want to see a man! I need some food to nourish and refresh my mind, and get this silliness instead. I will turn the page to see if there is anything better on the other side.

Sophie sat at the table and sewed something. I looked out of the window and amused myself by watching the passers-by. Suddenly a flunkey entered and announced a visitor—"Mr Teploft."

"Show him in!" said Sophie, and began to embrace me. "Ah! Meggy, Meggy, do you know who that is? He is dark, and belongs to the Royal Household; and what eyes he has! Dark and brilliant as fire."

Sophie hastened into her room. A minute later a young gentleman with black whiskers entered. He went to the mirror, smoothed his hair, and looked round the room. I turned away and sat down in my place. Sophie entered and returned his bow in a friendly manner.

I pretended to observe nothing, and continued to look out of the window. But I leant my head a little on one side to hear what they were talking about. Ah, my dear! what silly things they discussed—how a lady executed the wrong figure in dancing; how a certain Boboff, with his expansive shirt-frill, had looked like a stork and nearly fallen down; how a certain Lidina imagined she had blue eyes when they were really green, etc.

I do not know, my dear, what special charm she finds in her Mr Teploff, and why she is so delighted with him.

It seems to me myself that there is something wrong here. It is impossible that this Teploff should bewitch her. We will see further.

If this gentleman of the Household pleases her, then she must also be pleased, according to my view, with that official who sits in her papa's writing-room. Ah, my dear, if you know what a figure he is! A regular tortoise!

What official does she mean?

He has an extraordinary name. He always sits there and mends the pens. His hair looks like a truss of hay. Her papa always employs him instead of a servant.

I believe this abominable little beast is referring to me. But what has my hair got to do with hay?

Sophie can never keep from laughing when she sees him.

You lie, cursed dog! What a scandalous tongue! As if I did not know that it is envy which prompts you, and that here there is treachery at work—yes, the treachery of the chief clerk. This man hates me implacably; he has plotted against me, he is always seeking to injure me. I'll look through one more letter; perhaps it will make the matter clearer.

Fidel, my dear, pardon me that I have not written for so long. I was floating in a dream of delight. In truth, some author remarks, 'Love is a second life.' Besides, great changes are going on in the house. The young chamberlain is always here. Sophie is wildly in love with him. Her papa is quite contented. I heard from Gregor, who sweeps the floor, and is in the habit of talking to himself, that the marriage will soon be celebrated. Her papa will at any rate get his daughter married to a general, a colonel, or a chamberlain.

My lord! I can read no more. It is all about chamberlains and generals. I should like myself to be a general—not in order to sue for her hand and all that—no, not at all; I should like to be a general merely in order to see people wriggling, squirming, and hatching plots before me.

And then I should like to tell them that they are both of them not worth spitting on. But it is vexatious! I tear the foolish dog's letters up in a thousand pieces.

December 3rd.

—It is not possible that the marriage should take place; it is only idle gossip. What does it signify if he is a chamberlain! That is only a dignity, not a substantial thing which one can see or handle. His chamberlain's office will not procure him a third eye in his forehead. Neither is his nose made of gold; it is just like mine or anyone else's nose. He does not eat and cough, but smells and sneezes with it. I should like to get to the bottom of the mystery—whence do all these distinctions come? Why am I only a titular councillor?

Perhaps I am really a count or a general, and only appear to be a titular councillor. Perhaps I don't even know who and what I am. How many cases there are in history of a simple gentleman, or even a burgher or peasant, suddenly turning out to be a great lord or baron? Well, suppose that I appear suddenly in a general's uniform, on the right shoulder an epaulette, on the left an epaulette, and a blue sash across my breast, what sort of a tune would my beloved sing then? What would her papa, our director, say? Oh, he is ambitious! He is a freemason, certainly a freemason; however much he may conceal it, I have found it out. When he gives anyone his hand, he only reaches out two fingers. Well, could not I this minute be nominated a general or a superintendent? I should like to know why I am a titular councillor—why just that, and nothing more?

December 6th.

—Today I have been reading papers the whole morning. Very strange things are happening in Spain. I have not understood them all. It is said that the throne is vacant, the representatives of the people are in difficulties about finding an occupant, and riots are taking place.

All this appears to me very strange. How can the throne be vacant? It is said that it will be occupied by a woman. A woman cannot sit on a throne. That is impossible. Only a king can sit on a throne. They say that there is no king there, but that is not possible. There cannot be a kingdom without a king. There must be a king, but he is hidden away somewhere. Perhaps he is actually on the spot, and only some domestic complications, or fears of the neighbouring Powers, France and other countries, compel him to remain in concealment; there might also be other reasons.

December 8th.
—I was nearly going to the office, but various considerations kept me from doing so. I keep on thinking about these Spanish affairs. How is it possible that a woman should reign? It would not be allowed, especially by England. In the rest of Europe the political situation is also critical; the Emperor of Austria

These events, to tell the truth, have so shaken and shattered me, that I could really do nothing all day. Mavra told me that I was very absent-minded at table. In fact, in my absent-mindedness I threw two plates on the ground so that they broke in pieces.

After dinner I felt weak, and did not feel up to making abstracts of reports. I lay most of the time on my bed, and thought of the Spanish affairs.

April 43rd, 2000.
—Today is a day of splendid triumph. Spain has a king; he has been found, and I am he. I discovered it today; all of a sudden it came upon me like a flash of lightning.

I do not understand how I could imagine, that I am a titular councillor. How could such a foolish idea enter my head? It was fortunate that it occurred to no one to shut me up in an asylum. Now it is all clear, and as plain as a pikestaff. Formerly—I don't know why—everything seemed veiled in a kind of mist. That is, I believe, because people think that the human brain is in the head. Nothing of the sort; it is carried by the wind from the Caspian Sea.

For the first time I told Mavra who I am. When she learned that the king of Spain stood before her, she struck her hands together over her head, and nearly died of alarm. The stupid thing had never seen the king of Spain before!

I comforted her, however, at once by assuring her that I was not angry with her for having hitherto cleaned my boots badly. Women are stupid things; one cannot interest them in lofty subjects. She was frightened because she thought all kings of Spain were like Philip II. But I explained to her that there was a great difference between me and him. I did not go to the office. Why the devil should I? No, my dear friends, you won't get me there again! I am not going to worry myself with your infernal documents any more.

Marchember 86. Between day and night.
—Today the office-messenger came and summoned me, as I had not been there for three weeks. I went just for the fun of the thing. The chief clerk thought I would bow humbly before him, and make excuses; but I looked at him quite indifferently, neither angrily nor mildly, and sat down quietly at my place as though I noticed no one. I looked at all this rabble of scribblers, and thought, "If you only knew who is sitting among you! Good heavens! what a to-do you would make. Even the chief clerk would bow himself to the earth before me as he does now before the director.'

A pile of reports was laid before me, of which to make abstracts, but I did not touch them with one finger.

After a little time there was a commotion in the office, and there a report went round that the director was coming. Many of the clerks vied with each other to attract his notice; but I did not stir. As he came through our room, each one hastily buttoned up his coat; but I had no idea of doing anything of the sort. What is the director to me? Should I stand up before him? Never. What sort of a director is he? He is a bottle-stopper, and no director. A quite ordinary, simple bottle-stopper—nothing more. I felt quite amused as they gave me a document to sign.

They thought I would simply put down my name—"So-and-so, Clerk." Why not? But at the top of the sheet, where the director generally writes his name, I inscribed "Ferdinand Yin." in bold characters. You should have seen what a reverential silence ensued. But I made a gesture with my hand, and said, "Gentlemen, no ceremony please!" Then I went out, and took my way straight to the director's house.

He was not at home. The flunkey wanted not to let me in, but I talked to him in such a way that he soon dropped his arms.

I went straight to Sophie's dressing-room. She sat before the mirror. When she saw me, she sprang up and took a step backwards; but I did not tell her that I was the king of Spain.

But I told her that a happiness awaited her, beyond her power to imagine; and that in spite of all our enemies' devices we should be united. That was all which I wished to say to her, and I went out. Oh, what cunning creatures these women are! Now I have found out what woman really is. Hitherto no one knew whom a woman really loves; I am the first to discover it—she loves the devil. Yes, joking apart, learned men write nonsense when they pronounce that she is this and that; she loves the devil—that is all. You see a woman looking through her lorgnette from a box in the front row. One thinks she is watching that stout gentleman who wears an order. Not a bit of it! She is watching the devil who stands behind his back. He has hidden himself there, and beckons to her with his finger. And she marries him—actually—she marries him!

That is all ambition, and the reason is that there is under the tongue a little blister in which there is a little worm of the size of a pin's head. And this is constructed by a barber in Bean Street; I don't remember his name at the moment, but so much is certain that, in conjunction with a midwife, he wants to spread Mohammedanism all over the world, and that in consequence of this a large number of people in France have already adopted the faith of Islam.

No date. The day had no date.

—I went for a walk incognito on the Nevski Prospect. I avoided every appearance of being the king of Spain. I felt it below my dignity to let myself be recognized by the whole world, since I must first present myself at court. And I was also restrained by the fact that I have at present no Spanish national costume. If I could only get a cloak! I tried to have a consultation with a tailor, but these people are real asses! Moreover, they neglect their business, dabble in speculation, and have become loafers. I will have a cloak made out of my new official uniform which I have only worn twice. But to prevent this botcher of a tailor spoiling it, I will make it myself with closed doors, so that no one sees me. Since the cut must be altogether altered, I have used the scissors myself.

I don't remember the date. The devil knows what month it was.

—The cloak is quite ready. Mavra exclaimed aloud when I put it on. I will, however, not present myself at court yet; the Spanish deputation has not yet arrived. It would not be befitting if I appeared without them. My appearance would be less imposing. From hour to hour I expect them.

The 1st.

—The extraordinary long delay of the deputies in coming astonishes me. What can possibly keep them? Perhaps France has a hand in the matter; it is certainly hostilely inclined. I went to the post office to inquire whether the Spanish deputation had come. The postmaster is an extraordinary blockhead who knows nothing. "No," he said to me, "there is no Spanish deputation here; but if you want to send them a letter, we will forward it at the fixed rate." The deuce! What do I want with a letter? Letters are nonsense. Letters are written by apothecaries. . . .

Madrid, 30th Februariary.

—So I am in Spain after all! It has happened so quickly that I could hardly take it in. The Spanish deputies came early this morning, and I got with them into the carriage. This unexpected promptness seemed to me strange. We drove so quickly that in half an hour we were at the Spanish frontier. Over all Europe now there are cast-iron roads, and the steamers go very fast. A wonderful country, this Spain!

As we entered the first room, I saw numerous persons with shorn heads. I guessed at once that they must be either grandees or soldiers, at least to judge by their shorn heads.

The Chancellor of the State, who led me by the hand, seemed to me to behave in a very strange way; he pushed me into a little room and said, "Stay here, and if you call yourself "King Ferdinand" again, I will drive the wish to do so out of you."

I knew, however, that that was only a test, and I reasserted my conviction; on which the Chancellor gave me two such severe blows with a stick on the back, that I could have cried out with the pain. But I restrained myself, remembering that this was a usual ceremony of old—time chivalry when one was inducted into a high position, and in Spain the laws of chivalry prevail up to the present day. When I was alone, I determined to study State affairs; I discovered that Spain and China are one and the same country, and it is only through ignorance that people regard them as separate kingdoms. I advice everyone urgently to write down the word "Spain" on a sheet of paper; he will see that it is quite the same as China.

But I feel much annoyed by an event which is about to take place tomorrow; at seven o'clock the earth is going to sit on the moon. This is foretold by the famous English chemist, Wellington. To tell the truth, I often felt uneasy when I thought of the excessive brittleness and fragility of the moon. The moon is generally repaired in Hamburg, and very imperfectly. It is done by a lame cooper, an obvious blockhead who has no idea how to do it. He took waxed thread and olive-oil—hence that pungent smell over all the earth which compels people to hold their noses. And this makes the moon so fragile that no men can live on it, but only noses. Therefore we cannot see our noses, because they are on the moon.

When I now pictured to myself how the earth, that massive body, would crush our noses to dust, if it sat on the moon, I became so uneasy, that I immediately put on my shoes and stockings and hastened into the council-hall to give the police orders to prevent the moon sitting on the earth.

The grandees with the shorn heads, whom I met in great numbers in the hall, were very intelligent people, and when I exclaimed, "Gentlemen! let us save the moon, for the earth is going to sit on it," they all set to work to fulfill my imperial wish, and many of them clambered up the wall in order to take the moon down. At that moment the Imperial Chancellor came in. As soon as he appeared, they all scattered, but I alone, as king, remained. To my astonishment, however, the Chancellor beat me with the stick and drove me to my room. So powerful are ancient customs in Spain!

January in the same year, following after February.

—I can never understand what kind of a country this Spain really is. The popular customs and rules of court etiquette are quite extraordinary. I do not understand them at all, at all. Today my head was shorn, although I exclaimed as loudly as I could, that I did not want to be a monk. What happened afterwards, when they began to let cold water trickle on my head, I do not know. I have never experienced such hellish torments. I nearly went mad, and they had difficulty in holding me. The significance of this strange custom is entirely hidden from me. It is a very foolish and unreasonable one.

Nor can I understand the stupidity of the kings who have not done away with it before now. Judging by all the circumstances, it seems to me as though I had fallen into the hands of the Inquisition, and as though the man whom I took to be the Chancellor was the Grand Inquisitor. But yet I cannot understand how the king could fall into the hands of the Inquisition. The affair may have been arranged by France—especially Polignac—he is a hound, that Polignac! He has sworn to compass my death, and now he is hunting me down. But I know, my friend, that you are only a tool of the English. They are clever fellows, and have a finger in every pie. All the world knows that France sneezes when England takes a pinch of snuff.

The 25th.

—Today the Grand Inquisitor came into my room; when I heard his steps in the distance, I hid myself under a chair. When he did not see me, he began to call. At first he called "Poprishchin!" I made no answer. Then he called "Axanti Ivanovitch! Titular Councillor! Nobleman!" I still kept silence. "Ferdinand the Eighth, King of Spain!" I was on the point of putting out my head, but I thought, "No, brother, you shall not deceive me! You shall not pour water on my head again!"

But he had already seen me and drove me from under the chair with his stick. The cursed stick really hurts one. But the following discovery compensated me for all the pain, i.e. that every cock has his Spain under his feathers. The Grand Inquisitor went angrily away, and threatened me with some punishment or other. I felt only contempt for his powerless spite, for I know that he only works like a machine, like a tool of the English.

34st Marstch. February, 349.

—No, I no longer have the power to endure. God! what are they going to do with me? They pour cold water on my head. They take no notice of me, and seem neither to see nor hear. Why do they torture me? What do they want from one so wretched as myself? What can I give them? I possess nothing. I cannot bear all their tortures; my head aches as though everything were turning round in a circle. Save me! Carry me away! Give me three steeds swift as the wind! Mount your seat, coachman, ring bells, gallop horses, and carry me straight out of this world. Farther, ever farther, till nothing more is to be seen!

Ah! the heaven bends over me already; a star glimmers in the distance; the forest with its dark trees in the moonlight rushes past; a bluish mist floats under my feet; music sounds in the cloud; on the one side is the sea, on the other, Italy; beyond I also see Russian peasants' houses. Is not my parents' house there in the distance? Does not my mother sit by the window? Mother, mother, save your unhappy son! Let a tear fall on his aching head! See how they torture him! Press the poor orphan to your bosom! He has no rest in this world; they hunt him from place to place.

Mother, mother, have pity on your sick child! And do you know that the Bey of Algiers has a wart under his nose?

—1835

Ivan Turgenev
(1818-83)

Diary of a Superfluous Man
Translated from the Russian by Constance Garnett

Village of Sheep's Springs, *March* 20, 18—.

The doctor has just left me. At last I have got at something definite! For all his cunning, he had to speak out at last. Yes, I am soon, very soon, to die. The frozen rivers will break up, and with the last snow I shall, most likely, swim away . . . whither? God knows! To the ocean too. Well, well, since one must die, one may as well die in the spring. But isn't it absurd to begin a diary a fortnight, perhaps, before death? What does it matter? And by how much are fourteen days less than fourteen years, fourteen centuries? Beside eternity, they say, all is nothingness—yes, but in that case eternity, too, is nothing. I see I am letting myself drop into metaphysics; that's a bad sign—am I not rather faint-hearted, perchance? I had better begin a description of some sort. It's damp and windy out of doors.

I'm forbidden to go out. What can I write about, then? No decent man talks of his maladies; to write a novel is not in my line; reflections on elevated topics are beyond me; descriptions of the life going on around me could not even interest me; while I am weary of doing nothing, and too lazy to read. Ah, I have it, I will write the story of all my life for myself. A first-rate idea! Just before death it is a suitable thing to do, and can be of no harm to anyone. I will begin.

I was born thirty years ago, the son of fairly well-to-do landowners. My father had a passion for gambling; my mother was a woman of character . . . a very virtuous woman. Only, I have known no woman whose moral excellence was less productive of happiness. She was crushed beneath the weight of her own virtues, and was a source of misery to everyone, from herself upwards. In all the fifty years of her life, she never once took rest, or sat with her hands in her lap; she was forever fussing and bustling about like an ant, and to absolutely no good purpose, which cannot be said of the ant. The worm of restlessness fretted her night and day. Only once I saw her perfectly tranquil, and that was the day after her death, in her coffin. Looking at her, it positively seemed to me that her face wore an expression of subdued amazement; with the half-open lips, the sunken cheeks, and meekly-staring eyes, it seemed expressing, all over, the words, 'How good to be at rest!' Yes, it is good, good to be rid, at last, of the wearing sense of life, of the persistent, restless consciousness of existence! But that's neither here nor there.

I was brought up badly and not happily. My father and mother both loved me; but that made things no better for me. My father was not, even in his own house, of the slightest authority or consequence, being a man openly abandoned to a shameful and ruinous vice; he was conscious of his degradation, and not having the strength of will to give up his darling passion, he tried at least, by his invariably amiable and humble demeanor and his unswerving submissiveness, to win the condescending consideration of his exemplary wife. My mother certainly did bear her trial with the superb and majestic long-suffering of virtue, in which there is so much of egoistic pride. She never reproached my father for anything, gave him her last penny, and paid his debts without a word. He exalted her as a paragon to her face and behind her back, but did not like to be at home, and caressed me by stealth, as though he were afraid of contaminating me by his presence.

But at such times his distorted features were full of such kindness, the nervous grin on his lips was replaced by such a touching smile, and his brown eyes, encircled by fine wrinkles, shone with such love, that I could not help pressing my cheek to his, which was wet and warm with tears. I wiped away those tears with my handkerchief, and they flowed again without effort, like water from a brimming glass. I fell to crying, too, and he comforted me, stroking my back and kissing me all over my face with his quivering lips. Even now, more than twenty years after his death, when I think of my poor father, dumb sobs rise into my throat, and my heart beats as hotly and bitterly and aches with as poignant a pity as if it had long to go on beating, as if there were anything to be sorry for!

My mother's behavior to me, on the contrary, was always the same, kind, but cold. In children's books one often comes across such mothers, sermonizing and just. She loved me, but I did not love her. Yes! I fought shy of my virtuous mother, and passionately loved my vicious father.

But enough for today. It's a beginning, and as for the end, whatever it may be, I needn't trouble my head about it. That's for my illness to see to.

March 21.

Today it is marvelous weather. Warm, bright; the sunshine frolicking gaily on the melting snow; everything shining, steaming, dripping; the sparrows chattering like mad things about the drenched, dark hedges.

Sweetly and terribly, too, the moist air frets my sick chest. Spring, spring is coming! I sit at the window and look across the river into the open country. O nature! nature! I love thee so, but I came forth from thy womb good for nothing—not fit even for life. There goes a cock-sparrow, hopping along with outspread wings; he chirrups, and every note, every ruffled feather on his little body, is breathing with health and strength. . . .

What follows from that? Nothing. He is well and has a right to chirrup and ruffle his wings; but I am ill and must die—that's all. It's not worthwhile to say more about it. And tearful invocations to nature are mortally absurd. Let us get back to my story.

I was brought up, as I have said, very badly and not happily. I had no brothers or sisters. I was educated at home. And, indeed, what would my mother have had to occupy her, if I had been sent to a boarding-school or a government college? That's what children are for—that their parents may not be bored. We lived for the most part in the country, and some-times went to Moscow. I had tutors and teachers, as a matter of course; one, in particular, has remained in my memory, a dried-up, tearful German, Rickmann, an exceptionally mournful creature, cruelly maltreated by destiny, and fruit-lessly consumed by an intense pining for his far-off fatherland. Sometimes, near the stove, in the fearful stuffiness of the close ante-room, full of the sour smell of stale kvas, my un-shaved man-nurse, Vassily, nicknamed Goose, would sit, playing cards with the coachman, Potap, in a new sheepskin, white as foam, and superb tarred boots, while in the next room Rickmann would sing, behind the partition—

Herz, mein Herz, warum so traurig?
Was bekümmert dich so sehr?
'Sist ja schön im fremden Lande—
Herz, mein Herz—was willst du mehr?'

After my father's death we moved to Moscow for good. I was twelve years old. My father died in the night from a stroke. I shall never forget that night. I was sleeping soundly, as children generally do; but I remember, even in my sleep, I was aware of a heavy gasping noise at regular intervals. Sud-denly I felt some one taking hold of my shoulder and poking me. I opened my eyes and saw my nurse. 'What is it?' 'Come along, come along, Alexey Mihalitch is dying.' . . . I was out of bed and away like a mad thing into his bedroom. I looked:

my father was lying with his head thrown back, all red, and gasping fearfully. The servants were crowding round the door with terrified faces; in the hall someone was asking in a thick voice: 'Have they sent for the doctor?' In the yard outside, a horse was being led from the stable, the gates were creaking, a tallow candle was burning in the room on the floor, my mother was there, terribly upset, but not oblivious of the proprieties, nor of her own dignity. I flung myself on my father's bosom, and hugged him, faltering: 'Papa, papa. . .' He lay motionless, screwing up his eyes in a strange way. I looked into his face—an unendurable horror caught my breath; I shrieked with terror, like a roughly captured bird—they picked me up and carried me away. Only the day before, as though aware his death was at hand, he had caressed me so passionately and despondently.

A sleepy, unkempt doctor, smelling strongly of spirits, was brought. My father died under his lancet, and the next day, utterly stupefied by grief, I stood with a candle in my hands before a table, on which lay the dead man, and listened senselessly to the bass sing-song of the deacon, interrupted from time to time by the weak voice of the priest. The tears kept streaming over my cheeks, my lips, my collar, my shirt-front. I was dissolved in tears; I watched persistently, I watched intently, my father's rigid face, as though I expected something of him; while my mother slowly bowed down to the ground, slowly rose again, and pressed her fingers firmly to her forehead, her shoulders, and her chest, as she crossed herself. I had not a single idea in my head; I was utterly numb, but I felt something terrible was happening to me. . . . Death looked me in the face that day and took note of me.

We moved to Moscow after my father's death for a very simple cause: all our estate was sold up by auction for debts—that is, absolutely all, except one little village, the one in which I am at this moment living out my magnificent existence. I must admit that, in spite of my youth at the time, I grieved over the sale of our home, or rather, in reality, I grieved over our garden. Almost my only bright memories are associated with our garden. It was there that one mild spring evening I buried my best friend, an old bob-tailed, crook-pawed dog, Trix. It was there that, hidden in the long grass, I used to eat stolen apples—sweet, red, Novgorod apples they were. There, too, I saw for the first time, among the ripe raspberry bushes, the housemaid Klavdia, who, in spite of her turned-up nose and habit of giggling in her kerchief, aroused such a tender passion in me that I could hardly breathe, and stood faint and tongue-tied in her presence; and once at Easter, when it came to her turn to kiss my seignorial hand, I almost flung myself at her feet to kiss her down-trodden goat-skin slippers. My God! Can all that be twenty years ago? It seems not long ago that I used to ride on my shaggy chestnut pony along the old fence of our garden, and, standing up in the stirrups, used to pick the two-colored poplar leaves. While a man is living he is not conscious of his own life; it becomes audible to him, like a sound, after the lapse of time.

Oh, my garden, oh, the tangled paths by the tiny pond! Oh, the little sandy spot below the tumbledown dike, where I used to catch gudgeons! And you tall birch-trees, with long hanging branches, from beyond which came floating a peasant's mournful song, broken by the uneven jolting of the cart, I send you my last farewell!. . . On parting with life, to you alone I stretch out my hands. Would I might once more inhale the fresh, bitter fragrance of the wormwood, the sweet scent of the mown buckwheat in the fields of my native place! Would I might once more hear far away the modest tinkle of the cracked bell of our parish church; once more lie in the cool shade under the oak sapling on the slope of the familiar ravine; once more watch the moving track of the wind, flitting, a dark wave over the golden grass of our meadow!. . . Ah, what's the good of all this? But I can't go on today. Enough till tomorrow.

March 22.

Today it's cold and overcast again. Such weather is a great deal more suitable. It's more in harmony with my task. Yesterday, quite inappropriately, stirred up a multitude of useless emotions and memories within me. This shall not occur again. Sentimental out-breaks are like liquorice; when first you suck it, it's not bad, but afterwards it leaves a very nasty taste in the mouth. I will set to work simply and serenely to tell the story of my life. And so, we moved to Moscow. . . .

But it occurs to me, is it really worthwhile to tell the story of my life?

No, it certainly is not. . . . My life has not been different in any respect from the lives of numbers of other people. The parental home, the university, the government service in the lower grades, retirement, a little circle of friends, decent poverty, modest pleasures, unambitious pursuits, moderate desires—kindly tell me, is that new to any one? And so I will not tell the story of my life, especially as I am writing for my own pleasure; and if my past does not afford even me any sensation of great pleasure or great pain, it must be that there is nothing in it deserving of attention. I had better try to describe my own character to myself. What manner of man am I?. . . It may be observed that no one asks me that question—admitted. But there, I'm dying, by Jove!—I'm dying, and at the point of death I really think one may be excused a desire to find out what sort of a queer fish one really was after all.

Thinking over this important question, and having, moreover, no need whatever to be too bitter in my expressions in regard to myself, as people are apt to be who have a strong conviction of their valuable qualities, I must admit one thing. I was a man, or perhaps I should say a fish, utterly superfluous in this world. And that I propose to show tomorrow, as I keep coughing today like an old sheep, and my nurse, Terentyevna, gives me no peace: 'Lie down, my good sir,' she says, 'and drink a little tea.'. . . I know why she keeps on at me:

she wants some tea herself. Well! she's welcome! Why not let the poor old woman extract the utmost benefit she can from her master at the last . . . as long as there is still the chance?

March 23.

Winter again. The snow is falling in flakes. Superfluous, superfluous. . . . That's a capital word I have hit on. The more deeply I probe into myself, the more intently I review all my past life, the more I am convinced of the strict truth of this expression. Superfluous—that's just it. To other people that term is not applicable. . . . People are bad, or good, clever, stupid, pleasant, and disagreeable; but superfluous . . . no. Understand me, though: the universe could get on without those people too. . . no doubt; but uselessness is not their prime characteristic, their most distinctive attribute, and when you speak of them, the word 'superfluous' is not the first to rise to your lips. But I . . . there's nothing else one can say about me; I'm superfluous and nothing more. A supernumerary, and that's all. Nature, apparently, did not reckon on my appearance, and consequently treated me as an unexpected and uninvited guest. A facetious gentleman, a great devotee of preference, said very happily about me that I was the forfeit my mother had paid at the game of life. I am speaking about myself calmly now, without any bitterness. . . . It's all over and done with! Throughout my whole life I was constantly finding my place taken, perhaps because I did not look for my place where I should have done. I was apprehensive, reserved, and irritable, like all sickly people. Moreover, probably owing to excessive self-consciousness, perhaps as the result of the generally unfortunate cast of my personality, there existed between my thoughts and feelings, and the expression of those feelings and thoughts, a sort of inexplicable, irrational, and utterly insuperable barrier; and whenever I made up my mind to overcome this obstacle by force, to break down this barrier, my gestures, the expression of my face, my whole being, took on an appearance of painful constraint. I not only seemed, I positively became unnatural and affected. I was conscious of this myself, and hastened to shrink back into myself. Then a terrible commotion was set up within me. I analyzed myself to the last thread, compared myself with others, recalled the slightest glances, smiles, words of the people to whom I had tried to open myself out, put the worst construction on everything, laughed vindictively at my own pretensions to 'be like everyone else,'—and suddenly, in the midst of my laughter, collapsed utterly into gloom, sank into absurd dejection, and then began again as before—went round and round, in fact, like a squirrel on its wheel. Whole days were spent in this harassing, fruitless exercise. Well now, tell me, if you please, to whom and for what is such a man of use? Why did this happen to me? what was the reason of this trivial fretting at myself?—who knows? who can tell?

I remember I was driving once from Moscow in the diligence. It was a good road, but the driver, though he had four horses harnessed abreast, hitched on another, alongside of them. Such an unfortunate, utterly useless, fifth horse— fastened somehow on to the front of the shaft by a short stout cord, which mercilessly cuts his shoulder, forces him to go with the most unnatural action, and gives his whole body the shape of a comma—always arouses my deepest pity. I remarked to the driver that I thought we might on this occasion have got on without the fifth horse. . . . He was silent a moment, shook his head, lashed the horse a dozen times across his thin back and under his distended belly, and with a grin responded: 'Ay, to be sure; why do we drag him along with us? What the devil's he for?' And here am I too dragged along. But, thank goodness, the station is not far off.

Superfluous. . . . I promised to show the justice of my opinion, and I will carry out my promise. I don't think it necessary to mention the thousand trifles, everyday incidents and events, which would, however, in the eyes of any thinking man, serve as irrefutable evidence in my support—I mean, in support of my contention. I had better begin straight away with one rather important incident, after which probably there will be no doubt left of the accuracy of the term superfluous. I repeat: I do not intend to indulge in minute details, but I cannot pass over in silence one rather serious and significant fact, that is, the strange behavior of my friends (I too used to have friends) whenever I met them, or even called on them. They used to seem ill at ease; as they came to meet me, they would give a not quite natural smile, look, not into my eyes nor at my feet, as some people do, but rather at my cheeks, articulate hurriedly, 'Ah! how are you, Tchulkaturin!' (such is the surname fate has burdened me with) or 'Ah! here's Tchulkaturin!' turn away at once and positively remain stockstill for a little while after, as though trying to recollect something. I used to notice all this, as I am not devoid of penetration and the faculty of observation; on the whole I am not a fool; I sometimes even have ideas come into my head that are amusing, not absolutely commonplace. But as I am a superfluous man with a padlock on my inner self, it is very painful for me to express my idea, the more so as I know beforehand that I shall express it badly. It positively sometimes strikes me as extraordinary the way people manage to talk, and so simply and freely. . . . It's marvelous, really, when you think of it. Though, to tell the truth, I too, in spite of my padlock, sometimes have an itch to talk. But I did actually utter words only in my youth; in riper years I almost always pulled myself up. I would murmur to myself: 'Come, we'd better hold our tongue.' And I was still. We are all good hands at being silent; our women especially are great in that line. Many an exalted Russian young lady keeps silent so strenuously that the spectacle is calculated to produce a faint shudder and cold sweat even in any one prepared to face it. But that's not the point, and it's not for me to criticize others. I proceed to my promised narrative.

A few years back, owing to a combination of circumstances, very insignificant in themselves, but very important for me, it was my lot to spend six months in the district town O——. This town is all built on a slope, and very uncomfortably built, too. There are reckoned to be about eight hundred inhabitants in it, of exceptional poverty; the houses are hardly worthy of the name; in the chief street, by way of an apology for a pavement, there are here and there some huge white slabs of rough-hewn limestone, in consequence of which even carts drive round it instead of through it. In the very middle of an astoundingly dirty square rises a diminutive yellowish edifice with black holes in it, and in these holes sit men in big caps making a pretence of buying and selling. In this place there is an extraordinarily high striped post sticking up into the air, and near the post, in the interests of public order, by command of the authorities, there is kept a cartload of yellow hay, and one government hen struts to and fro. In short, existence in the town of O—— is truly delightful. During the first days of my stay in this town, I almost went out of my mind with boredom. I ought to say of myself that, though I am, no doubt, a superfluous man, I am not so of my own seeking; I'm morbid myself, but I can't bear anything morbid. . . . I'm not even averse to happiness—indeed, I've tried to approach it right and left. . . . And so it is no wonder that I too can be bored like any other mortal. I was staying in the town of O—— on official business.

Terentyevna has certainly sworn to make an end of me. Here's a specimen of our conversation:—

> Terentyevna: Oh—oh, my good sir! what are you forever writing for? it's bad for you, keeping all on writing.
>
> I: But I'm dull, Terentyevna.
>
> She: Oh, you take a cup of tea now and lie down. By God's mercy you'll get in a sweat and maybe doze a bit.

I: But I'm not sleepy.

She: Ah, sir! why do you talk so? Lord have mercy on you! Come, lie down, lie down; it's better for you.

I: I shall die anyway, Terentyevna!

She: Lord bless us and save us! . . . Well, do you want a little tea?

I: I shan't live through the week, Terentyevna!

She: Eh, eh! good sir, why do you talk so? . . . Well, I'll go and heat the samovar.

Oh, decrepit, yellow, toothless creature! Am I really, even in your eyes, not a man?

March 24. Sharp frost.

On the very day of my arrival in the town of O——, the official business, above referred to, brought me into contact with a certain Kirilla Matveitch Ozhogin, one of the chief functionaries of the district; but I became intimate, or, as it is called, 'friends' with him a fortnight later. His house was in the principal street, and was distinguished from all the others by its size, its painted roof, and the lions on its gates, lions of that species extraordinarily resembling unsuccessful dogs, whose natural home is Moscow. From those lions alone, one might safely conclude that Ozhogin was a man of property. And so it was; he was the owner of four hundred peasants; he entertained in his house all the best society of the town of O——, and had a reputation for hospitality. At his door was seen the mayor with his wide chestnut-colored droshky and pair—an exceptionally bulky man, who seemed as though cut out of material that had been laid by for a long time. The other officials, too, used to drive to his receptions: the attorney, a yellowish, spiteful creature; the land surveyor, a wit—of German extraction, with a Tartar face; the inspector of means of communication—a soft soul, who sang songs, but a scandalmonger; a former marshal of the district—a gentleman with dyed hair, crumpled shirt front, and tight trousers, and that lofty expression of face so characteristic of men who have stood on trial. There used to come also two landowners, inseparable friends, both no longer young and indeed a little the worse for wear, of whom the younger was continually crushing the elder and putting him to silence with one and the same reproach. 'Don't you talk, Sergei Sergeitch! What have you to say? Why, you spell the word cork with two *k*'s in it. . . . Yes, gentlemen,' he would go on, with all the fire of conviction, turning to the bystanders, 'Sergei Sergeitch spells it not cork, but kork.' And everyone present would laugh, though probably not one of them was conspicuous for special accuracy in orthography, while the luckless Sergei Sergeitch held his tongue, and with a faint smile bowed his head. But I am forgetting that my hours are numbered, and am letting myself go into too minute descriptions. And so, without further beating about the bush,—Ozhogin was married, he had a daughter, Elizaveta Kirillovna, and I fell in love with this daughter.

Ozhogin himself was a commonplace person, neither good-looking nor bad-looking; his wife resembled an aged chicken; but their daughter had not taken after her parents. She was very pretty and of a bright and gentle disposition. Her clear grey eyes looked out kindly and directly from under childishly arched brows; she was almost always smiling, and she laughed too, pretty often. Her fresh voice had a very pleasant ring; she moved freely, rapidly, and blushed gaily. She did not dress very stylishly, only plain dresses suited her. I did not make friends quickly as a rule, and if I were at ease with any one from the first—which, however, scarcely ever occurred—it said, I must own, a great deal for my new acquaintance. I did not know at all how to behave with women, and in their presence I either scowled and put on a morose air, or grinned in the most idiotic way, and in my embarrassment turned my tongue round and round in my mouth. With

Elizaveta Kirillovna, on the contrary, I felt at home from the first moment. It happened in this way.

I called one day at Ozhogin's before dinner, asked, 'At home?' was told, 'The master's at home, dressing; please to walk into the drawing-room.' I went into the drawing-room; I beheld standing at the window, with her back to me, a girl in a white gown, with a cage in her hands. I was, as my way was, somewhat taken aback; however, I showed no sign of it, but merely coughed, for good manners. The girl turned round quickly, so quickly that her curls gave her a slap in the face, saw me, bowed, and with a smile showed me a little box half full of seeds. 'You don't mind?' I, of course, as is the usual practice in such cases, first bowed my head, and at the same time rapidly crooked my knees, and straightened them out again (as though someone had given me a blow from behind in the legs, a sure sign of good breeding and pleasant, easy manners), and then smiled, raised my hand, and softly and carefully brandished it twice in the air. The girl at once turned away from me, took a little piece of board out of the cage, began vigorously scraping it with a knife, and suddenly, without changing her attitude, uttered the following words: 'This is papa's parrot. . . . Are you fond of parrots?' 'I prefer siskins,' I answered, not without some effort. 'I like siskins, too; but look at him, isn't he pretty? Look, he's not afraid.' (What surprised me was that I was not afraid.) 'Come closer. His name's Popka.' I went up, and bent down. 'Isn't he really sweet?' She turned her face to me; but we were standing so close together, that she had to throw her head back to get a look at me with her clear eyes. I gazed at her; her rosy young face was smiling all over in such a friendly way that I smiled too, and almost laughed aloud with delight. The door opened; Mr. Ozhogin came in. I promptly went up to him, and began talking to him very unconstrainedly. I don't know how it was, but I stayed to dinner, and spent the whole evening with them; and next day the Ozhogins' footman, an elongated, dull-eyed person, smiled upon me as a friend of the family when he helped me off with my overcoat.

To find a haven of refuge, to build oneself even a temporary nest, to feel the comfort of daily intercourse and habits, was a happiness I, a superfluous man, with no family associations, had never before experienced. If anything about me had had any resemblance to a flower, and if the comparison were not so hackneyed, I would venture to say that my soul blossomed from that day. Everything within me and about me was suddenly transformed! My whole life was lighted up by love, the whole of it, down to the paltriest details, like a dark, deserted room when a light has been brought into it. I went to bed, and got up, dressed, ate my breakfast, and smoked my pipe—differently from before. I positively skipped along as I walked, as though wings were suddenly sprouting from my shoulders. I was not for an instant, I remember, in uncertainty with regard to the feeling Elizaveta Kirillovna inspired in me. I fell passionately in love with her from the first day, and from the first day I knew I was in love. During the course of three weeks I saw her every day. Those three weeks were the happiest time in my life; but the recollection of them is painful to me. I can't think of them alone; I cannot help dwelling on what followed after them, and the most intense bitterness slowly takes possession of my softened heart.

When a man is very happy, his brain, as is well known, is not very active. A calm and delicious sensation, the sensation of satisfaction, pervades his whole being; he is swallowed up by it; the consciousness of personal life vanishes in him—he is in beatitude, as badly educated poets say. But when, at last, this 'enchantment' is over, a man is sometimes vexed and sorry that, in the midst of his bliss, he observed himself so little; that he did not, by reflection, by recollection, redouble and prolong his feelings . . . as though the 'beatific' man had time, and it were worth his while to reflect on his sensations! The happy man is what the fly is in the sunshine. And so it is that, when I recall those three weeks, it is almost impossible for me to retain in my mind any exact and definite impression, all the more so as during that time nothing very remarkable took place between us. . . . Those twenty days are present to my imagination as something warm, and young, and fragrant, a sort of streak of light in my dingy, greyish life. My memory becomes all at once remorselessly clear and trustworthy, only from the instant when, to use the phrase of badly-educated writers, the blows of destiny began to fall upon me.

Yes, those three weeks. . . . Not but what they have left some images in my mind. Sometimes when it happens to me to brood a long while on that time, some memories suddenly float up out of the darkness of the past—like stars which suddenly come out against the evening sky to meet the eyes straining to catch sight of them. One country walk in a wood has remained particularly distinct in my memory. There were four of us, old Madame Ozhogin, Liza, I, and a certain Bizmyonkov, a petty official of the town of O——, a light-haired, good-natured, and harmless person. I shall have more to say of him later. Mr. Ozhogin had stayed at home; he had a headache, from sleeping too long. The day was exquisite; warm and soft. I must observe that pleasure-gardens and pic-nic-parties are not to the taste of the average Russian. In district towns, in the so-called public gardens, you never meet a living soul at any time of the year; at the most, some old woman sits sighing and moaning on a green garden seat, broiling in the sun, not far from a sickly tree—and that, only if there is no greasy little bench in the gateway near. But if there happens to be a scraggy birchwood in the neighborhood of the town, tradespeople and even officials gladly make excursions thither on Sundays and holidays, with samovars, pies, and melons; set all this abundance on the dusty grass, close by the road, sit round, and eat and drink tea in the sweat of their brows till evening. Just such a wood there was at that time a mile and a half from the town of O——. We repaired there after dinner, duly drank our fill of tea, and then all four began to wander about the wood. Bizmyonkov walked with Madame Ozhogin on his arm, I with Liza on mine. The day was already drawing to evening. I was at that time in the very fire of first love (not more than a fortnight had passed since our first meeting), in that condition of passionate and concentrated adoration, when your whole soul innocently and unconsciously follows every movement of the beloved being, when you can never have enough of her presence, listen enough to her voice, when you smile with the look of a child convalescent after sickness, and a man of the smallest experience cannot fail at the first glance to recognize a hundred yards off what is the matter with you. Till that day I had never happened to have Liza on my arm. We walked side by side, stepping slowly over the green grass. A light breeze, as it were, flitted about us between the white stems of the birches, every now and then flapping the ribbon of her hat into my face. I incessantly followed her eyes, until at last she turned gaily to me and we both smiled at each other. The birds were chirping approvingly above us, the blue sky peeped caressingly at us through the delicate foliage. My head was going round with excess of bliss. I hasten to remark, Liza was not a bit in love with me. She liked me; she was never shy with any one, but it was not reserved for me to trouble her childlike peace of mind. She walked arm in arm with me, as she would with a brother. She was seventeen then. . . . And meanwhile, that very evening, before my eyes, there began that soft inward ferment which precedes the metamorphosis of the child into the woman. . . . I was witness of that transformation of the whole being, that guileless bewilderment, that agitated dreaminess; I was the first to detect the sudden softness of the glance, the sudden ring in the voice—and oh, fool! oh, superfluous man! For a whole week I had the face to imagine that I, I was the cause of this transformation!

This was how it happened.

We walked rather a long while, till evening, and talked little. I was silent, like all inexperienced lovers, and she, probably, had nothing to say to me. But she seemed to be pondering over something, and shook her head in a peculiar way, as she pensively nibbled a leaf she had picked. Sometimes she started walking ahead, so resolutely. . .then all at once stopped, waited for me, and looked round with lifted eyebrows and a vague smile. On the previous evening we had read together. *The Prisoner of the Caucasus*. With what eagerness she had listened to me, her face propped in both hands, and her bosom pressed against the table! I began to speak of our yesterday's reading; she flushed, asked me whether I had given the parrot any hemp-seed before starting, began humming some little song aloud, and all at once was silent again. The copse ended on one side in a rather high and abrupt precipice; below coursed a winding stream, and beyond it, over an immense expanse, stretched the boundless prairies, rising like waves, spreading wide like a table-cloth, and broken here and there by ravines. Liza and I were the first to come out at the edge of the wood; Bizmyonkov and the elder lady were behind. We came out, stood still, and involuntarily we both half shut our eyes; directly facing us, across a lurid mist, the vast, purple sun was setting. Half the sky was flushed and glowing; red rays fell slanting on the meadows, casting a crimson reflection even on the side of the ravines in shadow, lying in gleams of fire on the stream, where it was not hidden under the overhanging bushes, and, as it were, leaning on the bosom of the precipice and the copse. We stood, bathed in the blazing brilliance. I am not capable of describing all the impassioned solemnity of this scene. They say that by a blind man the color red is imagined as the sound of a trumpet. I don't know how far this comparison is correct, but really there was something of a challenge in this glowing gold of the evening air, in the crimson flush on sky and earth. I uttered a cry of rapture and at once turned to Liza. She was looking straight at the sun. I remember the sunset glow was reflected in little points of fire in her eyes. She was overwhelmed, deeply moved. She made no response to my exclamation; for a long while she stood, not stirring, with drooping head. . . . I held out my hand to her; she turned away from me, and suddenly burst into tears. I looked at her with secret, almost delighted amazement. . . . The voice of Bizmyonkov was heard a couple of yards off. Liza quickly wiped her tears and looked with a faltering smile at me. The elder lady came out of the copse leaning on the arm of her flaxen-headed escort; they, in their turn, admired the view. The old lady addressed some question to Liza, and I could not help shuddering, I remember, when her daughter's broken voice, like cracked glass, sounded in reply. Meanwhile the sun had set, and the afterglow began to fade. We turned back. Again I took Liza's arm in mine. It was still light in the wood, and I could clearly distinguish her features. She was confused, and did not raise her eyes. The flush that overspread her face did not vanish; it was as though she were still standing in the rays of the setting sun. . . . Her hand scarcely touched my arm. For a long while I could not frame a sentence; my heart was beating so violently. Through the trees there was a glimpse of the carriage in the distance; the coachman was coming at a walking pace to meet us over the soft sand of the road.

'Lizaveta Kirillovna,' I brought out at last, 'what did you cry for?'

'I don't know,' she answered, after a short silence. She looked at me with her soft eyes still wet with tears—her look struck me as changed, and she was silent again.

'You are very fond, I see, of nature,' I pursued. That was not at all what I meant to say, and the last words my tongue scarcely faltered out to the end. She shook her head. I could not utter another word. . . . I was waiting for something . . . not an avowal—how was that possible? I waited for a confiding glance, a question. . . . But Liza looked at the ground, and kept silent. I repeated once more in a whisper: 'Why was it?' and received no reply. She had grown, I saw that, ill at ease, almost ashamed.

A quarter of an hour later we were sitting in the carriage driving to the town. The horses flew along at an even trot; we were rapidly whirled along through the darkening, damp air. I suddenly began talking, more than once addressing first Bizmyonkov, and then Madame Ozhogin. I did not look at Liza, but I could see that from her corner in the carriage her eyes did not once rest on me. At home she roused herself, but would not read with me, and soon went off to bed. A turning-point, that turning-point I have spoken of, had been reached by her. She had ceased to be a little girl, she too had begun . . . like me . . . to wait for something. She had not long to wait.

But that night I went home to my lodgings in a state of perfect ecstasy. The vague half presentiment, half suspicion, which had been arising within me, had vanished. The sudden constraint in Liza's manner towards me I ascribed to maidenly bashfulness, timidity. . . . Hadn't I read a thousand times over in many books that the first appearance of love always agitates and alarms a young girl? I felt supremely happy, and was already making all sorts of plans in my head.

If someone had whispered in my ear then: 'You're raving, my dear chap! that's not a bit what's in store for you. What's in store for you is to die all alone, in a wretched little cottage, amid the insufferable grumbling of an old hag who will await your death with impatience to sell your boots for a few coppers. . .'!

Yes, one can't help saying with the Russian philosopher—'How's one to know what one doesn't know?'

Enough for today.

March 25. A white winter day.

I have read over what I wrote yesterday, and was all but tearing up the whole manuscript. I think my story's too spun out and too sentimental. However, as the rest of my recollections of that time presents nothing of a pleasurable character, except that peculiar sort of consolation which Lermontov had in view when he said there is pleasure and pain in irritating the sores of old wounds, why not indulge oneself? But one must know where to draw the line. And so I will continue without any sort of sentimentality.

During the whole of the week after the country excursion, my position was in reality in no way improved, though the change in Liza became more noticeable every day. I interpreted this change, as I have said before, in the most favourable way for me. . . . The misfortune of solitary and timid people—who are timid from self-consciousness—is just that, though they have eyes and indeed open them wide, they see nothing, or see everything in a false light, as though through colored spectacles. Their own ideas and speculations trip them up at every step. At the commencement of our acquaintance, Liza behaved confidingly and freely with me, like a child; perhaps there may even have been in her attitude to me something more than mere childish liking. . . . But after this strange, almost instantaneous change had taken place in her, after a period of brief perplexity, she felt constrained in my presence; she unconsciously turned away from me, and was at the same time melancholy and dreamy. . . . She was waiting . . . for what? She did not know . . . while I . . . I, as I have said above, was delighted at this change. . . . Yes, by God, I was ready to expire, as they say, with rapture. Though I am prepared to allow that anyone else in my place might have been deceived. . . . Who is free from vanity? I need not say that all this was only clear to me in the course of time, when I had to lower my clipped and at no time over-powerful wings.

The misunderstanding that had arisen between Liza and me lasted a whole week—and there is nothing surprising in that: it has been my lot to be a witness of misunderstandings that have lasted for years and years. Who was it said, by the way, that truth alone is powerful? Falsehood is just as living as truth, if not more so. To be sure, I recollect that even during that week I felt from time to time an uneasy gnawing astir within me . . . but solitary people like me, I say again, are as incapable of understanding what is going on within them as what is taking place before their eyes. And, besides, is love a natural feeling? Is it natural for man to love? Love is a sickness; and for sickness there is no law. Granting that there was at times an unpleasant pang in my heart; well, everything inside me was turned upside down. And how is one to know in such circumstances, what is all right and what is all wrong? and what is the cause, and what the significance, of each separate symptom? But, be that as it may, all these misconceptions, presentiments, and hopes were shattered in the following manner.

One day—it was in the morning about twelve o'clock—I had hardly entered Mr. Ozhogin's hall, when I heard an unfamiliar, mellow voice in the drawing-room, the door opened, and a tall and slim man of five-and-twenty appeared in the doorway, escorted by the master of the house. He rapidly put on a military overcoat which lay on the slab, and took cordial leave of Kirilla Matveitch. As he brushed past me, he carelessly touched his foraging cap, and vanished with a clink of his spurs.

'Who is that?' I asked Ozhogin.

'Prince N., 'the latter responded, with a preoccupied face; 'sent from Petersburg to collect recruits. But where are the servants?' he went on in a tone of annoyance; 'no one handed him his coat.'

We went into the drawing-room.

'Has he been here long?' I inquired.

'Arrived yesterday evening, I'm told. I offered him a room here, but he refused. He seems a very nice fellow, though.'

'Has he been long with you?'

'About an hour. He asked me to introduce him to Olimpiada Nikitishna.'

'And did you introduce him?'

'Of course.'

'And Lizaveta Kirillovna, too, did he . . .'

'He made her acquaintance, too, of course.'

I was silent for a space.

'Has he come here for long, do you know?'

'Yes, I believe he has to be here for a fortnight.'

And Kirilla Matveitch hurried away to dress. I walked several times up and down the drawing-room. I don't recollect that Prince N.'s arrival made any special impression on me at the time, except that feeling of hostility which usually possesses us on the appearance of any new person in our domestic circle. Possibly there was mingled with this feeling something too of the nature of envy—of a shy and obscure person from Moscow towards a brilliant officer from Petersburg. 'The prince,' I mused, 'is an upstart from the capital; he'll look down upon us. . . .' I had not seen him for more than an instant, but I had had time to perceive that he was good-looking, clever, and at his ease. After pacing the room for some time, I stopped at last before a looking-glass, pulled a comb out of my pocket, gave a picturesque carelessness to my hair, and, as sometimes happens, became suddenly absorbed in the contemplation of my own face. I remember my attention centered anxiously about my nose; the soft and undefined outlines of that feature afforded me no great satisfaction, when suddenly in the dark depths of the sloping mirror, which reflected almost the whole room, the door opened, and the slender figure of Liza appeared. I don't know why I did not stir, and kept the same expression on my face. Liza craned her head forward, looked intently at me, and raising her eyebrows, biting her lips, and holding her breath as any one does who is glad at not being noticed, she cautiously drew back and stealthily drew the door to after her. The door creaked slightly. Liza started and stood rooted to the spot. . . I still kept from stirring . . . she pulled the handle again and vanished. There was no possibility of doubt: the expression of Liza's face at the sight of my figure, that expression in which nothing could be detected except a desire to get away again successfully, to escape a disagreeable interview, the quick flash of delight I had time to catch in her eyes when she fancied she really had managed to creep away unnoticed—it all spoke too clearly; that girl did not love me. For a long, long while I could not take my eyes off that motionless, dumb door, which was once more a patch of white in the looking-glass. I tried to smile at my own long face—dropped my head, went home again, and flung myself on the sofa. I felt extraordinarily heavy at heart, so much so that I could not cry . . . and, besides, what was there to cry about. . .? 'Is it possible?' I repeated incessantly, lying, as though I were murdered, on my back with my hands folded on my breast—'is it possible?'. . .Don't you think that's rather good, that 'is it possible?'

March 26. Thaw.

When, next day, after long hesitation and with a low sinking at my heart, I went into the Ozhogins' familiar drawing-room, I was no longer the same man as they had known during the last three weeks. All my old peculiarities, which I had begun to get over, under the influence of a new feeling, reappeared and took possession of me, like proprietors returning to their house. People of my sort are usually guided, not so much by positive facts, as by their own impressions: I, who no longer ago than the day before had been dreaming of the 'raptures of love returned,' was that day no less convinced of my 'unhappiness,' and was absolutely despairing, though I was not myself able to find any rational ground for my despair. I could not as yet be jealous of Prince N., and whatever his qualities might be, his mere arrival was not sufficient to extinguish Liza's good-will towards me at once. . . . But stay, was there any good-will on her part? I recalled the past. 'What of the walk in the wood?' I asked myself. 'What of the expression of her face in the glass?' 'But,' I went on, 'the walk in the wood, I think . . . Fie on me! my God, what a wretched creature I am!' I said at last, out loud. Of such sort were the unphrased, incomplete thoughts that went round and round a thousand times over in a monotonous whirl in my head. I repeat, I went back to the Ozhogins' the same hypersensitive, suspicious, constrained creature I had been from my childhood up. . . .

I found the whole family in the drawing-room; Bizmyonkov was sitting there, too, in a corner. Everyone seemed in high good-humor; Ozhogin, in particular, positively beamed, and his first word was to tell me that Prince N. had spent the whole of the previous evening with them. Liza gave me a tranquil greeting. 'Oh,' said I to myself; 'now I understand why you're in such spirits.' I must own the prince's second visit puzzled me. I had not anticipated it. As a rule fellows like me anticipate everything in the world, except what is bound to occur in the natural order of things; I sulked and put on the air of an injured but magnanimous person; I tried to punish Liza by showing my displeasure, from which one must conclude I was not yet completely desperate after all. They do say that in some cases when one is really loved, it's positively of use to torment the adored one; but in my position it was indescribably stupid. Liza, in the most innocent way, paid no attention to me. No one but Madame Ozhogin observed my solemn taciturnity, and she inquired anxiously after my health. I replied, of course, with a bitter smile, that I was thankful to say I was perfectly well. Ozhogin continued to expatiate on the subject of their visitor; but noticing that I responded reluctantly, he addressed himself principally to

Bizmyonkov, who was listening to him with great attention, when a servant suddenly came in, announcing the arrival of Prince N. Our host jumped up and ran to meet him; Liza, upon whom I at once turned an eagle eye, flushed with delight, and made as though she would move from her seat. The prince came in, all agreeable perfume, gaiety, cordiality. . . .

As I am not composing a romance for a gentle reader, but simply writing for my own amusement, it stands to reason I need not make use of the usual dodges of our respected authors. I will say straight out without further delay that Liza fell passionately in love with the prince from the first day she saw him, and the prince fell in love with her too—partly from having nothing to do, and partly from a propensity for turning women's heads, and also owing to the fact that Liza really was a very charming creature. There was nothing to be wondered at in their falling in love with each other. He had certainly never expected to find such a pearl in such a wretched shell (I am alluding to the God-forsaken town of O——), and she had never in her wildest dreams seen anything in the least like this brilliant, clever, fascinating aristocrat.

After the first courtesies, Ozhogin introduced me to the prince, who was very affable in his behavior to me. He was as a rule very affable with everyone; and in spite of the immeasurable distance between him and our obscure provincial circle, he was clever enough to avoid being a source of constraint to any one, and even to make a show of being on our level, and only living at Petersburg, as it were, by accident.

That first evening. . . . Oh, that first evening! In our happy days of childhood our teachers used to describe and set up before us as an example the manly fortitude of the young Spartan, who, having stolen a fox and hidden it under his tunic, without uttering one shriek let it devour all his entrails, and so preferred death itself to disgrace. . . . I can find no better comparison for my indescribable sufferings during the evening on which I first saw the prince by Liza's side. My continual forced smile and painful vigilance, my idiotic silence, my miserable and ineffectual desire to get away—all that was doubtless something truly remarkable in its own way. It was not one wild beast alone gnawing at my vitals; jealousy, envy, the sense of my own insignificance, and helpless hatred were torturing me. I could not but admit that the prince really was a very agreeable young man. . . . I devoured him with my eyes; I really believe I forgot to blink as usual, as I stared at him. He talked not to Liza alone, but all he said was of course really for her. He must have felt me a great bore. He most likely guessed directly that it was a discarded lover he had to deal with, but from sympathy for me, and also a profound sense of my absolute harmlessness, he treated me with extraordinary gentleness. You can fancy how this wounded me! In the course of the evening I tried, I remember, to smooth over my mistake. I positively (don't laugh at me, whoever you may be, who chance to look through these lines—especially as it was my last illusion. . .) . . . I, positively, in the midst of my different sufferings, imagined all of a sudden that Liza wanted to punish me for my haughty coldness at the beginning of my visit, that she was angry with me and only flirting with the prince from pique. . . . I seized my opportunity and with a meek but gracious smile, I went up to her, and muttered—'Enough, forgive me, not that I'm afraid . . .' and suddenly, without awaiting her reply, I gave my features an extraordinarily cheerful and free-and-easy expression, with a set grin, passed my hand above my head in the direction of the ceiling (I wanted, I remember, to set my cravat straight), and was even on the point of pirouetting round on one foot, as though to say, 'All is over, I am happy, let's all be happy,'—I did not, however, execute this maneuver, as I was afraid of losing my balance, owing to an unnatural stiffness in my knees. . . . Liza failed absolutely to understand me; she looked in my face with amazement, gave a hasty smile, as though she wanted to get rid of me as quickly as possible, and again approached the prince. Blind and deaf as I was, I could not but be inwardly aware that she was not in the least angry, and was not annoyed with me at that instant: she simply never gave me a thought. The blow was a final one. My last hopes were shattered with a crash, just as a block of ice, thawed by the sunshine of spring, suddenly falls into tiny morsels. I was utterly defeated at the first skirmish, and, like the Prussians at Jena, lost everything at once in one day. No, she was not angry with me! . . .

Alas, it was quite the contrary! She too—I saw that—was being swept off her feet by the torrent. Like a young tree, already half torn from the bank, she bent eagerly over the stream, ready to abandon to it forever the first blossom of her spring and her whole life. A man whose fate it has been to be the witness of such a passion, has lived through bitter moments if he has loved himself and not been loved. I shall forever remember that devouring attention, that tender gaiety, that innocent self-oblivion, that glance, still a child's and already a woman's, that happy, as it were flowering smile that never left the half-parted lips and glowing cheeks. . . . All that Liza had vaguely foreshadowed during our walk in the wood had come to pass now—and she, as she gave herself up utterly to love, was at once stiller and brighter, like new wine, which ceases to ferment because its full maturity has come. . . .

I had the fortitude to sit through that first evening and the subsequent evenings . . . all to the end! I could have no hope of anything. Liza and the prince became every day more devoted to each other . . . But I had absolutely lost all sense of personal dignity, and could not tear myself away from the spectacle of my own misery. I remember one day I tried not to go, swore to myself in the morning that I would stay at home, and at eight o'clock in the evening (I usually set off at seven) leaped up like a madman, put on my hat, and ran breathless into Kirilla Matveitch's drawing-room. My position was excessively absurd. I was obstinately silent; sometimes for whole days together I did not utter a sound. I was, as I have said already, never distinguished for eloquence; but now everything I had in my mind took flight, as it were, in the presence of the prince, and I was left bare and bereft. Besides, when I was alone, I set my wretched brain working so hard, slowly going over everything I had noticed or surmised during the preceding day, that when I went back to the Ozhogins' I scarcely had energy left to observe again. They treated me considerately, as a sick person; I saw that. Every morning I adopted some new, final resolution, for the most part painfully hatched in the course of a sleepless night. At one time I made up my mind to have it out with Liza, to give her friendly advice . . . but when I chanced to be alone with her, my tongue suddenly ceased to work, froze as it were, and we both, in great discomfort, waited for the entrance of some third person. Another time I meant to run away, of course forever, leaving my beloved a letter full of reproaches, and I even one day began this letter; but the sense of justice had not yet quite vanished in me. I realized that I had no right to reproach any one for anything, and I flung what I had written in the fire. Then I suddenly offered myself up wholly as a sacrifice, gave Liza my benediction, praying for her happiness, and smiled in meek and friendly fashion from my corner at the prince. But the cruel-hearted lovers not only never thanked me for my self-sacrifice, they never even noticed me, and were, apparently, quite ready to dispense with my smiles and my blessings. . . .

Then, in wrath, I suddenly flew into quite the opposite mood. I swore to myself, wrapping my cloak about me like a Spaniard, to rush out from some dark corner and stab my lucky rival, and with brutal glee I imagined Liza's despair. . . . But, in the first place, such corners were few in the town of O——; and, secondly—the wooden fence, the street lamp, the policeman in the distance. . . . No! in such corners it was somehow far more suitable to sell buns and oranges than to shed human blood. I must own that, among other means of deliverance, as I very vaguely expressed it in my colloquies with myself, I did entertain the idea of having recourse to Ozhogin himself . . . of calling the attention of that nobleman to the perilous situation of his daughter, and the mournful consequences of her indiscretion. . . .

I even once began speaking to him on a certain delicate subject; but my remarks were so indirect and misty, that after listening and listening to me, he suddenly, as it were, waking up, rubbed his hand rapidly and vigorously all over his face, not sparing his nose, gave a snort, and walked away from me. It is needless to say that in resolving on this step I persuaded myself that I was acting from the most disinterested motives, was desirous of the general welfare, and was doing my duty as a friend of the house. . . . But I venture to think that even had Kirilla Matveitch not cut short my outpourings, I should in any case not have had courage to finish my monologue. At times I set to work with all the solemnity of some sage of antiquity, weighing the qualities of the prince; at times I comforted myself with the hope that it was all of no consequence, that Liza would recover her senses, that her love was not real love . . . oh, no! In short, I know no idea that I did not worry myself with at that time. There was only one resource which never, I candidly admit, entered my head: I never once thought of taking my life. Why it did not occur to me I don't know. . . . Possibly, even then, I had a presentiment I should not have long to live in any case.

It will be readily understood that in such unfavorable circumstances my manner, my behavior with people, was more than ever marked by unnaturalness and constraint. Even Madame Ozhogin—that creature dull-witted from her birth up—began to shun me, and at times did not know in what way to approach me. Bizmyonkov, always polite and ready to do services, avoided me. I fancied even at that time that I had in him a companion in misfortune—that he too loved Liza.

But he never responded to my hints, and altogether showed a reluctance to converse with me. The prince behaved in a very friendly way to him; the prince, one might say, respected him. Neither Bizmyonkov nor I was any obstacle to the prince and Liza; but he did not shun them as I did, nor look savage nor injured—and readily joined them when they desired it. It is true that on such occasions he was not conspicuous for any special mirthfulness; but his good-humor had always been somewhat subdued in character.

In this fashion about a fortnight passed by. The prince was not only handsome and clever: he played the piano, sang, sketched fairly well, and was a good hand at telling stories. His anecdotes, drawn from the highest circles of Petersburg society, always made a great impression on his audience, all the more so from the fact that he seemed to attach no importance to them. . . .

The consequence of this, if you like, simple accomplishment of the prince's was that in the course of his not very protracted stay in the town of O—— he completely fascinated all the neighborhood. To fascinate us poor dwellers in the steppes is at all times a very easy task for anyone coming from higher spheres. The prince's frequent visits to the Ozhogins (he used to spend his evenings there) of course aroused the jealousy of the other worthy gentry and officials of the town. But the prince, like a clever person and a man of the world, never neglected a single one of them; he called on all of them; to every married lady and every unmarried miss he addressed at least one flattering phrase, allowed them to feed him on elaborately solid edibles, and to make him drink wretched wines with magnificent names; and conducted himself, in short, like a model of caution and tact. Prince N—— was in general a man of lively manners, sociable and genial by inclination, and in this case incidentally from prudential motives also; he could not fail to be a complete success in everything.

Ever since his arrival, all in the house had felt that the time had flown by with unusual rapidity; everything had gone off beautifully. Papa Ozhogin, though he pretended that he noticed nothing, was doubtless rubbing his hands in private at the idea of such a son-in-law. The prince, for his part, managed matters with the utmost sobriety and discretion, when, all of a sudden, an unexpected incident. . . .

Till tomorrow. Today I'm tired. These recollections irritate me even at the edge of the grave. Terentyevna noticed today that my nose has already begun to grow sharp; and that, they say, is a bad sign.

March 27. Thaw continuing.

Things were in the position described above: the prince and Liza were in love with each other; the old Ozhogins were waiting to see what would come of it; Bizmyonkov was present at the proceedings—there was nothing else to be said of him. I was struggling like a fish on the ice, and watching with all my might,—I remember that at that time I set myself the task of preventing Liza at least from falling into the snares of a seducer, and consequently began paying particular attention to the maidservants and the fateful 'back stairs'—though, on the other hand, I often spent whole nights in dreaming with what touching magnanimity I would one day hold out a hand to the betrayed victim and say to her, 'The traitor has deceived thee; but I am thy true friend . . . let us forget the past and be happy!'—when sudden and glad tidings overspread the whole town. The marshal of the district proposed to give a great ball in honor of their respected guest, on his private estate Gornostaevka. All the official world, big and little, of the town of O—— received invitations, from the mayor down to the apothecary, an excessively emaciated German, with ferocious pretensions to a good Russian accent, which led him into continually and quite inappropriately employing racy colloquialisms. . . . Tremendous preparations were, of course, put in hand. One purveyor of cosmetics sold sixteen dark-blue jars of pomatum, which bore the inscription *à la jesmin.* The young ladies provided themselves with tight dresses, agonizing in the waist and jutting out sharply over the stomach; the mammas put formidable erections on their heads by way of caps; the busy papas were half dead with the bustle. The longed-for day arrived at last. I was among those invited. From the town to Gornostaevka was reckoned between seven and eight miles. Kirilla Matveitch offered me a seat in his coach; but I refused. . . . In the same way children, who have been punished, wishing to pay their parents out, refuse their favorite dainties at table. Besides, I felt that my presence would be felt as a constraint by Liza. Bizmyonkov took my place. The prince drove in his own carriage, and I in a wretched little droshky, hired for an immense sum for this solemn occasion. I am not going to describe that ball. Everything about it was just as it always is. There was a band, with trumpets extraordinarily out of tune, in the gallery; there were country gentlemen, greatly flustered, with their inevitable families, mauve ices, viscous lemonade; servants in boots trodden down at heel and knitted cotton gloves; provincial lions with spasmodically contorted faces, and so on and so on. And all this little world was revolving round its sun—round the prince. Lost in the crowd, unnoticed even by the young ladies of eight-and-forty, with red pimples on their brows and blue flowers on the top of their heads, I stared incessantly, first at the prince, then at Liza. She was very charmingly dressed and very pretty that evening. They only twice danced together (it is true, he danced the mazurka with her); but it seemed, to me at least, that there was a sort of secret, continuous communication between them. Even while not looking at her, while not speaking to her, he was still, as it were, addressing her, and her alone. He was handsome and brilliant and charming with other people—for her sake only. She was apparently conscious that she was the queen of the ball, and that she was loved. Her face at once beamed with childlike delight and innocent pride, and was suddenly illuminated by another, deeper feeling. Happiness radiated from her. I observed all this. . . . It was not the first time I had watched them. . . . At first this wounded me intensely; afterwards it, as it were, touched me; but, finally, it infuriated me. I suddenly felt extraordinarily wrathful, and, I remember, was extraordinarily delighted at this new sensation, and even conceived a certain respect for myself. 'We'll show them we're not crushed yet,' I said to myself. When the first inviting notes of the mazurka sounded, I looked about me with composure, and with a cool and easy air approached a long-faced young lady with a red and shiny nose, a mouth that stood awkwardly open, as though it had come unbuttoned, and a scraggy neck that recalled the handle of a bass-viol. I went up to her, and, with a perfunctory scrape of my heels, invited her to the dance. She was wearing a dress of faded rosebud pink, not full-blown rose color; on her head quivered a striped and dejected beetle of some sort on a thick bronze pin; and altogether this lady was, if one may so express it, soaked through and through with a sort of sour ennui and inveterate lack of success. From the very commencement of the evening she had not once stirred from her seat; no one had thought of asking her to dance. One flaxen-headed youth of sixteen had, through lack of a partner, been on the point of addressing this lady, and had taken a step in her direction, but had thought better of it, stared at her, and hurriedly dived into the crowd. You can fancy with what joyful amazement she agreed to my proposal! I led her in triumph right across the ballroom, picked out two chairs, and sat down with her in the ring of the mazurka, among ten couples, almost opposite the prince, who had, of course, been offered the first place. The prince, as I have said already, was dancing with Liza. Neither I nor my partner was disturbed by invitations; consequently, we had plenty of time for conversation. To tell the truth, my partner was not conspicuous for her capacity for the utterance of words in consecutive speech; she used her mouth principally for the achievement of a strange downward smile such as I had never till then beheld; while she raised her eyes upward, as though some unseen force were pulling her face in two. But I did not feel her lack of eloquence. Happily I felt full of wrath, and my partner did not make me shy. I fell to finding fault with everything and everyone in the world, with especial emphasis on town-bred youngsters and Petersburg dandies; and went to such lengths at last, that my partner gradually ceased smiling, and instead of turning her eyes upward, began suddenly—from astonishment, I suppose—to squint, and that so strangely, as though she had for the first time observed the fact that she had a nose on her face. And one of the lions, referred to above, who was sitting next me, did not once take his eyes off me; he positively turned to me with the expression of an actor on the stage, who has waked up in an unfamiliar place, as though he would say, 'Is it really you!' While I poured forth this tirade, I still, however, kept watch on the prince and Liza. They were continually invited; but I suffered less when they were both dancing; and even when they were sitting side by side, and smiling as they talked to each other that sweet smile which hardly leaves the faces of happy lovers, even then I was not in such torture; but when Liza flitted across the room with some desperate dandy of an hussar, while the prince with her blue gauze scarf on his knees followed her dreamily with his eyes, as though delighting in his conquest;—then, oh! then, I went through intolerable agonies, and in my anger gave vent to such spiteful observations, that the pupils of my partner's eyes simply fastened on her nose!

Meanwhile the mazurka was drawing to a close. They were beginning the figure called *la confidente*. In this figure the lady sits in the middle of a circle, chooses another lady as her confidant, and whispers in her ear the name of the gentleman with whom she wishes to dance.

Her partner conducts one after another of the dancers to her; but the lady, who is in the secret, refuses them, till at last the happy man fixed on beforehand arrives. Liza sat in the middle of the circle and chose the daughter of the host, one of those young ladies of whom one says, 'God help them!'. . . The prince proceeded to discover her choice. After presenting about a dozen young men to her in vain (the daughter of the house refused them all with the most amiable of smiles), he at last turned to me.

Something extraordinary took place within me at that instant; I, as it were, twitched all over, and would have refused, but got up and went along. The prince conducted me to Liza. . . . She did not even look at me; the daughter of the house shook her head in refusal, the prince turned to me, and, probably incited by the goose-like expression of my face, made me a deep bow. This sarcastic bow, this refusal, transmitted to me through my triumphant rival, his careless smile, Liza's indifferent inattention, all this lashed me to frenzy. . . . I moved up to the prince and whispered furiously, 'You think fit to laugh at me, it seems?'

The prince looked at me with contemptuous surprise, took my arm again, and making a show of re-conducting me to my seat, answered coldly, 'I?'

'Yes, you!' I went on in a whisper, obeying, however—that is to say, following him to my place; 'you; but I do not intend to permit any empty-headed Petersburg up-start——'

The prince smiled tranquilly, almost condescendingly, pressed my arm, whispered, 'I understand you; but this is not the place; we will have a word later,' turned away from me, went up to Bizmyonkov, and led him up to Liza. The pale little official turned out to be the chosen partner. Liza got up to meet him.

Sitting beside my partner with the dejected beetle on her head, I felt almost a hero. My heart beat violently, my breast heaved gallantly under my starched shirt front, I drew deep and hurried breaths, and suddenly gave the local lion near me such a magnificent glare that there was an involuntary quiver of his foot in my direction. Having disposed of this person, I scanned the whole circle of dancers. . . . I fancied two or three gentlemen were staring at me with some perplexity; but, in general, my conversation with the prince had passed unnoticed. . . . My rival was already back in his chair, perfectly composed, and with the same smile on his face. Bizmyonkov led Liza back to her place. She gave him a friendly bow, and at once turned to the prince, as I fancied, with some alarm. But he laughed in response, with a graceful wave of his hand, and must have said something very agreeable to her, for she flushed with delight, dropped her eyes, and then bent them with affectionate reproach upon him.

The heroic frame of mind, which had suddenly developed in me, had not disappeared by the end of the mazurka; but I did not indulge in any more epigrams or 'quizzing.' I contented myself with glancing occasionally with gloomy severity at my partner, who was obviously beginning to be afraid of me, and was utterly tongue-tied and continuously blinking by the time I placed her under the protection of her mother, a very fat woman with a red cap on her head. Having consigned the scared maiden lady to her natural belongings, I turned away to a window, folded my arms, and began to await what would happen. I had rather long to wait. The prince was the whole time surrounded by his host—surrounded, simply, as England is surrounded by the sea,—to say nothing of the other members of the marshal's family and the rest of the guests. And besides, he could hardly go up to such an insignificant person as me and begin to talk without arousing a general feeling of surprise. This insignificance, I remember, was positively a joy to me at the time. 'All right,' I thought, as I watched him courteously addressing first one and then another highly respected personage, honored by his notice, if only for an 'instant's flash,' as the poets say;—'all right, my dear . . . you'll come to me soon—I've insulted you, anyway.' At last the prince, adroitly escaping from the throng of his adorers, passed close by me, looked somewhere between the window and my hair, was turning away, and suddenly stood still, as though he had recollected something. 'Ah, yes!' he said, turning to me with a smile, 'by the way, I have a little matter to talk to you about.'

Two country gentlemen, of the most persistent, who were obstinately pursuing the prince, probably imagined the 'little matter' to relate to official business, and respectfully fell back. The prince took my arm and led me apart. My heart was thumping at my ribs.

'You, I believe,' he began, emphasizing the word *you*, and looking at my chin with a contemptuous expression, which, strange to say, was supremely becoming to his fresh and handsome face, 'you said something abusive to me?'

'I said what I thought,' I replied, raising my voice.

'Sh . . . quietly,' he observed; 'decent people don't bawl. You would like, perhaps, to fight me?'

'That's your affair,' I answered, drawing myself up.

'I shall be obliged to challenge you,' he remarked carelessly, 'if you don't withdraw your expressions. . . .'

'I do not intend to withdraw from anything,' I rejoined with pride.

'Really?' he observed, with an ironical smile.

'In that case,' he continued, after a brief pause, 'I shall have the honor of sending my second to you tomorrow.'

'Very good,'I said in a voice, if possible, even more indifferent.

The prince gave a slight bow.

'I cannot prevent you from considering me empty-headed,' he added, with a haughty droop of his eyelids; 'but the Princes N—— cannot be upstarts. Good-bye till we meet, Mr. . . . Mr. Shtukaturin.'

He quickly turned his back on me, and again approached his host, who was already beginning to get excited.

Mr. Shtukaturin! . . . My name is Tchulkaturin. . . . I could think of nothing to say to him in reply to this last insult, and could only gaze after him with fury. 'Till tomorrow,' I muttered, clenching my teeth, and I at once looked for an officer of my acquaintance, a cavalry captain in the Uhlans, called Koloberdyaev, a desperate rake, and a very good fellow. To him I related, in few words, my quarrel with the prince, and asked him to be my second. He, of course, promptly consented, and I went home.

I could not sleep all night—from excitement, not from cowardice. I am not a coward. I positively thought very little of the possibility confronting me of losing my life—that, as the Germans assure us, highest good on earth. I could think only of Liza, of my ruined hopes, of what I ought to do. 'Ought I to try to kill the prince?' I asked myself; and, of course, I wanted to kill him—not from revenge, but from a desire for Liza's good. 'But she will not survive such a blow,' I went on. 'No, better let him kill me!' I must own it was an agreeable reflection, too, that I, an obscure provincial person, had forced a man of such consequence to fight a duel with me.

The morning light found me still absorbed in these reflections; and, not long after it, appeared Koloberdyaev.

'Well,' he asked me, entering my room with a clatter, 'where's the prince's second?' 'Upon my word,' I answered with annoyance, 'it's seven o'clock at the most; the prince is still asleep, I should imagine.' 'In that case,' replied the cavalry officer, in nowise daunted, 'order some tea for me. My head aches from yesterday evening. . . . I've not taken my clothes off all night. Though, indeed,' he added with a yawn, 'I don't as a rule often take my clothes off.'

Some tea was given him. He drank off six glasses of tea and rum, smoked four pipes, told me he had on the previous day bought, for next to nothing, a horse the coachman refused to drive, and that he was meaning to drive her out with one of her forelegs tied up, and fell asleep, without undressing, on the sofa, with a pipe in his mouth. I got up and put my papers to rights. One note of invitation from Liza, the one note I had received from her, I was on the point of putting in my bosom, but on second thoughts I flung it in a drawer. Koloberdyaev was snoring feebly, with his head hanging from the leather pillow. . . . For a long while, I remember, I scrutinized his unkempt, daring, careless, and good-natured face. At ten o'clock the man announced the arrival of Bizmyonkov. The prince had chosen him as second.

We both together roused the soundly sleeping cavalry officer. He sat up, stared at us with dim eyes, in a hoarse voice demanded vodka. He recovered himself, and exchanging greetings with Bizmyonkov, he went with him into the next room to arrange matters. The consultation of the worthy seconds did not last long. A quarter of an hour later, they both came into my bedroom. Koloberdyaev announced to me that 'we're going to fight today at three o'clock with pistols.' In silence I bent my head, in token of my agreement. Bizmyonkov at once took leave of us, and departed. He was rather pale and inwardly agitated, like a man unused to such jobs, but he was, nevertheless, very polite and chilly. I felt, as it were, conscience-stricken in his presence, and did not dare look him in the face. Koloberdyaev began telling me about his horse. This conversation was very welcome to me. I was afraid he would mention Liza. But the good-natured cavalry officer was not a gossip, and, moreover, he despised all women, calling them, God knows why, green stuff. At two o'clock we had lunch, and at three we were at the place fixed upon—the very birch copse in which I had once walked with Liza, a couple of yards from the precipice.

We arrived first; but the prince and Bizmyonkov did not keep us long waiting. The prince was, without exaggeration, as fresh as a rose; his brown eyes looked out with excessive cordiality from under the peak of his cap. He was smoking a cigar, and on seeing Koloberdyaev shook his hand in a friend-ly way.

Even to me he bowed very genially. I was conscious, on the contrary, of being pale, and my hands, to my terrible vexation, were slightly trembling . . . my throat was parched. . . . I had never fought a duel before. 'O God!' I thought; 'if only that ironical gentleman doesn't take my agi-tation for timidity!' I was inwardly cursing my nerves; but glancing, at last, straight in the prince's face, and catching on his lips an almost imperceptible smile, I suddenly felt furious again, and was at once at my ease. Meanwhile, our seconds were fixing the barrier, measuring out the paces, loading the pistols. Koloberdyaev did most; Bizmyonkov rather watched him. It was a magnificent day—as fine as the day of that ever-memorable walk. The thick blue of the sky peeped, as then, through the golden green of the leaves. Their lisping seemed to mock me. The prince went on smoking his cigar, leaning with his shoulder against the trunk of a young lime-tree. . . .

'Kindly take your places, gentlemen; ready,' Koloberdyaev pronounced at last, handing us pistols.

The prince walked a few steps away, stood still, and, turn-ing his head, asked me over his shoulder, 'You still refuse to take back your words, then?'

I tried to answer him; but my voice failed me, and I had to content myself with a contemptuous wave of the hand. The prince smiled again, and took up his position in his place. We began to approach one another. I raised my pistol, was about to aim at my enemy's chest—but suddenly tilted it up, as though someone had given my elbow a shove, and fired. The prince tottered, and put his left hand to his left temple—a thread of blood was flowing down his cheek from under the white leather glove, Bizmyonkov rushed up to him.

'It's all right,' he said, taking off his cap, which the bullet had pierced; 'since it's in the head, and I've not fallen, it must be a mere scratch.'

He calmly pulled a cambric handkerchief out of his pocket, and put it to his blood-stained curls.

I stared at him, as though I were turned to stone, and did not stir.

'Go up to the barrier, if you please!' Koloberdyaev observed severely.

I obeyed.

'Is the duel to go on?' he added, addressing Bizmyonkov.

Bizmyonkov made him no answer. But the prince, without taking the handkerchief from the wound, without even giving himself the satisfaction of tormenting me at the barrier, replied with a smile. 'The duel is at an end,' and fired into the air. I was almost crying with rage and vexation. This man by his magnanimity had utterly trampled me in the mud; he had completely crushed me. I was on the point of making objections, on the point of demanding that he should fire at me. But he came up to me, and held out his hand.

'It's all forgotten between us, isn't it?' he said in a friendly voice.

I looked at his blanched face, at the blood-stained hand-kerchief, and utterly confounded, put to shame, and annihilated, I pressed his hand.

'Gentlemen!' he added, turning to the seconds, 'everything, I hope, will be kept secret?'

'Of course!' cried Koloberdyaev; 'but, prince, allow me . . .'

And he himself bound up his head.

The prince, as he went away, bowed to me once more. But Bizmyonkov did not even glance at me. Shattered—morally shattered—went homewards with Koloberdyaev.

'Why, what's the matter with you?' the cavalry captain asked me. 'Set your mind at rest; the wound's not serious. He'll be able to dance by tomorrow, if you like. Or are you sorry you didn't kill him? You're wrong, if you are; he's a first-rate fellow.'

'What business had he to spare me!' I muttered at last.

'Oh, so that's it!' the cavalry captain rejoined tranquilly. . . 'Ugh, you writing fellows are too much for me!'

I don't know what put it into his head to consider me an author.

I absolutely decline to describe my torments during the evening following upon that luckless duel. My vanity suffered indescribably. It was not my conscience that tortured me; the consciousness of my imbecility crushed me. 'I have given myself the last decisive blow by my own act!' I kept repeating, as I strode up and down my room. 'The prince, wounded by me, and forgiving me. . . Yes, Liza is now his. Now nothing can save her, nothing can hold her back on the edge of the abyss.' I knew very well that our duel could not be kept secret, in spite of the prince's words; in any case, it could not remain a secret for Liza.

'The prince is not such a fool,' I murmured in a frenzy of rage, 'as not to profit by it.'. . . But, meanwhile, I was mistaken. The whole town knew of the duel and of its real cause next day, of course. But the prince had not blabbed of it; on the contrary, when, with his head bandaged and an explanation ready, he made his appearance before Liza, she had already heard everything. . . . Whether Bizmyonkov had betrayed me, or the news had reached her by other channels, I cannot say. Though, indeed, can anything ever be concealed in a little town? You can fancy how Liza received him, how all the family of the Ozhogins received him! As for me, I suddenly became an object of universal indignation and loathing, a monster, a jealous bloodthirsty madman. My few acquaintances shunned me as if I were a leper. The authorities of the town promptly addressed the prince, with a proposal to punish me in a severe and befitting manner. Nothing but the persistent and urgent entreaties of the prince himself averted the calamity that menaced me. That man was fated to annihilate me in every way. By his generosity he had shut, as it were, a coffin-lid down upon me. It's needless to say that the Ozhogins' doors were at once closed against me. Kirilla Matveitch even sent me back a bit of pencil I had left in his house. In reality, he, of all people, had no reason to be angry with me. My 'insane' (that was the expression current in the town) jealousy had pointed out, defined, so to speak, the relations of the prince to Liza. Both the old Ozhogins themselves and their fellow-citizens began to look on him almost as betrothed to her. This could not, as a fact, have been quite to his liking. But he was greatly attracted by Liza; and meanwhile, he had not at that time attained his aims. With all the adroitness of a clever man of the world, he took advantage of his new position, and promptly entered, as they say, into the spirit of his new part. . . .

But I!. . . For myself, for my future, I renounced all hopes, at that time. When suffering reaches the point of making our whole being creak and groan, like an overloaded cart, it ought to cease to be ridiculous . . . but no! laughter not only accompanies tears to the end, to exhaustion, to the impossibility of shedding more—it even rings and echoes, where the tongue is dumb, and complaint itself is dead. . . . And so, as in the first place I don't intend to expose myself as ridiculous, even to myself, and secondly as I am fearfully tired, I will put off the continuation, and please God the conclusion, of my story till tomorrow. . . .

March 29.

A slight frost; yesterday it was thawing._

Yesterday I had not the strength to go on with my diary; like Poprishchin, I lay, for the most part, on my bed, and talked to Terentyevna. What a woman! Sixty years ago she lost her first betrothed from the plague, she has outlived all her children, she is inexcusably old, drinks tea to her heart's desire, is well fed, and warmly clothed; and what do you suppose she was talking to me about, all day yesterday? I had sent another utterly destitute old woman the collar of an old livery, half moth-eaten, to put on her vest (she wears strips over the chest by way of vest) . . . and why wasn't it given to her? 'But I'm your nurse; I should think. . . Oh . . . oh, my good sir, it's too bad of you . . . after I've looked after you as I have!' . . . and so on. The merciless old woman utterly wore me out with her reproaches. . . . But to get back to my story.

And so, I suffered like a dog, whose hindquarters have been run over by a wheel. It was only then, only after my banishment from the Ozhogins' house, that I fully realized how much happiness a man can extract from the contemplation of his own unhappiness. O men! pitiful race, indeed!

. . . But, away with philosophical reflections. . . . I spent my days in complete solitude, and could only by the most roundabout and even humiliating methods find out what was passing in the Ozhogins' household, and what the prince was doing. My man had made friends with the cousin of the latter's coachman's wife. This acquaintance afforded me some slight relief, and my man soon guessed, from my hints and little presents, what he was to talk about to his master when he pulled his boots off every evening. Sometimes I chanced to meet some one of the Ozhogins' family, Bizmyonkov, or the prince in the street. . . . To the prince and to Bizmyonkov I bowed, but I did not enter into conversation with them. Liza I only saw three times: once, with her mamma, in a fashionable shop; once, in an open carriage with her father and mother and the prince; and once, in church. Of course, I was not impudent enough to approach her, and only watched her from a distance. In the shop she was very much preoccupied, but cheerful. . . . She was ordering something for herself, and busily matching ribbons. Her mother was gazing at her, with her hands folded on her lap, and her nose in the air, smiling with that foolish and devoted smile which is only permissible in adoring mothers. In the carriage with the prince, Liza was . . .I shall never forget that meeting! The old people were sitting in the back seats of the carriage, the prince and Liza in the front. She was paler than usual; on her cheek two patches of pink could just be seen. She was half facing the prince; leaning on her straight right arm (in the left hand she was holding a sunshade), with her little head drooping languidly, she was looking straight into his face with her expressive eyes. At that instant she surrendered herself utterly to him, entrusted herself to him forever. I had not time to get a good look at his face—the carriage galloped by too quickly,—but I fancied that he too was deeply touched.

The third time I saw her in church. Not more than ten days had passed since the day when I met her in the carriage with the prince, not more than three weeks since the day of my duel. The business upon which the prince had come to O—— was by now completed. But he still kept putting off his departure. At Petersburg, he was reported to be ill. In the town, it was expected every day that he would make a proposal in form to Kirilla Matveitch. I was myself only awaiting this final blow to go away forever. The town of O—— had grown hateful to me. I could not stay indoors, and wandered from morning to night about the suburbs. One grey, gloomy day, as I was coming back from a walk, which had been cut short by the rain, I went into a church. The evening service had only just begun, there were very few people; I looked round me, and suddenly, near a window, caught sight of a familiar profile. For the first instant, I did not recognize it: that pale face, that spiritless glance, those sunken cheeks— could it be the same Liza I had seen a fortnight before? Wrapped in a cloak, without a hat on, with the cold light from the broad white window falling on her from one side, she was gazing fixedly at the holy image, and seemed striving to pray, striving to awake from a sort of listless stupor. A red-cheeked, fat little page with yellow trimmings on his chest was standing behind her, and, with his hands clasped behind his back, stared in sleepy bewilderment at his mistress. I trembled all over, was about to go up to her, but stopped short. I felt choked by a torturing presentiment. Till the very end of the evening service, Liza did not stir. All the people went out, a beadle began sweeping out the church, but still she did not move from her place. The page went up to her, said something to her, touched her dress; she looked round, passed her hand over her face, and went away. I followed her home at a little distance, and then returned to my lodging.

'She is lost!' I cried, when I had got into my room.

As a man, I don't know to this day what my sensations were at that moment. I flung myself, I remember, with clasped hands, on the sofa and fixed my eyes on the floor. But I don't know—in the midst of my woe I was, as it were, pleased at something. . . . I would not admit this for anything in the world, if I were not writing only for myself. . . . I had been tormented, certainly, by terrible, harassing suspicions . . .and who knows, I should, perhaps, have been greatly disconcerted if they had not been fulfilled. 'Such is the heart of man!' some middle-aged Russian teacher would exclaim at this point in an expressive voice, while he raises a fat forefinger, adorned with a cornelian ring. But what have we to do with the opinion of a Russian teacher, with an expressive voice and a cornelian on his finger?

Be that as it may, my presentiment turned out to be well founded. Suddenly the news was all over the town that the prince had gone away, presumably in consequence of a summons from Petersburg; that he had gone away without making any proposal to Kirilla Matveitch or his wife, and that Liza would have to deplore his treachery till the end of her days. The prince's departure was utterly unexpected, for only the evening before his coachman, so my man assured me, had not the slightest suspicion of his master's intentions. This piece of news threw me into a perfect fever. I at once dressed, and was on the point of hastening to the Ozhogins', but on thinking the matter over I considered it more seemly to wait till the next day. I lost nothing, however, by remaining at home. The same evening, there came to see me in all haste a certain Pandopipopulo, a wandering Greek, stranded by some chance in the town of O——, a scandalmonger of the first magnitude, who had been more indignant with me than any one for my duel with the prince. He did not even give my man time to announce him; he fairly burst into my room, warmly pressed my hand, begged my pardon a thousand times, called me a paragon of magnanimity and courage, painted the prince in the darkest colors, censured the old Ozhogins, who, in his opinion, had been punished as they deserved, made a slighting reference to Liza in passing, and hurried off again, kissing me on my shoulder. Among other things, I learned from him that the prince, *en vrai grand seigneur*, on the eve of his departure, in response to a delicate hint from Kirilla Matveitch, had answered coldly that he had no intention of deceiving any one, and no idea of marrying, had risen, made his bow, and that was all. . . . Next day I set off to the Ozhogins'. The shortsighted footman leaped up from his bench on my appearance, with the rapidity of lightning. I bade him announce me; the footman hurried away and returned at once. 'Walk in,' he said; 'you are begged to go in.' I went into Kirilla Matveitch's study. . . . The rest tomorrow.

March 30. Frost.

And so I went into Kirilla Matveitch's study. I would pay any one handsomely, who could show me now my own face at the moment when that highly respected official, hurriedly flinging together his dressing-gown, approached me with outstretched arms. I must have been a perfect picture of modest triumph, indulgent sympathy, and boundless magnanimity. . . . I felt myself something in the style of Scipio Africanus. Ozhogin was visibly confused and cast down, he avoided my eyes, and kept fidgeting about. I noticed, too, that he spoke unnaturally loudly, and in general expressed himself very vaguely. Vaguely, but with warmth, he begged my forgiveness, vaguely alluded to their departed guest, added a few vague generalities about deception and the instability of earthly blessings, and, suddenly feeling the tears in his eyes, hastened to take a pinch of snuff, probably in order to deceive me as to the cause of his tearfulness. . . . He used the Russian green snuff, and it's well known that that article forces even old men to shed tears that make the human eye look dull and senseless for several minutes.

I behaved, of course, very cautiously with the old man, inquired after the health of his wife and daughter, and at once artfully turned the conversation on to the interesting subject of the rotation of crops. I was dressed as usual, but the feeling of gentle propriety and soft indulgence which filled me gave me a fresh and festive sensation, as though I had on a white waistcoat and a white cravat. One thing agitated me, the thought of seeing Liza. . . . Ozhogin, at last, proposed of his own accord to take me up to his wife. The kind-hearted but foolish woman was at first terribly embarrassed on seeing me; but her brain was not capable of retaining the same impression for long, and so she was soon at her ease. At last I saw Liza . . . she came into the room. . . .

I had expected to find in her a shamed and penitent sinner, and had assumed beforehand the most affectionate and reassuring expression of face. . . . Why lie about it? I really loved her and was thirsting for the happiness of forgiving her, of holding out a hand to her; but to my unutterable astonishment, in response to my significant bow, she laughed coldly, observed carelessly, 'Oh, is that you?' and at once turned away from me. It is true that her laugh struck me as forced, and in any case did not accord well with her terribly thin face . . . but, all the same, I had not expected such a reception. . . . I looked at her with amazement . . . what a change had taken place in her! Between the child she had been and the woman before me, there was nothing in common. She had, as it were, grown up, straightened out; all the features of her face, especially her lips, seemed defined . . . her gaze had grown deeper, harder, and gloomier. I stayed on at the Ozhogins' till dinner-time. She got up, went out of the room, and came back again, answered questions with composure, and designedly took no notice of me. She wanted, I saw, to make me feel that I was not worth her anger, though I had been within an ace of killing her lover. I lost patience at last; a malicious allusion broke from my lips. . . . She started, glanced swiftly at me, got up, and going to the window, pronounced in a rather shaky voice, 'You can say anything you like, but let me tell you that I love that man, and always shall love him, and do not consider that he has done me any injury, quite the contrary.' . . . Her voice broke, she stopped . . . tried to control herself, but could not, burst into tears, and went out of the room. . . . The old people were much upset. . . . I pressed the hands of both, sighed, turned my eyes heavenward, and withdrew.

I am too weak, I have too little time left, I am not capable of describing in the same detail the new range of torturing reflections, firm resolutions, and all the other fruits of what is called inward conflict, that arose within me after the renewal of my acquaintance with the Ozhogins. I did not doubt that Liza still loved, and would long love, the prince . . . but as one reconciled to the inevitable, and anxious myself to conciliate, I did not even dream of her love. I desired only her affection, I desired to gain her confidence, her respect, which, we are assured by persons of experience, forms the surest basis for happiness in marriage. . . . Unluckily, I lost sight of one rather important circumstance, which was that Liza had hated me ever since the day of the duel. I found this out too late. I began, as before, to be a frequent visitor at the house of the Ozhogins. Kirilla Matveitch received me with more effusiveness and affability than he had ever done. I have even ground for believing that he would at that time have cheerfully given me his daughter, though I was certainly not a match to be coveted. Public opinion was very severe upon him and Liza, while, on the other hand, it extolled me to the skies. Liza's attitude to me was unchanged. She was, for the most part, silent; obeyed, when they begged her to eat, showed no outward signs of sorrow, but, for all that, was wasting away like a candle. I must do Kirilla Matveitch the justice to say that he spared her in every way. Old Madame Ozhogin only ruffled up her feathers like a hen, as she looked at her poor nestling. There was only one person Liza did not shun, though she did not talk much even to him, and that was Bizmyonkov. The old people were rather short, not to say rude, in their behavior to him. They could not forgive him for having been second in the duel. But he went on going to see them, as though he did not notice their unamiability. With me he was very chilly, and—strange to say—I felt, as it were, afraid of him. This state of things went on for a fortnight. At last, after a sleepless night, I resolved to have it out with Liza, to open my heart to her, to tell her that, in spite of the past, in spite of all possible gossip and scandal, I should consider myself only too happy if she would give me her hand, and restore me her confidence. I really did seriously imagine that I was showing what they call in the school reading-books an unparalleled example of magnanimity, and that, from sheer amazement alone, she would consent. In any case, I resolved to have an explanation and to escape, at last, from suspense.

Behind the Ozhogins' house was a rather large garden, which ended in a little grove of lime-trees, neglected and overgrown. In the middle of this thicket stood an old summer-house in the Chinese style: a wooden paling separated the garden from a blind alley. Liza would sometimes walk, for hours together, alone in this garden. Kirilla Matveitch was aware of this, and forbade her being disturbed or followed; let her grief wear itself out, he said. When she could not be found indoors, they had only to ring a bell on the steps at dinner-time and she made her appearance at once, with the same stubborn silence on her lips and in her eyes, and some little leaf crushed up in her hand. So, noticing one day that she was not in the house, I made a show of going away, took leave of Kirilla Matveitch, put on my hat, and went out from the hall into the courtyard, and from the courtyard into the street, but promptly darted in at the gate again with extraordinary rapidity and hurried past the kitchen into the garden. Luckily no one noticed me. Without losing time in deliberation, I went with rapid steps into the grove. In a little path before me was standing Liza. My heart beat violently. I stood still, drew a deep sigh, and was just on the point of going up to her, when suddenly she lifted her hand without turning round, and began listening. . . . From behind the trees, in the direction of the blind alley, came a distinct sound of two knocks, as though someone were tapping at the paling. Liza clapped her hands together, there was heard the faint creak of the gate, and out of the thicket stepped Bizmyonkov. I hastily hid behind a tree. Liza turned towards him without speaking. . . . Without speaking, he drew her arm in his, and the two walked slowly along the path together. I looked after them in amazement. They stopped, looked round, disappeared behind the bushes, reappeared again, and finally went into the summer-house. This summer-house was a diminutive round edifice, with a door and one little window. In the middle stood an old one-legged table, overgrown with fine green moss; two discolored deal benches stood along the sides, some distance from the damp and darkened walls. Here, on exceptionally hot days, in bygone times, perhaps once a year or so, they had drunk tea. The door did not quite shut, the window-frame had long ago come out of the window, and hung disconsolately, only attached at one corner, like a bird's broken wing. I stole up to the summer-house, and peeped cautiously through the chink in the window. Liza was sitting on one of the benches, with her head drooping. Her right hand lay on her knees, the left Bizmyonkov was holding in both his hands. He was looking sympathetically at her.

'How do you feel today?' he asked her in a low voice.

'Just the same,' she answered, 'not better, nor worse.—The emptiness, the fearful emptiness!' she added, raising her eyes dejectedly.

Bizmyonkov made her no answer.

'What do you think,' she went on: 'will he write to me once more?'

'I don't think so, Lizaveta Kirillovna!'

She was silent.

'And after all, why should he write? He told me everything in his first letter. I could not be his wife; but I have been happy . . . not for long . . . I have been happy . . .'

Bizmyonkov looked down.

'Ah,' she went on quickly, 'if you knew how I loathe that Tchulkaturin . . . I always fancy I see on that man's hands . . . his blood.' (I shuddered behind my chink.) 'Though indeed,' she added, dreamily, 'who knows, perhaps, if it had not been for that duel. . . . Ah, when I saw him wounded I felt at once that I was altogether his.'

'Tchulkaturin loves you,' observed Bizmyonkov.

'What is that to me? I don't want any one's love.'. . . . She stopped and added slowly, 'Except yours. Yes, my friend, your love is necessary to me; except for you, I should be lost. You have helped me to bear terrible moments . . .'

She broke off . . . Bizmyonkov began with fatherly tenderness stroking her hand.

'There's no help for it! What is one to do! what is one to do, Lizaveta Kirillovna!' he repeated several times.

'And now indeed,' she went on in a lifeless voice, 'I should die, I think, if it were not for you. It's you alone that keep me up; besides, you remind me of him. . . . You knew all about it, you see. Do you remember how fine he was that day. . . . But forgive me; it must be hard for you. . . .'

'Go on, go on! Nonsense! Bless you!' Bizmyonkov interrupted her.

She pressed his hand.

'You are very good, Bizmyonkov,' she went on; 'you are good as an angel. What can I do! I feel I shall love him to the grave. I have forgiven him, I am grateful to him. God give him happiness! May God give him a wife after his own heart'—and her eyes filled with tears—'if only he does not forget me, if only he will sometimes think of his Liza!—Let us go,' she added, after a brief silence.

Bizmyonkov raised her hand to his lips.

'I know,' she began again hotly, 'everyone is blaming me now, everyone is throwing stones at me. Let them! I wouldn't, any way, change my misery for their happiness . . . no! no!. . . He did not love me for long, but he loved me! He never deceived me, he never told me I should be his wife; I never dreamed of it myself. It was only poor papa hoped for it. And even now I am not altogether unhappy; the memory remains to me, and however fearful the results . . . I'm stifling here . . . it was here I saw him the last time. . . . Let's go into the air.'

They got up. I had only just time to skip on one side and hide behind a thick lime-tree. They came out of the summer-house, and, as far as I could judge by the sound of their steps, went away into the thicket. I don't know how long I went on standing there, without stirring from my place, plunged in a sort of senseless amazement, when suddenly I heard steps again. I started, and peeped cautiously out from my hiding-place. Bizmyonkov and Liza were coming back along the same path. Both were greatly agitated, especially Bizmyonkov.

I fancied he was crying. Liza stopped, looked at him, and distinctly uttered the following words: 'I do consent, Bizmyonkov. I would never have agreed if you were only trying to save me, to rescue me from a terrible position, but you love me, you know everything—and you love me. I shall never find a trustier, truer friend. I will be your wife.'

Bizmyonkov kissed her hand: she smiled at him mournfully and moved away towards the house. Bizmyonkov rushed into the thicket, and I went my way. Seeing that Bizmyonkov had apparently said to Liza precisely what I had intended to say to her, and she had given him precisely the reply I was longing to hear from her, there was no need for me to trouble myself further. Within a fortnight she was married to him. The old Ozhogins were thankful to get any husband for her.

Now, tell me, am I not a superfluous man? Didn't I play throughout the whole story the part of a superfluous person? The prince's part . . . of that it's needless to speak; Bizmyonkov's part, too, is comprehensible. . . . But I—with what object was I mixed up in it?. . . A senseless fifth wheel to the cart!. . . Ah, it's bitter, bitter for me!. . . But there, as the barge-haulers say, 'One more pull, and one more yet,'—one day more, and one more yet, and there will be no more bitter nor sweet for me.

March 31.

I'm in a bad way. I am writing these lines in bed. Since yesterday evening there has been a sudden change in the weather. Today is hot, almost a summer day. Everything is thawing, breaking up, flowing away. The air is full of the smell of the opened earth, a strong, heavy, stifling smell. Steam is rising on all sides. The sun seems beating, seems smiting everything to pieces. I am very ill, I feel that I am breaking up.

I meant to write my diary, and, instead of that, what have I done? I have related one incident of my life. I gossiped on, slumbering reminiscences were awakened and drew me away. I have written, without haste, in detail, as though I had years before me. And here now, there's no time to go on. Death,

death is coming. I can hear her menacing *crescendo*. The time is come . . . the time is come!. . .

And indeed, what does it matter? Isn't it all the same whatever I write? In sight of death the last earthly cares vanish. I feel I have grown calm; I am becoming simpler, clearer. Too late I've gained sense!. . . It's a strange thing! I have grown calm—certainly, and at the same time . . . I'm full of dread. Yes, I'm full of dread. Half hanging over the silent, yawning abyss, I shudder, turn away, with greedy intentness gaze at everything about me. Every object is doubly precious to me. I cannot gaze enough at my poor, cheerless room, saying farewell to each spot on my walls. Take your fill for the last time, my eyes. Life is retreating; slowly and smoothly she is flying away from me, as the shore flies from the eyes of one at sea. The old yellow face of my nurse, tied up in a dark kerchief, the hissing samovar on the table, the pot of geranium in the window, and you, my poor dog, Tresór, the pen I write these lines with, my own hand, I see you now . . . here you are, here. . . . Is it possible . . . can it be, today . . . I shall never see you again! It's hard for a live creature to part with life! Why do you fawn on me, poor dog? why do you come putting your forepaws on the bed, with your stump of a tail wagging so violently, and your kind, mournful eyes fixed on me all the while? Are you sorry for me? or do you feel already that your master will soon be gone? Ah, if I could only keep my thoughts, too, resting on all the objects in my room! I know these reminiscences are dismal and of no importance, but I have no other. 'The emptiness, the fearful emptiness!' as Liza said.

O my God, my God! Here I am dying. . . . A heart capable of loving and ready to love will soon cease to beat. . . . And can it be it will be still forever without having once known happiness, without having once expanded under the sweet burden of bliss? Alas! it's impossible, impossible, I know. . . . If only now, at least, before death—for death after all is a sacred thing, after all it elevates any being—if any kind, sad, friendly voice would sing over me a farewell song of my own sorrow, I could, perhaps, be resigned to it. But to die stupidly, stupidly. . . .

I believe I'm beginning to rave.

Farewell, life! farewell, my garden! and you, my lime-trees! When the summer comes, do not forget to be clothed with flowers from head to foot . . . and may it be sweet for people to lie in your fragrant shade, on the fresh grass, among the whispering chatter of your leaves, lightly stirred by the wind. Farewell, farewell! Farewell, everything and forever!

Farewell, Liza! I wrote those two words, and almost laughed aloud. This exclamation strikes me as taken out of a book. It's as though I were writing a sentimental novel and ending up a despairing letter. . . .

Tomorrow is the first of April. Can I be going to die tomorrow? That would be really too unseemly. It's just right for me, though . . .

How the doctor did chatter today.

April 1.

It is over. . . . Life is over. I shall certainly die today. It's hot outside . . . almost suffocating . . . or is it that my lungs are already refusing to breathe? My little comedy is played out. The curtain is falling.

Sinking into nothing, I cease to be superfluous . . .

Ah, how brilliant that sun is! Those mighty beams breathe of eternity . . .

Farewell, Terentyevna!. . . This morning as she sat at the window she was crying . . . perhaps over me . . . and perhaps because she too will soon have to die. I have made her promise not to kill Tresór.

It's hard for me to write. . . . I will put down the pen. . . . It's high time; death is already approaching with ever-increasing rumble, like a carriage at night over the pavement;

it is here, it is flitting about me, like the light breath which made the prophet's hair stand up on end.

I am dying. . . . Live, you who are living,

> And about the grave
> May youthful life rejoice,
> And nature heedless
> Glow with eternal beauty.

Note by the Editor.—Under this last line was a head in profile with a big streak of hair and moustaches, with eyes *en face*, and eyelashes like rays; and under the head someone had written the following words:

> 'This manuscript was read
> And the Contents of it Not Approved
> By Peter Zudotyeshin
> My My My
> My dear Sir,
> Peter Zudotyeshin,
> Dear Sir.

But as the handwriting of these lines was not in the least like the handwriting in which the other part of the manuscript was written, the editor considers that he is justified in concluding that the above lines were added subsequently by another person, especially since it has come to his (the editor's) knowledge that Mr. Tchulkaturin actually did die on the night between the 1st and 2nd of April in the year 18—, at his native place, Sheep's Springs.

—1850

Leo Tolstoy
(1828-1910)

Lucerne
From the Recollections of Prince Nekhliudof
Translated from the Russian by Nathan Haskell Dole

July 20, 1857.

Yesterday evening I arrived at Lucerne, and put up at the best inn there, the Schweitzerhof. "Lucerne, the chief city of the canton, situated on the shore of the Vierwaldstattersee," says Murray, "is one of the most romantic places of Switzerland: here cross three important highways, and it is only an hour's distance by steamboat to Mount Righi, from which is obtained one of the most magnificent views in the world."

Whether that be true or no, other guides say the same thing, and consequently at Lucerne there are throngs of travelers of all nationalities, especially the English.

The magnificent five-storied building of the Hotel Schweitzerhof is situated on the quay, at the very edge of the lake, where in olden times there used to be the crooked covered wooden bridge with chapels on the corners and pictures on the roof. Now, thanks to the tremendous inroad of Englishmen, with their necessities, their tastes, and their money, they have torn down the old bridge, and in its place erected a granite quay, straight as a stick. On the quay they have built straight, quadrangular five-storied houses; in front of the houses they have set out two rows of lindens and provided them with supports, and between the lindens is the usual supply of green benches.

This is the promenade; and here back and forth stroll the Englishwomen in their Swiss straw hats, and the Englishmen in simple and comfortable attire, and rejoice in their work. Possibly these quays and houses and lindens and Englishmen would be excellent in their way anywhere else, but here they seem discordant amid this strangely magnificent, and at the same time indescribably harmonious and smiling nature.

As soon as I went up to my room, and opened the window facing the lake, the beauty of the sheet of water, of the mountains, and of the sky, at the first moment literally dazzled and overwhelmed me. I experienced an inward unrest, and the necessity of expressing in some manner the feelings that suddenly filled my soul to overflowing. I felt a desire to embrace, powerfully to embrace, someone, to tickle him, or to pinch him; in short to do to him and to myself something extraordinary.

It was seven o'clock in the evening. The rain had been falling all day, but now it had cleared.

The lake, iridescent as melted sulfur, and dotted with boats, which left behind them vanishing trails, spread out before my windows smooth, motionless as it were, between the variegated green shores. Farther away it was contracted between two monstrous headlands, and, darkling, set itself against and disappeared behind a confused pile of mountains, clouds, and glaciers. In the foreground stretched a panorama of moist, fresh green shores, with reeds, meadows, gardens, and villas. Farther away, the dark green wooded heights, crowned with the ruins of feudal castles; in the background, the rolling, pale lilac-colored vista of mountains, with fantastic peaks built up of crags and pallid snow-capped summits. And everything was bathed in a fresh, transparent azure atmosphere, and kindled by the warm rays of the setting sun, bursting forth through the riven skies.

Not on the lake or on the mountains or in the skies was there a single completed line, a single unmixed color, a single moment of repose; everywhere motion, irregularity, fantasy, endless conglomeration and variety of shades and lines; and above all, a calm, a softness, a unity, and the inevitability of beauty.

And here amid this indeterminate, kaleidoscopic, unfettered loveliness, before my very window, stretched stupidly, compelling the gaze, the white line of the quay, the lindens with their supports, and the green seats—miserable, tasteless creations of human ingenuity, not subordinated, like the distant villas and ruins, to the general harmony of the beautiful scene, but on the contrary brutally opposed to it . . .

Constantly, though against my will, my eyes were attracted to that horribly straight line of the quay; and mentally I should have liked to get rid of it, to demolish it like a black spot which should disfigure the nose beneath one's eye.

But the quay with the sauntering Englishmen remained where it was, and I involuntarily tried to find a point of view where it would be out of my sight. I succeeded in finding such a view; and till dinner was ready I took delight, alone by myself in this incomplete and therefore the more enjoyable feeling of oppression that one experiences in the solitary contemplation of natural beauty.

About half-past seven I was called to dinner. Two long tables, accommodating at least a hundred persons, were spread in the great, magnificently decorated dining-room on the first floor. The silent gathering of the guests lasted three minutes—the rustle of women's gowns, the soft steps, the softly spoken words addressed to the courtly and elegant waiters. And all the places were occupied by ladies and gentlemen dressed elegantly, even richly, and for the most part in perfect taste.

As is apt to be the case in Switzerland, the majority of the guests were English, and this gave the ruling characteristics of the common table: that is, a strict decorum regarded as an obligation, a reserve founded not in pride but in the absence of any necessity for social relationship, and finally a uniform sense of satisfaction felt by each in the comfortable and agreeable gratification of his wants.

On all sides gleamed the whitest laces, the whitest collars, the whitest teeth—natural and artificial—the whitest complexions and hands. But the faces, many of which were very handsome, bore the expression merely of individual prosperity, and absolute absence of interest in all that surrounded them unless it bore directly on their own individual selves; and the white hands, glittering with rings or protected by mitts, moved only for the purpose of straightening collars, cutting meat, or filling wine-glasses; no soul-felt emotion was betrayed in these actions.

Occasionally members of some one family would exchange remarks in subdued voices, about the excellence of such and such a dish or wine, or about the beauty of the view from Mount Righi.

Individual tourists, whether men or women, sat beside one another in silence, and did not even seem to see one another. If it happened occasionally that, out of this five-score human beings, two spoke to each other, the topic of their conversation was certain to be the weather, or the ascent of the Righi.

Knives and forks scarcely rattled on the plates, so perfect was the observance of propriety; and no one dared to convey peas and vegetables to the mouth otherwise than on the fork. The waiters, involuntarily subdued by the universal silence, asked in a whisper what wine you would be pleased to order.

Such dinners always depress me: I dislike them, and before they are over I become blue. It always seems to me as if I had done something wrong; just as when I was a boy I was set upon a chair in consequence of some naughtiness and bidden ironically, "Now rest a little while, my dear young fellow." And all the time my young blood was pulsing through my veins, and in the other room I could hear the merry shouts of my brothers.

I used to try to rebel against this feeling of being choked down, which I experienced at such dinners, but in vain. All these dead-and-alive faces have an irresistible influence over me, and I myself become also as one dead. I have no desires, I have no thoughts; I do not even observe.

At first I attempted to enter into conversation with my neighbors; but I got no response beyond the phrases which had probably been repeated in that place a hundred thousand times, a hundred thousand times by the same persons.

And yet these people were by no means all stupid and feelingless; but evidently many of them, though they seemed so dead, led self-centered lives, just as I did, and in many cases far more complicated and interesting ones than my own. Why, then, should they deprive themselves of one of the greatest enjoyments of life—the enjoyment that comes from the intercourse of man with man?

How different it used to be in our *pension* at Paris, where twenty of us, belonging to as many different nationalities, professions, and individualities, met together at a common table, and, under the influence of the Gallic sociability, found the keenest zest!

There, immediately, from one end of the table to the other, the conversation, sandwiched with witticisms and puns, though often in a broken speech, became general. There everyone, without being solicitous for the proprieties, said whatever came into his head. There we had our own philosopher, our own disputant, our own *bel esprit*, our own butt—all common property.

There, immediately after dinner, we would move the table to one side, and, without paying too much attention to rhythm, take to dancing the polka on the dusty carpet, and often keep it up till evening. There, though we were rather flirtatious, and not overwise or dignified, still we were human beings.

And the Spanish countess with romantic proclivities, and the Italian *abbate*, who insisted on declaiming from the "Divine Comedy" after dinner, and the American doctor who had the *entrée* into the Tuileries, and the young dramatic author with his long hair, and the pianist who, according to her own account, had composed the best polka in existence, and the unhappy widow who was a beauty, and wore three rings on every finger—all of us enjoyed this society, which, though somewhat superficial, was human and pleasant. And we each carried away from it hearty recollections of the others, superficial or serious, as the case might be.

But at these English *table-d'hote* dinners, as I look at all these laces, ribbons, jewels, pomaded locks, and silken gowns, I often think how many living women would be happy, and would make others happy, with these adornments.

Strange to think how many friends and lovers—most fortunate friends and lovers—are, perhaps, sitting side by side without knowing it! And God knows why they never come to this knowledge, and never give each other this happiness, which they might so easily give, and which they so long for.

I began to feel depressed, as usual, after such a dinner; and, without waiting for dessert, I sallied out in the most gloomy frame of mind for a constitutional through the city. My melancholy frame of mind was not relieved, but was rather confirmed, by the narrow, muddy streets without lanterns, the shuttered shops, the encounters with drunken workmen, and with women hastening after water, or in bonnets, glancing around them as they glided down the alleys or along the walls.

It was perfectly dark in the streets when I returned to the hotel without casting a glance about me, or having an idea in my head. I hoped that sleep would put an end to my melancholy. I experienced that horrible spiritual chill, loneliness, and heaviness, which sometimes, without any reason, beset those who are just arrived in any new place.

Looking down at my feet, I walked along the quay to the Schweitzerhof, when suddenly my ear was struck by the strains of a peculiar but thoroughly agreeable and sweet music.

These strains had an immediately enlivening effect on me. It was as if a bright, cheerful light had poured into my soul. I felt contented, gay. My slumbering attention was awakened again to all surrounding objects; and the beauty of the night and the lake, to which, till then, I had been indifferent, suddenly came over me with quickening force like something new.

I involuntarily took in at a glance the dark sky with gray clouds flecking its deep blue, now lighted by the rising moon, the glassy, dark green lake, with its surface reflecting the lighted windows, and far away the snowy mountains; and I heard the croaking of the frogs over on the Froschenburg shore, and the dewy fresh call of the quail.

Directly in front of me, in the spot whence the sounds of music had first come, and which still especially attracted my attention, I saw, amid the semi-darkness on the street, a throng of people standing in a semicircle, and in front of the crowd, at a little distance, a small man in dark clothes.

Behind the throng and the man, there stood out harmoniously against the blue, ragged sky, gray and blue, the black tops of a few Lombardy poplars in some garden, and, rising majestically on high, the two stern spires that stand on the towers of the ancient cathedral.

I drew nearer, and the strains became more distinct. At some distance I could clearly distinguish the full accords of a guitar, sweetly swelling in the evening air, and several voices, which, while taking turns with one another, did not sing any definite theme, but gave suggestions of one in places wherever the melody was most pronounced.

The theme was in somewhat the nature of a mazurka, sweet and graceful. The voices sounded now near at hand, now far distant; now a bass was heard, now a tenor, now a falsetto such as the Tyrolese warblers are wont to sing.

It was not a song, but the graceful, masterly sketch of a song. I could not comprehend what it was, but it was beautiful.

Those voluptuous, soft chords of the guitar, that sweet, gentle melody, that solitary figure of the man in black, amid the fantastic environment of the dark lake, the gleaming moon, and the twin spires of the cathedral rising in majestic silence, and the black tops of the poplars—all was strange and perfectly beautiful, or at least seemed so to me.

All the confused, arbitrary impressions of life suddenly became full of meaning and beauty. It seemed to me as if a fresh fragrant flower had sprung up in my soul. In place of the weariness, dullness, and indifference toward everything in the world, which I had been feeling the moment before, I experienced a necessity for love, a fullness of hope, and an unbounded enjoyment of life.

"What does thou desire, what doest thou long for?" an inner voice seemed to say. "Here it is. Thou art surrounded on all sides by beauty and poetry. Breathe it in, in full, deep draughts, as long as thou hast strength. Enjoy it to the full extent of thy capacity 'Tis all thine, all blessed!" . . . .

I drew nearer. The little man was, as it seemed, a traveling Tyrolese. He stood before the windows of the hotel, one leg advanced, his head thrown back; and, as he thrummed on the guitar, he sang his graceful song in all those different voices.

I immediately felt an affection for this man, and a gratefulness for the change which he had brought about in me.

The singer, as far as I was able to judge, was dressed in an old black coat. He had short black hair, and he wore a civilian's hat which was no longer new. There was nothing artistic in his attire, but his clever and youthfully gay motions and pose, together with his diminutive stature, formed a pleasing and at the same time pathetic spectacle.

On the steps, in the windows, and on the balconies of the brilliantly lighted hotel, stood ladies handsomely decorated and attired, gentlemen with polished collars, porters and lackeys in gold-embroidered liveries; in the street, in the semicircle of the crowd, and farther along on the sidewalk, among the lindens, were gathered groups of well-dressed waiters, cooks in white caps and aprons, and young girls wandering about with arms about each others' waists.

All, it seemed, were under the influence of the same feeling as I myself experienced. All stood in silence around the singer, and listened attentively. Silence reigned, except in the pauses of the song, when there came from far away across the waters the regular click of a hammer, and from the Froschenburg shore rang in fascinating, monotone the voices of the frogs, interrupted by the mellow, monotonous call of the quail.

The little man in the darkness, in the midst of the street, poured out his heart like a nightingale, in couplet after couplet, song after song. Though I had come close to him, his singing continued to give me greater and greater gratification.

His voice, which was of great power, was extremely pleasant and tender; the taste and feeling for rhythm which he displayed in the control of it were extraordinary, and proved that he had great natural gifts.

After he sung each couplet, he invariably repeated the theme in variation, and it was evident that all his graceful variations came to him at the instant, spontaneously.

Among the crowd, and above on the Schweitzerhof, and nearby on the boulevard, were heard frequent murmurs of approval, though generally the most respectful silence reigned.

The balconies and the windows kept filling more and more with handsomely dressed men and women leaning on their elbows, and picturesquely illuminated by the lights in the house.

Promenaders came to a halt, and in the darkness on the quay stood men and women in little groups. Near me, at some distance from the common crowd, stood an aristocratic cook and lackey, smoking their cigars. The cook was forcibly impressed by the music, and at every high falsetto note enthusiastically nodded his head to the lackey, and nudged him with his elbow with an expression of astonishment which seemed to say, "How he sings! hey?"

The lackey, by whose undissimulated smile I could mark the depth of feeling he experienced, replied to the cook's nudges by shrugging his shoulders, as if to show that it was hard enough for him to be made enthusiastic, and that he had heard much better music.

In one of the pauses of his song, while the minstrel was clearing his throat, I asked the lackey who he was, and if he often came there.

"Twice in the summer he comes here," replied the lackey. "He is from Aargau; he gets his livelihood by begging."

"Tell me, do many like him come round here?" I asked.

"Oh, yes," replied the lackey, not comprehending the full force of what I asked; but immediately after, recollecting himself, he added, "Oh, no. This one is the only one I ever heard here. No one else."

At this moment the little man had finished his first song, was briskly twanging his guitar, and said something in his German patois, which I could not understand, but which brought forth a hearty round of laughter from the surrounding throng.

"What was that he said?" I asked.

"He said his throat is dried up, he would like some wine," replied the lackey, who was standing near me.

"What? is he rather fond of the glass?"

"Yes, all that sort of people are," replied the lackey, smiling and pointing at the minstrel.

The minstrel took off his cap, and swinging his guitar went toward the hotel. Raising his head, he addressed the ladies and gentlemen standing by the windows and on the balconies, saying in a half-Italian, half-German accent, and with the same intonation as jugglers use in speaking to their audiences:

"Messieurs et mesdames, si vous croyez que je gagne quelque chose, vous vous trompez: je ne suis qu'un pauvre tiaple."

He stood in silence a moment, but as no one gave him anything, he once more took up his guitar, and said:

"A présent, messieurs et mesdames, je vous chanterai l'air du Righi."

His hotel audience made no response, but stood in expectation of the coming song. Below on the street a laugh went round, probably in part because he had expressed himself so strangely, and in part because no one had given him anything.

I gave him a few centimes, which he deftly changed from one hand to the other, and bestowed them in his vest-pocket; and then, replacing his cap, began once more to sing; it was the graceful, sweet Tyrolese melody which he had called *l'air du Righi*.

This song, which formed the last on his program, was even better than the preceding, and from all sides in the wondering throng were heard sounds of approbation.

He finished. Again he swung his guitar, took off his cap, held it out in front of him, went two or three steps nearer to the windows, and again repeated his stock phrase: *"Messieurs et mesdames, si vous croyez que je gagne quelque chose,"* which he evidently considered to be very shrewd and witty. But in his voice and motions I perceived now a certain irresolution and childish timidity which were especially touching in a person of such diminutive stature.

This elegant public, still picturesquely grouped in the lighted windows and on the balconies, were shining in their rich attire. A few conversed in soberly discreet tones, apparently about the singer who was standing there below them with outstretched hand; others gazed down with attentive curiosity on the little black figure. On one balcony could be heard a young girl's merry, ringing laughter.

In the crowd below the talk and laughter kept growing louder and louder.

The singer for the third time repeated his phrase, but in a still weaker voice, and did not even end the sentence; and again he stretched his hand with his cap, but instantly drew it back. Again, not one of those brilliantly dressed scores of people standing to listen to him threw him a penny.

The crowd laughed heartlessly.

The little singer, so it seemed to me, shrunk more into himself, took his guitar into his other hand, lifted his cap, and said:

"*Messieurs et mesdames, je vous remercie, et je vous souhais une bonne nuit.*"

Then he put on his hat.

The crowd cackled with laughter and satisfaction. The handsome ladies and gentlemen, calmly exchanging remarks, withdrew gradually from the balconies. On the boulevard the promenading began once more. The street, which had been still during the singing, assumed its wonted liveliness; a few men, however, stood at some distance, and, without approaching the singer, looked at him and laughed.

I heard the little man muttering something between his teeth, as he turned away; and I saw him, apparently growing more and more diminutive, start toward the city with brisk steps. The promenaders, who had been looking at him, followed him at some distance, still making merry at his expense. . . .

My mind was in a whirl; I could not comprehend what it all meant; and still standing in the same place, I gazed abstractedly into the darkness after the little man, who was fast disappearing, as he went with ever increasing swiftness with long strides into the city, followed by the merrymaking promenaders.

I was overmastered by a feeling of pain, of bitterness, and, above all, of shame for the little man, for the crowd, for myself, as if it were I who had asked for money and received none; as if it were I who had been turned to ridicule.

Without looking any longer, feeling my heart oppressed, I also hurried with long strides toward the entrance of the Schweitzerhof. I could not explain the feeling that overmastered me; only there was something like a stone, from which I could not free myself, weighing down my soul and oppressing me.

At the stately, well-lighted entrance I met the Swiss, who politely made way for me. An English family was also at the door. A portly, handsome, tall gentleman, with black sidewhiskers, in a black hat, and with a plaid on one arm, while in his hand he carried a costly cane, came out slowly, and full of importance. Leaning on his arm was a lady, who wore a raw silk gown and a bonnet with bright ribbons and the most charming laces. With them was a pretty, fresh-looking young lady, in a graceful Swiss hat, with a feather, *à la mousquetaire*; from under it escaped long, light yellow curls, softly encircling her fair face. In front of them skipped a buxom girl of ten, with round, white knees which showed from under her thin embroideries. "What a lovely night!" the lady was saying in a sweet, happy voice, as I passed them.

"Oh, yes," growled the Englishman, lazily; and it was evident that he found it so enjoyable to be alive in the world, that it was too much trouble even to speak.

And it seemed as if all of them alike found it so comfortable and easy, so light and free, to be alive in the world, their faces and motions expressed such perfect indifference to the lives of everyone else, and such absolute confidence, that it was to them that the Swiss made way, and bowed so profoundly, and that when they returned they would find clean, comfortable beds and rooms, and that all this was bound to be, and was their indefeasible right, that I could not help contrasting them with the wandering minstrel, who, weary, perhaps hungry, full of shame, was retreating before the laughing crowd. And then, suddenly, I comprehended what it was that oppressed my heart with such a load of heaviness, and I felt an indescribable anger against these people.

Twice I walked up and down past the Englishman, and each time, without turning out for him, my elbow punched him, which gave me a feeling of indescribable satisfaction; and then, darting down the steps, I hastened through the darkness in the direction taken by the little man on his way to the city.

Overtaking three men, walking together, I asked them where the singer was; they laughed, and pointed straight ahead. There he was, walking alone with brisk steps; no one was with him; all the time, as it seemed to me, he was indulging in bitter monologue.

I caught up with him, and proposed to him to go somewhere with me and drink a bottle of wine. He kept on with his rapid walk, and looked at me indignantly; but when it dawned on him what I meant, he halted.

"Well, I will not refuse, if you are so kind," said he; "here is a little *café*. We can go in there. It's very ordinary," he added, pointing to a drinking-salon that was still open.

His expression "very ordinary" involuntarily suggested to my mind the idea of not going to a very ordinary *café*, but to go to the Schweitzerhof, where those who had been listening to him were. Notwithstanding the fact that several times he showed a sort of timid disquietude at the idea of going to the Schweitzerhof, declaring that it was too fashionable for him there, still I insisted on carrying out my purpose; and he, already pretending the he was not in the least abashed, and gaily swinging his guitar, went back with me across the quay.

A few loiterers who had happened along as I was talking with the minstrel, and had stopped to hear what I had to say, now, after arguing among themselves, followed us to the very entrance of the hotel, evidently expecting from the Tyrolese some further demonstration.

I ordered a bottle of wine of a waiter whom I met in the hall. The waiter smiled and looked at us, and went by without answering. The head waiter, to whom I addressed myself with the same order, listened to me and, measuring the minstrel's modest little figure from head to foot, sternly ordered the waiter to take us to the room at the left.

The room at the left was a barroom for simple people. In the corner of this room, a hunchbacked maid was washing dishes. The whole furniture consisted of bare wooden tables and benches.

The waiter who came to serve us looked at us with a supercilious smile, thrust his hands in his pockets, and exchanged some remarks with the humpbacked dishwasher. He evidently tried to give us to understand that he felt himself immeasurably higher than the minstrel, both in dignity and social position, so that he considered it not only an indignity, but actually ridiculous, that he was called on to serve us.

"Do you wish *vin ordinaire?*" he asked, with a knowing look, winking toward my companion and switching his napkin from one hand to the other.

"Champagne, and your very best," said I, endeavoring to assume my haughtiest and most imposing appearance.

But neither my champagne, nor my endeavor to look haughty and imposing, had the least effect on the servant; he smiled incredulously, loitered a moment or two gazing at us, took time enough to glance at his gold watch, and with leisurely steps, as if going out for a walk, left the room.

Soon he returned with the wine, bringing two other waiters with him. These two sat down near the dishwasher, and gazed at us with amused attention and a bland smile, just as parents gaze at their children when they are gently playing. Only the humpbacked dishwasher, it seemed to me, did not look at us scornfully but sympathetically.

Though it was trying and awkward to lunch with the minstrel, and to play the entertainer, under the fire of all these waiters' eyes, I tried to do my duty with as little constraint as possible. In the lighted room I could see him better. He was a small but symmetrically built and muscular man, though almost a dwarf in stature; he had bristly black hair, teary big black eyes, bushy eyebrows, and a thoroughly pleasant, attractively shaped mouth. He had little side-whiskers, his hair was short, his attire was very simple and mean. He was not over-clean, was ragged and sunburnt, and in general had the look of a laboring-man. He was far more like a poor tradesman than an artist.

Only in his ever humid and brilliant eyes, and in his firm mouth, was there any sign of originality or genius. By his face it might be conjectured that his age was between twenty-five and forty; in reality, he was thirty- seven.

Here is what he related to me, with good-natured readiness and evident sincerity, of his life. He was a native of Aargau. In early childhood he had lost father and mother; other relatives he had none. He had never owned any property. He had been apprenticed to a carpenter; but twenty- two years previously one of his arms had been attacked by caries, which had prevented him from ever working again.

From childhood he had been fond of singing, and he began to be a singer. Occasionally strangers had given him money. With this he had learned his profession, bought his guitar, and now for eighteen years he had been wandering about through Switzerland and Italy, singing before hotels. His whole luggage consisted of his guitar, and a little purse in which, at the present time, there was only a franc and a half. That would have to suffice for supper and lodgings this night.

Every year now for eighteen years he had made the round of the best and most popular resorts of Switzerland—Zurich, Lucerne, Interlaken, Chamounix, etc.; by the way of the St. Bernard he would go down into Italy, and return over the St. Gotthard, or through Savoy. Just at present it was rather hard for him to walk, as he had caught a cold, causing him to suffer from some trouble in his legs—he called it *Gliederzucht*, or rheumatism—which grew more severe from year to year; and, moreover, his voice and eyes had grown weaker. Nevertheless, he was on his way to Interlaken, Aix- les-Bains, and thence over the little St. Bernard to Italy, which he was very fond of. It was evident that on the whole he was well content with his life.

When I asked him why he returned home, if he had any relatives there, or a house and land, his mouth parted in a gay smile, and he replied, *"Oui, le sucre est bon, il est doux pour les enfants!"* and he winked at the servants.

I did not catch his meaning, but the group of servants burst out laughing.

"No, I have nothing of the sort, but still I should always want to go back," he explained to me. "I go home because there is always a something that draws one to one's native place."

And once more he repeated with a shrewd, self-satisfied smile, his phrase, *"Oui, le sucre est bon,"* and then laughed good-naturedly.

The servants were very much amused, and laughed heartily; only the hunchbacked dishwasher looked earnestly from her big kindly eyes at the little man, and picked up his cap for him, when, as we talked, he once knocked it off the bench. I have noticed that wandering minstrels, acrobats, even jugglers, delight in calling themselves artists, and several times I hinted to my comrade that he was an artist; but he did not at all accept this designation, but with perfect simplicity looked on his work as a means of existence.

When I asked him if he had not himself written the songs which he sang, he showed great surprise at such a strange question, and replied that the words of whatever he sang were all of old Tyrolese origin.

"But how about that song of the Righi? I think that cannot be very ancient," I suggested.

"Oh, that was composed about fifteen years ago. There was a German in Basle; he was a clever man; it was he who composed it. A splendid song. You see he composed it especially for travelers."

And he began to repeat the words of the Righi song, which he liked so well, translated them into French as he went along.

> If you wish to go to Righi,
> you will not need shoes to Wegis
> (for you go that far by steamboat).
> But from Wegis take a stout staff,
> also on your arm a maiden.
> Drink a glass of wine on starting,
> only do not drink too freely,
> for if you desire to drink here,
> you must earn the right to, first.

"Oh! a splendid song!" he exclaimed, as he finished. The servants, evidently, also found the song much to their mind, because they came up closer to us.

"Yes, but who was it composed the music?" I asked.

"Oh, no one at all; you know you must have something new when you are going to sing for strangers."

When the ice was brought, and I had given my comrade a glass of champagne, he seemed somewhat ill at ease, and, glancing at the servants, he turned and twisted on the bench.

We touched our glasses to the health of all artists; he drank half a glass, then he seemed to be collecting his ideas, and knit his brows in deep thought.

"It is long since I have tasted such wine, *je ne vous dis que ça*. In Italy the *vino d'Asti* is excellent, but this is still better. Ah! Italy; it is splendid to be there!" he added.

"Yes, there they know how to appreciate music and artists," said I, trying to bring him round to the evening's mischance before the Schweitzerhof.

"No," he replied. "There, as far as music is concerned, I cannot give anybody satisfaction. The Italians are themselves musicians—none like them in the world; but I know only Tyrolese songs. They are something of a novelty to them, though."

"Well, you find rather more generous gentlemen there, don't you?" I went on to say, anxious to make him share in my resentment against the guests of the Schweitzerhof. "There it would not be possible to find a big hotel frequented by rich people, where, out of a hundred listening to an artist's singing, not one would give him anything."

My question utterly failed of the effect that I expected. It did not enter his head to be indignant with them; on the contrary, he saw in my remark an implied slur on his talent which had failed of its reward, and he hastened to set himself right before me. "It is not every time that you get anything," he remarked; "sometimes one isn't in good voice, or you are tired; now today I have been walking ten hours, and singing almost all the time. That is hard. And these important aristocrats do not always care to listen to Tyrolese songs."

"But still, how can they help giving?" I insisted. He did not comprehend my remark.

"That's nothing," he said; "but here the principal thing is, *on est tres* serré pour la police *that's what's the trouble. Here, according to these* republican laws, you are not allowed to sing; but in Italy you can go wherever you please, no one says a word. Here, if they want to let you, they let you; but if they don't want to, then they can throw you into jail."

"What? That's incredible!"

"Yes, it is true. If you have been warned once, and are found singing again, they may put you in jail. I was kept there three months once," he said, smiling as if that were one of his pleasantest recollections.

"Oh! that is terrible!" I exclaimed. "What was the reason?"

"That was in consequence of one of the new laws of the republic," he went on to explain, growing animated. "They cannot comprehend here that a poor fellow must earn his living somehow. If I were not a cripple, I would work. But what harm do I do to anyone in the world by my singing? What does it mean? The rich can live as they wish, but *un pauvre tiaple* like myself can't live at all. What does it mean by laws of the republic? If that is the way they run, then we don't want a republic. Isn't that so, my dear sir? We don't want a republic, but we want . . . we simply want . . . we want" . . . he hesitated a little, . . . "we want natural laws."

I filled up his glass.

"You are not drinking," I said.

He took the glass in his hand, and bowed to me.

"I know what you wish," he said, blinking his eyes at me, and threatening me with his finger. "You wish to make me drunk, so as to see what you can get out of me; but no, you shan't have that gratification."

"Why should I make you drunk?" I inquired. "All I wished was to give you a pleasure."

He seemed really sorry that he had offended me by interpreting my insistence so harshly. He grew confused, stood up, and touched my elbow.

"No, no," said he, looking at me with a beseeching expression in his moist eyes. "I was only joking."

And immediately after he made use of some horribly uncultivated slang expression, intended to signify that I was, nevertheless, a fine young man.

"*Je ne vous dis que ça,*" he said in conclusion.

In this fashion the minstrel and I continued to drink and converse; and the waiters continued to stare at us unceremoniously, and, as it seemed, to ridicule us.

In spite of the interest which our conversation aroused in me, I could not avoid taking notice of their behavior; and I confess I began to grow more and more angry.

One of the waiters arose, came up to the little man, and, looking at the top of his head, began to smile. I was already full of wrath against the inmates of the hotel, and had not yet had a chance to pour it out on any one; and now I confess I was in the highest degree irritated by this audience of waiters.

The Swiss, not removing his hat, came into the room, and sat down near me, leaning his elbows on the table. This last circumstance, which was so insulting to my dignity or my vainglory, completely enraged me, and gave an outlet for all the wrath which the whole evening long had been boiling within me. Why had he so humbly bowed when he had met me before, and now, because I was sitting with the traveling minstrel, did he come and take his place near me so rudely? I was entirely overmastered by that boiling, angry indignation which I enjoy in myself, which I sometimes endeavor to stimulate when it comes over me, because it has an exhilarating effect on me, and gives me, if only for a short time, a certain extraordinary flexibility, energy, and strength in all my physical and moral faculties.

I leaped to my feet.

"Whom are you laughing at?" I screamed at the waiter; and I felt my face turn pale, and my lips involuntarily set together.

"I am not laughing, I only . . . "replied the waiter, moving away from me.

"Yes, you are; you are laughing at this gentleman. And what right have you to come, and to take a seat here, when there are guests? Don't you dare to sit down!" The Swiss, muttering something, got up and turned to the door.

"What right have you to make sport of this gentleman, and to sit down by him, when he is a guest, and you are a waiter? Why didn't you laugh at me this evening at dinner, and come and sit down beside me? Because he is meanly dressed, and sings in the streets? Is that the reason? and because I have better clothes? He is poor, but he is a thousand times better than you are; that I am sure of, because he has never insulted any one, but you have insulted him."

"I didn't mean anything," replied my enemy, the waiter. "Did I disturb him by sitting down?"

The waiter did not understand me, and my German was wasted on him. The rude Swiss was about to take the waiter's part; but I fell upon him so impetuously that the Swiss pretended not to understand me, and waved his hand.

The hunchbacked dish-washer, either because she perceived my wrathful state, and feared a scandal, or possibly because she shared my views, took my part, and, trying to force her way between me and the porter, told him to hold his tongue, saying that I was right, but at the same time urging me to calm myself.

"*Der Herr hat Recht; Sie haben Recht,*" she said over and over again. The minstrel's face presented a most pitiable, terrified expression; and evidently he did not understand why I was angry, and what I wanted; and he urged me to let him go away as soon as possible.

But the eloquence of wrath burned within me more and more. I understood it all—the throng that had made merry at his expense, and his auditors who had not given him anything; and not for all the world would I have held my peace.

I believe that, if the waiters and the Swiss had not been so submissive, I should have taken delight in having a brush with them, or striking the defenseless English girl on the head with a stick. If at that moment I had been at Sevastopol, I should have taken delight in devoting myself to slaughtering and killing in the English trench.

"And why did you take this gentleman and me into this room, and not into the other? What?" I thundered at the Swiss, seizing him by the arm so that he could not escape from me. "What right had you to judge by his appearance that this gentleman must be served in this room, and not in that? Have not all guests who pay equal rights in hotels? Not only in a republic, but in all the world! Your scurvy republic! . . . Equality, indeed! You would not dare to take an Englishman into this room, not even those Englishmen who have heard this gentleman free of cost; that is, who have stolen from him, each one of them, the few centimes which ought to have been given to him. How did you dare to take us to this room?"

"That room is closed," said the porter.

"No," I cried, "that isn't true; it isn't closed."

"Then you know best."

"I know . . . I know that you are lying."

The Swiss turned his back on me.

"Eh! What is to be said?" he muttered.

"What is to be said?" I cried. "Now conduct us instantly into that room!"

In spite of the dishwasher's warning, and the entreaties of the minstrel, who would have preferred to go home, I insisted on seeing the head waiter, and went with my guest into the big dining room. The head waiter, hearing my angry voice, and seeing my menacing face, avoided a quarrel, and, with contemptuous servility, said that I might go wherever I pleased. I could not prove to the Swiss that he had lied, because he had hastened out of sight before I went into the hall.

The dining room was, in fact, open and lighted; and at one of the tables sat an Englishman and a lady, eating their supper. Although we were shown to a special table, I took the dirty minstrel to the very one where the Englishman was, and bade the waiter bring to us there the unfinished bottle.

The two guests at first looked with surprised, then with angry, eyes at the little man, who, more dead than alive, was sitting near me. They talked together in a low tone; then the lady pushed back her plate, her silk dress rustled, and both of them left the room. Through the glass doors I saw the Englishman saying something in an angry voice to the waiter, and pointing with his hand in our direction. The waiter put his head through the door, and looked at us. I waited with pleasurable anticipation for someone to come and order us out, for then I could have found a full outlet for all my indignation. But fortunately, thought at the time I felt injured, we were left in peace. The minstrel, who before had fought shy of the wine, now eagerly drank all that was left in the bottle, so that he might make his escape as quickly as possible.

He, however, expressed his gratitude with deep feeling, as it seemed to me, for his entertainment. His teary eyes grew still more humid and brilliant, and he made use of a most strange and complicated phrase of gratitude. But still very pleasant to me was the sentence in which he said that if everybody treated artists as I had been doing, it would be very good, and ended by wishing me all manner of happiness. We went out into the hall together. There stood the servants, and my enemy the Swiss apparently airing his grievances against me before them. All of them, I thought, looked at me as if I were a man who had lost his wits. I treated the little man exactly like an equal, before all that audience of servants; and then, with all the respect that I was able to express in my behavior, I took off my hat, and pressed his hand with its dry and hardened fingers.

The servants pretended not to pay the slightest attention to me. Only one of them indulged in a sarcastic laugh. As soon as the minstrel had bowed himself out, and disappeared in the darkness, I went up-stairs to my room, intending to sleep off all these impressions and the foolish, childish anger which had come upon me so unexpectedly. But, finding that I was too much excited to sleep, I once more went down into the street with the intention of walking until I should have recovered my equanimity, and, I must confess, with the secret hope that I might accidentally come across the porter or the waiter or the Englishman, and show them all their rudeness, and, most of all, their unfairness. But beyond the Swiss, who when he saw me turned his back, I met no one; and I began to promenade in absolute solitude back and forth along the quay.

"This is an example of the strange fate of poetry," said I to myself, having grown a little calmer. "All love it, all are in search of it; it is the only thing in life that men love and seek, and yet no one recognizes its power, no one prizes this best treasure of the world, and those who give it to men are not rewarded. Ask any one you please, ask all these guests of the Schweitzerhof, what is the most precious treasure in the world, and all, or ninety-nine out of a hundred, putting on a sardonic expression, will say that the best thing in the world is money.

"'Maybe, though, this does not please you, or coincide with your elevated ideas,' it will be urged; 'but what is to be done if human life is so constituted that money alone is capable of giving a man happiness? I cannot force my mind not to see the world as it is,' it will be added, 'that is, to see the truth.'

"Pitiable is your intellect, pitiable the happiness which you desire! And you yourselves, unhappy creatures, not knowing what you desire, . . . why have you all left your fatherland, your relatives, your money-making trades and occupations, and come to this little Swiss city of Lucerne? Why did you all this evening gather on the balconies, and in respectful silence listen to the little beggar's song? And if he had been willing to sing longer, you would have been silent and listened longer. What! could money, even millions of it, have driven you all from your country, and brought you all together in this little nook of Lucerne? Could money have gathered you all on the balconies to stand for half an hour silent and motionless? No! One thing compels you to do it, and will forever have a stronger influence than all the other impulses of life: the longing for poetry which you know, which you do not realize, but feel, always will feel as long as you have any human sensibilities. The word 'poetry' is a mockery to you; you make use of it as a sort of ridiculous reproach; you regard the love for poetry as something meant for children and silly girls, and you make sport of them for it. For yourselves you must have something more definite.

"But children look upon life in a healthy way; they recognize and love what man ought to love, and what gives happiness. But life has so deceived and perverted you, that you ridicule the only thing that you really love, and you seek for what you hate and for what gives you unhappiness.

"You are so perverted that you did not perceive what obligations you were under to the poor Tyrolese who rendered you a pure delight; but at the same time you feel needlessly obliged to humiliate yourselves before some lord, which gives you neither pleasure nor profit, but rather causes you to sacrifice your comfort and convenience. What absurdity! what incomprehensible lack of reason!

"But it was not this that made the most powerful impression on me this evening. This blindness to all that gives happiness, this unconsciousness of poetic enjoyment, I can almost comprehend, or at least I have become wonted to it, since I have almost everywhere met with it in the course of my life; the harsh, unconscious churlishness of the crowd was no novelty to me; whatever those who argue in favor of popular sentiment may say, the throng is a conglomeration of very possibly good people, but of people who touch each other only on their coarse animal sides, and express only the sickness and harshness of human nature. But how was it that you, children of a free, humane people, you Christians, you simply as human beings, repaid with coldness and ridicule the poor beggar who gave you a pure enjoyment? But no, in your country there are asylums for beggars. There are no beggars, there must be none; and there must be no feelings of sympathy, since that would be a confession that beggary existed.

"But he labored, he gave you enjoyment, he besought you to give him something of your superfluity in payment for his labor of which you took advantage. But you looked on him with a cool smile as on one of the curiosities in your lofty brilliant palaces; and though there were a hundred of you, favored with happiness and wealth, not one man or one woman among you gave him a *sou*. Abashed he went away from you, and the thoughtless throng, laughing, followed and ridiculed not you, but him, because you were cold, harsh, and dishonorable; because you robbed him in receiving the entertainment which he have you; for this you jeered *him*.

"On the 19th of July, 1857, in Lucerne, before the Schweitzerhof Hotel, in which were lodging very opulent people, a wandering beggar minstrel sang for half an hour his songs, and played his guitar. About a hundred people listened to him. The minstrel thrice asked all to give him something. No one person gave him a thing, and many made sport of him.

"This is not an invention, but an actual fact, as those who desire can find out for themselves by consulting the papers for the list of those who were at the Schweitzerhof on the 19th of July.

"This is an event which the historians of our time ought to describe in letters of inextinguishable flame. This even is more significant and more serious, and fraught with far deeper meaning, than the facts that are printed in newspapers and histories. That the English have killed several thousand Chinese because the Chinese would not sell them anything for money while their land is overflowing with ringing coins; that the French have killed several thousand Kabyles because the wheat grows well in Africa, and because constant war is essential for the drill of an army; that the Turkish ambassador in Naples must not be a Jew; and that the Emperor Napoleon walks about in Plombières, and gives his people the express assurance that he rules only in direct accordance with the will of the people—all these are words which darken or reveal something long known. But the episode that took place in Lucerne on the 19th of July seems to me something entirely novel and strange, and it is connected not with the everlastingly ugly side of human nature, but with a well-known epoch in the development of society. This fact is not for the history of human activities, but for the history of progress and civilization.

"Why is it that this inhuman fact, impossible in any German, French, or Italian country, is quite possible here where civilization, freedom, and equality are carried to the highest degree of development, where there are gathered together the most civilized travelers from the most civilized nations? Why is it that these people who, in their palaces, their meetings, and their societies, labor warmly for the condition of the celibate Chinese in India, about the spread of Christianity and culture in Africa, about the formation of societies for attaining all perfection—why is it that they should not find in their souls the simple, primitive feeling of human sympathy? Has such a feeling entirely disappeared, and has its place been taken by vainglory, ambition, and cupidity, governing these men in their palaces, meetings, and societies? Has the spreading of that reasonable, egotistical association of people, which we call civilization, destroyed and rendered nugatory the desire for instinctive and loving association? And is this that boasted equality for which so much innocent blood has been shed, and so many crimes have been perpetrated? Is it possible that nations, like children, can be made happy by the mere sound of the word 'equality'?

"Equality before the law? Does the whole life of a people revolve within the sphere of law? Only the thousandth part of it is subject to the law; the rest lies outside of it, in the sphere of the customs and intuitions of society.

"But in society the lackey is better dressed than the minstrel, and insults him with impunity. I am better dressed than the lackey, and insult him with impunity. The Swiss considers me higher, but the minstrel lower, than himself; when I made the minstrel my companion, he felt that he was on an equality with us both, and behaved rudely. I was impudent to the Swiss, and the Swiss acknowledged that he was inferior to me. The waiter was impudent to the minstrel, and the minstrel accepted the fact that he was inferior to the waiter.

"And is that government free, even though men seriously call it free, where a single citizen can be thrown into prison, because, without harming any one, without interfering with any one, he does the only thing he can to prevent himself from dying of starvation?

"A wretched, pitiable creature is man with his craving for positive solutions, thrown into this everlastingly tossing, limitless ocean of *good* and *evil*, of facts, of combinations and contradictions. For centuries men have been struggling and laboring to put the *good* on one side, the *evil* on the other. Centuries will pass, and no matter how much the unprejudiced mind may strive to decide where the balance lies between the *good* and the *evil*, the scales will refuse to tip the beam, and there will always be equal quantities of the *good* and the *evil* on each scale.

"If only man would learn to form judgments, and not indulge in rash and arbitrary thoughts, and not to make reply to questions that are propounded merely to remain forever unanswered! If only he would learn that; every thought is both a lie and a truth!—a lie from the one-sidedness and inability of man to recognize all truth; and true because it expresses one side of mortal endeavor. There are divisions in this everlastingly tumultuous, endless, endlessly confused chaos of the *good* and the *evil*. They have drawn imaginary lines over this ocean, and they contend that the ocean is really thus divided.

"But are there not millions of other possible subdivisions from absolutely different standpoints, in other planes? Certainly these novel subdivisions will be made in centuries to come, just as millions of different ones have been made in centuries past.

"Civilization is *good*, barbarism is *evil*; freedom, *good*, slavery, *evil*. Now this imaginary knowledge annihilates the instinctive, beatific, primitive craving for the *good* which is in human nature. And who will explain to me what is freedom, what is despotism, what is civilization, what is barbarism?

"Where are the boundaries that separate them? And whose soul possesses so absolute a standard of good and evil as to measure these fleeting, complicated facts? Whose intellect is so great as to comprehend and weigh all the facts in the irretrievable past? And who can find any circumstance in which *good* and *evil* do not exist together? And because I know that I see more of one than of the other, is it not because my standpoint is wrong? And who has the ability to separate himself so absolutely from life, even for a moment, as to look upon it independently from above?

"One, only one infallible Guide we have—the universal Spirit which penetrates all collectively and as units, which has endowed each of us with the craving for the right; the Spirit which commands the tree to grow toward the sun, which commands the flower in autumn-tide to scatter its seed, and which commands each one of us unconsciously to draw closer together. And this one unerring, inspiring voice rings out louder than the noisy, hasty development of civilization.

"Who is the greater man, and who the greater barbarian— that lord, who, seeing the minstrel's well-worn clothes, angrily left the table, who gave him not the millionth part of his possessions in payment of his labor, and now lazily sitting in his brilliant, comfortable room, calmly expresses his opinion

about the events that are happening in China, and justifies the massacres that have been done there; or the little minstrel, who, risking imprisonment, with a franc in his pocket, and doing no harm to any one, has been going about for a score of years, up hill and down dale, rejoicing men's hearts with his songs, though they have jeered at him, and almost cast him out of the pale of humanity; and who, in weariness and cold and shame, has gone off to sleep, no one knows where, on his filthy straw?"

At this moment, from the city, through the dead silence of the night, far, far away, I caught the sound of the little man's guitar and his voice.

"No," something involuntarily said to me, "you have no right to commiserate the little man, or to blame the lord for his well-being. Who can weigh the inner happiness which is found in the soul of each of these men? There he stands somewhere in the muddy road, and gazes at the brilliant moonlit sky, and gayly sings amid the smiling, fragrant night; in his soul there is no reproach, no anger, no regret. And who knows what is transpiring now in the hearts of all these men within those opulent, brilliant rooms? Who knows if they all have as much unencumbered, sweet delight in life, and as much satisfaction with the world, as dwells in the soul of that little man?

"Endless are the mercy and wisdom of Him who has permitted and formed all these contradictions. Only to thee, miserable little worm of the dust, audaciously, lawlessly attempting to fathom His laws, His designs—only to thee do they seem like contradictions.

"Full of love He looks down from His bright, immeasurable height, and rejoices in the endless harmony in which you all move in endless contradictions. In thy pride thou hast thought thyself able to separate thyself from the laws of the universe. No, thou also, with thy petty, ridiculous anger against the waiters—thou also hast disturbed the harmonious craving for the eternal and the infinite." . . .

—1857

ABOUT THE CONTRIBUTORS

Claud Field has translated into English a variety of texts by notable authors from around the world. Some of his most renowned work includes Meister Eckhart's *Sermons*, Abu Hamid al-Ghazali's *Confessions* and *The Alchemy of Happiness*, August Strindberg's *Historical Miniatures*, and Nikolai Gogol's collection, *The Mantle and Other Stories*.

Constance Garnett studied Latin, Greek and Russian at Cambridge University. She translated over seventy volumes of Russian literature by authors such as Chekhov, Dostoyevsky, Gogol, Tolstoy and Turgenev and she is generally considered responsible for making those authors available to English-speaking audiences.

Nathan Haskell Dole graduated from Harvard University and worked as a writer and journalist before translating works that were originally written in French, Italian, Russian and Spanish. Besides his distinguished translations of Leo Tolstoy and Armando Palacio Valdés, he has written over twenty volumes of original poetry and prose.

Sherman Sutherland received his PhD in English from Ohio University, where one of his concentrations was narratology, particularly with respect to temporal distance in first-person narratives. He has written poems, short stories and one novel. His next book, *Understanding Literary Theory*, will be available in December 2012. He currently teaches in Ohio.

www.ingramcontent.com/pod-product-compliance
Lightning Source LLC
Chambersburg PA
CBHW050028180626
46810CB00002B/627